Death in a Hammock

Death in a Hammock

Kinley Roby

Five Star • Waterville, Maine

First Edition
First Printing: May 2003

Published in 2003 in conjunction with Tekno Books and Ed Gorman.

Set in 11 pt. Plantin.

Printed in the United States on permanent paper.

ISBN 0-7862-5396-7 (hc : alk. paper)

For Barry N. Malzberg,
friend and mentor

Acknowledgements

To Bill Pronzini and Marcia Muller I want to express my gratitude for their generous help and encouragement. I also wish to express my thanks to the officers and staff of the Collier County Sheriff's Department for their patient help with a long list of technical matters.

Prologue

"It's for you," Jennifer said, pointing the phone at him.

She was tall and dark, with thick, heavy hair, and wore an expression of deep dissatisfaction on her otherwise handsome face.

"Who is it?" Harry asked, getting up from the supper table.

He took the phone from his wife as she walked past him without answering.

"Hello," he said and did not speak again until he said, "OK," and hung up.

"Well?" Jennifer asked coldly.

"There's a problem."

He walked back to the table, a fair-haired, solidly built man in his late thirties. He paused behind his chair, frowning with concern.

Their two children, Sarah seven and Clive four, went on eating, but Jennifer carefully laid her knife and fork across her plate. She placed her hands flat on the table as if she was bracing herself for an assault.

"What is it this time?" she asked.

"Jacob Stone just told the crowd in Whitney's Store he planned to go up into his north orchard when he got home and shoot one of his deer."

"His deer," Jennifer said with a short, bitter laugh. "The State's deer. I don't care whose deer they are. You're not going up there."

Harry looked at the children.

"Let's talk about this in the bedroom," he said quietly.

"Fine," she snapped.

"I have to go," he told her, closing the door.

"No, you don't. Jacob Stone is half crazy and he's dangerous."

"Deer season closed two days ago, Jennifer. You know it as well as I do."

It seemed to him that since coming to this post in western Maine, all they did was wrangle.

"What does that matter?" she demanded. "If you go up there, he'll shoot you. When I agreed to come to this godforsaken place, I did not agree to have you killed."

"Stone is not going to shoot me," Harry protested. "He's just trying to scare me off. If he succeeds, every man in this county will know I can't enforce the law. Their respect for me will be gone. If that happens, I'll be finished here as a warden."

"Good," she said, furious now. "Why are you keeping us in this godforsaken place anyway? The people despise us. There's not a decent school for Sarah within thirty miles and no hospital nearer than Rangeley. There's not even a movie theater to escape to. And now you tell me you have to risk your life to maintain respect. Wake up, Harry. You've got a wife and two children. It's time to come down from the tree house."

He stared at her for a moment, his face burning with anger. He knew backward and forward the argument about whether or not to stay here. They had been having it for months. Worse still, he knew she was at least partly right. Parmachenee Lake was almost off the map. But what hurt him and angered him was her refusal even to try to see the situation from his point of view. This was his hardship post. It was a test. If they got through it successfully, he was on his way to becoming a supervisor. After that, one advancement would follow another. He couldn't understand why she refused to see what it meant to him, to them.

"I'll be back as soon as I can," he said in a choked voice and left.

Still occupied with the sour thoughts his argument with Jennifer had bred in him, Harry stepped down from his 4x4 into the snow and caught his breath as the cold bit into him. He glanced up at the hill and at the slate gray sky above it, judging how much light he had left. Enough, he thought, to get up to that damned orchard before it was dark.

Despite Jennifer's warning, he stubbornly refused to admit Stone posed any physical threat. The farmer was a property rights nut as well as a bully who had to be faced down. The sooner he did it, the sooner he could get back to his supper. Quickly, he pulled on his mittens, snapped up the hood of his green parka, slipped on his backpack, and lifted his rifle from its rack behind the front seat.

His breath quickly rimed the fur trim on his hood as he set off across the field toward a stand of white pines covering the hill below Stone's orchard. At the edge of the woods some reluctance made him pause and look back at the road, deserted except for his van. The half-buried lines of barbed wire fencing stitching the fields did nothing to relieve the desolation of the snow-piled pastures, stony hills, and dense woods surrounding him. With a grunt of resignation he turned back to his task and plowed forward into the dark trees. He had gone only a few yards when he heard the flat, heavy slam of a rifle on the hill above him, followed by a second report.

"Damned fool," he said through his teeth and picked up his pace.

Fifteen minutes later Harry stepped out of the woods and waded through a drifted gap in the stone wall separating the pine trees from the orchard. Twenty yards above him, partly hidden by the bare apple trees, he saw a dark figure kneeling in the snow beside a short toboggan. Although it was not fully dark, Stone had lighted his hurricane lantern. It stood beside him on the toboggan, casting a yellow light on the snow. Harry began climbing, still unable to see what Stone was doing. Having covered half the distance separating them, he stopped and shouted, "Jacob, it's Harry Brock."

Stone got quickly to his feet, picking up his rifle as he straightened.

"Walk out of here, Brock," he called in a high, harsh voice.

Harry began climbing again.

"Can't do that, Jacob."

Stone lifted his rifle in a single, smooth motion and fired. Harry flinched away from the burning pain that seared the outside of his right shoulder. He clawed his gun out of the snow and was brushing off the scope when Stone fired again. The bullet struck a branch above Harry's head and showered him with bark and splintered wood.

"Jesus Loving Christ!" Harry rolled onto his knees. His shoulder felt as if it was on fire.

"Jacob." His shout was drowned by the blast of Stone's gun. His parka hood was yanked off his head as the slug tore through it.

Harry no longer doubted Stone was trying to kill him. The knowledge calmed him. He sank back onto his heels and shook off his right mitten. He raised the rifle, put the scope's crosshairs on Stone's left hip, and squeezed the trigger. Stone was reloading when the impact of the bullet flung him sprawling into the snow.

Harry stood up and worked the action on his rifle without

taking his eyes off the fallen man. Stone did not move. Harry desperately wanted to turn around and go back down the hill. But, instead, he picked up his mitten and forced himself to plow upward through the orchard to the place where Stone lay across the body of the buck he had been dressing out. Climbing the steep slope, he had been unable to see the deer. Now he stood over the two bodies, staring at their blood soaking into the snow.

A raven, returning late to its roost, saw the dead deer and the motionless figures of the men and swerved to take a closer look. The beat of its wings in the silence snapped the lock on Harry's mind. He looked up. The bird squawked in alarm and flapped swiftly away. Steeling himself, Harry knelt beside Stone and tried to find his pulse. There was none.

Stone lay on his left side. Very gently, Harry rolled him onto his back. Blood was still welling from the wound in his hip, but he was not bleeding as if an artery had been severed. Why was there no pulse? Harry put his ear close to Stone's open mouth but felt no breath. The open eyes stared unblinking at the heavy sky.

"You can't be dead," Harry said aloud.

Working rapidly, he unfastened Stone's belt and cut his blood-soaked trousers away from his hip. The entrance wound was small, and the exit wound at the top of his buttock was not much larger. The fact that both wounds were scarcely bleeding confirmed Harry's fear. Stone's heart was not beating.

Harry yanked off his pack, pulled out a roll of gauze bandage, and quickly packed the wounds. Then he unzipped Stone's jacket and, finding no more bleeding, got quickly to work trying to revive him. But his efforts were useless. Stone was well and truly dead.

Winded from his efforts, Harry crouched for a few

moments beside the dead man and tried without success to understand what had happened. Defeated, he pulled the cut trousers back together, zipped up Stone's jacket, and rolled him onto the toboggan. Then, sick at heart, he struggled to his feet and began the grim task of taking the dead man home.

Three days later Harry was arrested and arraigned on a charge of first-degree murder. Denied bail, he was sent to the Oxford County jail in South Paris, sixty miles to the south. His trial began the second week in January in an explosion of media attention.

Jacob Stone's death built into a bonfire the Maine public's always smoldering suspicion of uniformed authority. And Agnes Stone and her three children evoked statewide pity and outrage from the moment they appeared on television. Until he went on trial, the press and the rest of the media subjected Harry to an intense scrutiny almost wholly lacking in sympathy. They showed no interest in trying to understand why he had shot Jacob Stone.

The trial lasted three weeks. Jennifer Brock and the children came every day to listen and watch. Having tried and failed to find someone in Parmachenee Lake willing to look after them while she attended the trial, Jennifer was finally compelled to take them with her to South Paris to live in a motel. Unable to reach Harry, the reporters pursued Jennifer. And although it was state and not national media hounding her, the abuse was severe enough to put her on tranquilizers and make Clive revert to wetting the bed, something he had not done for over a year.

Agnes Stone and her three children were also in South Paris, housed at the state's expense on the other side of town in a somewhat fancier motel than the one Jennifer occupied. The media cast Agnes Stone in the role of the tragic victim. In contrast, they portrayed Jennifer as a co-conspirator in the cold-blooded murder of a poor, honest farmer struggling to feed his family. But that difference did nothing to ease Agnes Stone's grief or lessen the profound unease the shy, retiring country woman experienced whenever she stepped outside her motel.

One of the janitors working on the third floor of the County Courthouse, where the jury had been deliberating for nearly a week, heard the foreman tell the officer on duty they would be coming out shortly. The janitor stood his broom in a corner and hurried down the flights of creaking wooden stairs, telling everyone he met that the jury was coming out. News spread first through the Courthouse then spread on the icy wind and driving snow down Main Street and into the bars and shops and motel lobbies, sending reporters, TV camera crews, and curious citizens scurrying toward the Courthouse.

Two State Troopers drove Mrs. Stone and her three children to the Courthouse and shepherded them through the shouting reporters into the courtroom. Jennifer Brock, with Sarah and Clive in tow, arrived shortly after with Harry's lawyer. He got them through the ranks of reporters but not without some jostling and a lot of verbal abuse.

The overheated courtroom was already packed and noisy by the time Harry was led in and seated at the defendant's table. Once unshackled from his wrist and ankle chains, he turned to look for Jennifer and the children. Clive nodded solemnly, as did Sarah, who appeared to be on the verge of tears. Jennifer gave him a brief, tight-lipped nod and looked quickly away.

Harry let his gaze drift briefly over the crowded rows of people filling the court. He forced himself to look at Agnes

Stone and her two girls, both under five. The boy was ten and not her child but her dead husband's youngest brother. He had lived with them for most of his life.

Harry knew Agnes Stone could not have been more than thirty-five but she looked fifteen years older. Her thin, brown hair was already heavily streaked with white. She was small, pale, and sharp-featured and sat huddled in a curve of misery. The girls crowded against their mother. But the boy sat stiff-backed, a defiant expression on his narrow face, hard dark eyes looking angrily out at the world. Like Jacob, Harry thought with a sharp twist of the guilt that Stone's death had driven into his mind like a nail.

The boy caught Harry staring at him and glared back with a burning hatred. Harry turned away. What help could it be to the boy, he asked himself for possibly the hundredth time, to hear again and again that Harry had not intended to kill Jacob? How could it help him to know, as he now had to know, that his brother had publicly announced his decision to shoot a deer out of season and then tried to kill the man who came to arrest him?

What sense could the boy make of the fact that it was not malice but physics that caused the slug to shatter on his brother's hip bone, sending a piece of lead angling upward through Jacob's torso and ripping through his heart? The answer, Harry admitted, was self-evident in the boy's wild and hate-filled gaze.

The bailiff's hoarse voice called, "All rise!" The clatter of voices behind Harry sank to a murmur, and he heard the groan of the wind and the hiss of snow striking the windows in sudden bursts.

"You OK?" his lawyer asked him quietly as they got to their feet.

"Sure," Harry answered.

He was not all right. But it did not even occur to him to say so. The lawyer, skilled and thorough, had already explained to him what the jury's options were and what kinds of decisions they could plausibly reach. Harry knew them by heart, and the knowledge did not help. He felt he was, probably deservedly, beyond help.

The jury, five men and seven women, filed into their seats, the scuffling and scraping noises they made settling themselves sounded to Harry unnaturally loud. One of the jurors, a tall, white haired woman in a purple wool suit, remained standing, gripping a piece of paper in front of her with both hands.

"The defendant will rise."

Harry and his lawyer got to their feet. Despite the tightness in his throat, Harry felt that for him what was happening was without meaning. He had long since settled the issue of his guilt or innocence.

"Madam Foreman, has the jury reached a verdict?"

"We have, Your Honor."

"How find you?"

"We find the defendant not guilty on all counts."

A long, deep sigh that verged on a groan rose from the spectators, and was drowned instantly in a rising, keening, solitary cry. Harry turned to see Agnes Stone rising from her chair, her face twisted in pain, her children crowding in on her, their arms raised either to support her or pull her down. Harry could not bear to watch, and he twisted away. The judge pounded his gavel.

The cry died and Harry heard the judge saying something to him he could not hear. The gavel banged down again, and it was over.

"Congratulations," his lawyer was saying, pumping Harry's hand. "You're a free man. We won, fella. We won."

Harry was stunned. He had expected to be found guilty of everything for which he had been charged. With his mind on Jennifer and Clive and Sarah, he only half listened to his lawyer's final instructions. He wanted them in his arms, but he couldn't see them in the rapidly emptying room. Instead, he saw a burly, red-faced man in a black coat and a green wool hat pulled down over his ears push his way through the stragglers at the door and stride down the aisle toward him.

"You Harry Brock?"

"Yes."

"This is for you." He passed Harry a large yellow envelope.

"What is it? Who are you?"

"Your wife's lawyer. My card's in the envelope. What you've got there is a legal notice that she's filing for divorce."

Harry stared at him, unable to speak.

"Sorry, pal," the man said as he turned away. "Shit happens."

Chapter 1

May had begun hot, even for southwest Florida. But on the positive side, the heat had flushed the last of the snowbirds out of the sand traps and sent them winging north.

On this May morning Harry Brock, who had no intention of going anywhere north of Tequesta County, was painting on his lanai. Except for the mockingbird singing in the wisteria vine on the west corner of the veranda, the Hammock where his house was located was drenched in silence and heat. But Harry was oblivious to everything except the painting in front of him and the brush in his hand. For better light, he was working with his back to the door and had just stepped back to look at the painting when a harsh voice behind him barked, "Are you H. Brock?"

"Jesus!" Harry spun around, his sandals clattering like bones on the Mexican tile floor.

"Really," the woman peering through the screen said with a bitter laugh. "Then I've come to the wrong place."

"I exaggerated my divinity," Harry said warily, wondering if she was one of the religious cranks who sometime strayed onto the Hammock. "But I am Harry Brock," he added. "You scared the hell out of me."

Very few people found their way to his door, which was just the way he wanted it. He was strongly built, pushing fifty, of medium height, and deeply browned by the sun. His closely cropped hair, thinning on top, was a faded brown, salted with gray. He was wearing khaki shorts and a dark blue polo shirt.

"I thought you were deaf," she shot back. "You didn't hear me climb these steps."

"I don't get many visitors."

From the shadow of the porch, she was little more than a glowing outline through the screen. But beyond her he saw more clearly a little girl about four and a boy two or three years older listlessly kicking a ball across the small patch of lawn between the huge, moss-draped live oaks shading the house.

Oh, shit, he thought, all that's missing is the dog.

Resigned but still disgruntled, Harry turned and swirled the paint brush he was holding in a Mason jar of thinner, wiped it clean with a rag that looked like Joseph's coat, and tossed the brush and the cloth onto his work table.

She stepped back as he pushed open the door, and he got a good look at her. She was at least as tall as he was and straight-backed. She stood with her fists on her hips, and her scowl had trouble written all over it.

Her aggressive stance told him she probably wasn't trying to save his soul. Good. Maybe that meant he could get rid of her quickly. She appeared to be about thirty. When she turned her head briefly to check on the kids, he saw that her reddish blonde hair hung down her back in a single thick braid that brushed the pockets of her cut-off jeans. She wore battered white running shoes and a man's faded orange shirt several sizes too big for her, its tails knotted around her waist.

Good Will, he thought, trying hard not to feel sorry for her. She'd be a good-looking woman if she'd stop scowling. Looking at her more closely, he realized with an unwelcome bump of concern, she had the pinched look of someone who for some time had not had enough to eat. So did the kids.

"Come in," he said. He couldn't let them go without

offering to feed them.

"No thanks," she answered and glanced past him at his painting. "An artist," she said in the same hard voice.

"That might be stretching it. What can I do for you?"

"Your flowers look like plastic lawn ornaments."

The outrageousness of her comment made him laugh, and his anger evaporated. At the same time he noticed that she had extraordinarily vivid green eyes.

"I paint that way on purpose. Now, if you've finished insulting my picture, how can I help?"

She smiled thinly.

"I'm looking for Will Trachey. Do you know him?"

The smile vanished as suddenly as it had come.

He hesitated, glancing at the kids listlessly kicking their ball.

"I know him," he said, keeping his voice neutral.

As he spoke, he made a decision and stepped through the door into the blazing sunlight in front of the lanai and let it swing shut. She took another step back, but he sensed no fear in her.

"Run the risk that I'll attack you once we're in the house and bring those two kids inside," he said. "They look as if they've had all the sun they can take. There's cold milk and cookies. You might want something yourself. There's coffee and some donuts."

For a moment those remarkable eyes flared. Harry thought she might be going to pop him, but instead she nodded.

"Minna, Jesse," she called in a flat voice. "Come here."

"They look worn out," he said as the kids trailed toward them across the grass.

"That's because they are. They've been sleeping in the car."

She turned down the milk after smelling the carton and settled on Sprite. He made the coffee while she seated Minna and Jesse at the kitchen table and filled their glasses and doled out chocolate chip cookies from the jar Harry had given her. Then she stood with her arms folded, leaning a hip against the table, watching them eat.

While he opened a box of sugar donuts and got down cups and saucers, he studied her. She looked as worn out as the kids. And, unless he was mistaken, badly frightened as well. On the way to the kitchen she had scrutinized the rooms as if they might be booby trapped, and she hadn't let the kids touch the cookies until she'd tasted one.

"What's your name?" he asked.

She sat down with obvious reluctance while he filled their cups. "Katherine Trachey. Katherine with a K," she responded, picking up a donut. "I don't answer to K.T. or Katy or any of that crap."

Harry glanced at her left hand. No ring. She opened and closed the hand and looked from it to him. "I hocked it," she said aggressively.

He nodded. She didn't miss much, he thought with approval. He wondered what she was expecting from Willard Trachey other than pain and grief.

"Will live around here somewhere?" she demanded around a bite of the donut. "I saw his name on a mailbox back there on the road."

Outside the open kitchen window in a thick clump of sea grapes growing at the corner of the house, a pair of cardinals began chipping excitedly. The kids ran to look. By standing on tiptoe Minna could just see over the sill. Jesse was whispering to her and pointing at the bird.

"They're quiet kids," Harry said.

She nodded.

20

"You know where he lives?"

"I know."

"How do I get there?"

"I'll have to show you," he said. "But that's OK. I've painted enough lawn ornaments for today."

Her mouth twitched toward a smile that didn't reach her eyes.

"How complicated can a dirt road be?"

"It's hard to find, and if you're taking those kids out there, I'm going with you."

"You suggesting I can't take care of them properly?"

"No, Katherine. It's what might be out there if he isn't," Harry answered with more edge. "I'd have no grounds to comment on you as a mother, except to say I don't know why you shouldn't be a good one."

"This coffee tastes like varnish," she said after a pause, during which she studied him the way a dog might size up a cat it wanted to run.

"Don't drink it then," he said.

She gave him a fleeting smile and dusted the sugar off her hands. Then she turned and spoke to Minna and Jesse in the flat voice she used with them, "You kids finished with your pop and cookies?"

They both nodded. Harry looked at them and thought sadly he had yet to hear either of them laugh or even speak out loud. It might have been because they were tired, but he didn't think so. But then, it wasn't any of his business, was it?

"Minna, you come with me," Katherine said, pushing her chair back. "We're going to the bathroom. Jesse, you go after us."

Harry told her where to find it, and she left with Minna. Jesse went back to the window, where the cardinals were still chipping loudly. Harry joined him.

"The redbirds probably saw a rat snake," he said. "They make a fuss when one's around. You ever seen a rat snake?"

Jesse shook his head.

"You want to go out and see if we can find it?"

To Harry's surprise, the child turned and bolted through the door after his mother. When she came back carrying Minna, Harry told her what had happened.

"Good," she said. "He might live to grow up."

Harry wrestled down the impulse to tell her it was a damn poor idea to bring up a boy to fear and hate men.

When Jesse returned from the toilet, they all went outside. "Where's your car?" he asked when they reached the end of the path.

"Back towards the bridge a ways."

"Did you break down?"

"Ran out of gas."

"I've got a can in the garage. I'll get it."

"Is this place an island?" she asked when he came back and they set off along the road.

"More or less," he said. "But down here it's called a hammock. This one's called Bartram's Hammock, named after John Bartram, one of our early naturalists."

"I thought a hammock was a fish net strung between two trees."

"Good description. But to the Seminoles and maybe, farther back, the Tequestas, or even the Calusas, who, as far as we know, were the first people here, it meant home or cool place. The Indians liked living on hammocks. Their extra elevation keeps them from flooding very often, and the water surrounding them protects them from all but the worst fires."

Katherine pointed to the sparkle of water through the coffee bushes beyond the road and asked what it was.

"It's Puc Puggy Creek," he said. "You crossed it coming

in here. Puc Puggy is the name the Indians gave John Bartram. Actually, I don't think Bartram ever got this far south and west in Florida, but that doesn't matter. The Creek drains Stickpen Cypress Preserve. That has water in it all year round. Your husband's cabin is on the edge of the Stickpen."

"Jesus," Katherine said. "All I did was ask if this was an island."

"Listen and learn." Harry winked at the kids, who in their solemn way, appeared to be listening to him. "All the moisture means the Hammock can support a lot of trees, ferns, and other plants."

He waved his free hand over his head to indicate the tangle of trees and lianas under which they were walking. "Makes it a nice place to live. Lots of animals and birds. Warm in the winter, cool in summer. There are several springs in here that hold fresh water all through the dry season."

"And snakes, spiders, and flies."

"Those too."

They had reached her car, a heavily rusted gray Chevy Corsica. The front bumper on the rider's side was held up with a wire coat hanger. Harry poured gasoline into the tank, and told Katherine to crank the starter.

"Lots of snakes," he repeated, grinning at the kids.

"You ought to give guided tours of this place and charge a fee," Katherine responded, trying the engine without success.

"Let it rest a minute," he said. Then added with a straight face, "The engine, I mean."

She leaned back in the seat and looked at him, her expression softening.

"What's that accent I hear?" she asked.

"Maine," he said. "I've been down here twelve years, but I think I've got it for life."

"What did you do in Maine?"

"Game warden," he answered shortly.

"Now you paint pictures for a living?"

"Flattering suggestion. I'm a private investigator."

She made a face. "You married?"

"Not for a long time."

"Got any kids?"

"Two." He did not want a conversation about either his marriage or his children.

"Try the starter," he said quickly, before she could think of another damned question.

The motor caught. They drove back to his place in silence. He crossed the lawn to the safety of his old Land Rover with relief.

"You an antique car freak?" she called after him.

"You got it first try."

He pulled onto the sandy track in front of Katherine's car and drove off slowly to keep from covering her and the kids with dust. When he reached Tucker LaBeau's farm, he saw his old friend fitting new palm fronds into his hen house roof. He waved and Tucker pulled off his straw hat and waved back, his white hair floating in the sun.

The roof repair and Tucker's enthusiastic wave told Harry that Bonnie and Clyde, a pair of gray foxes who regarded Tucker's hens as their personal meat supply, had made another raid. Thinking about listening to Tucker describe the latest skirmish with the renegade foxes restored Harry's good humor.

A mile beyond Tucker's place, he turned off the road and scraped down the twisting, narrow track to Will Trachey's cabin. The track was almost smothered by Virginia creeper vines and wax myrtle bushes.

"What a shit hole," Katherine said in a loud voice, getting

out of her car and slamming the door.

He guessed her descriptive comment was for Trachey's benefit and grinned appreciatively, making sure the kids didn't see him. Most women, he thought, would have been flattened by what she appeared to have been through. But here she was on her feet and swinging. He liked that.

"There's probably worse places," he said.

"And worse cars. Mine, for instance."

She was staring at Will's late model shiny red Pontiac Firebird parked beside the cabin.

"That's for sure," he agreed as he studied the cabin huddled under the big fig tree.

"Well, where is the son-of-a-bitch? Willard," she yelled, "come out here."

Harry winced. Getting the reunion off to a warm start, he thought. But there was no answer.

"I'm going in there. Watch the kids."

"No," he told her firmly. "Let me go in first. You wait here."

She started to protest, but he walked away from her and kept going until he could see the back door. Nobody in sight. He retraced his steps until he could see the Stickpen water and Trachey's rickety boat landing. There was no boat tied to the cypress pilings or pulled onto the shore. Katherine stood glowering at him with her fists on her hips.

He went down to the landing and looked out across the slowly moving black water glinting under the silent trees. He turned toward the point where Puc Puggy Creek flowed out of the trees into the water meadow. Still no boat.

Something wasn't right. He began to feel very uneasy.

He pulled off his hat and ran his hand over his head. Where was Willard? He looked back at the landing. OK, there's no boat, he thought. He could be out in the Stickpen, but that wasn't likely. Trachey only went into the Stickpen to poach something or move drugs. It was the wrong time of year for most kinds of poaching and he hadn't heard any activity on the river overnight, so the drug option was pretty well eliminated.

"Come on, Brock," she called impatiently.

He heard her getting the kids out of the car and quickly walked back around the cabin. "I told you to wait."

She was striding towards him. "You afraid I'll find a woman in there? Hell, I used to come home from work and find them in my bed."

"I'm not worried about women. The people who come out here to see your husband are the kind you generally meet only in nightmares and Bruce Willis movies. And keep the kids away from the water. There's water moccasins down there."

"Christ!"

"I'll make it quick," he called as she ran back to the kids.

The screen door on the porch hung partly open, but he knocked on it anyway and shouted, "Willard, you in there? It's Harry Brock."

No answer. Half a dozen green and brown lizards were darting across the screen, snapping up emerald green blow flies swarming and buzzing around the door. High in the fig a mourning dove flapped noisily. Harry looked up, startled. He swore a little and went back to listening for sounds in the cabin. Nothing. Except for the dove calling, the cabin and the rest of the surrounding woods were silent as a painting.

Right, he told himself, taking a deep breath, let's go see what the bastard's up to.

He pushed open the door, scaring up a buzzing cloud of flies, and stepped quickly onto the porch. The cabin door was ajar. He crossed the porch, gave it a push, popped his head inside.

"God damn!" The stench drove him back onto the porch, his stomach trying to crawl into his throat. He ran along the porch to the nearest window and peered through the dusty glass. A long time ago he had found a trapper dead in his cabin. It was spring and the body had thawed. Harry knew what he was smelling.

Startled, he saw that the cabin had been wrecked. For a moment he thought a bear had broken into the place. But the destruction was too complete for even a marauding bear. The table and chairs were thrown over and smashed. The shelves along the walls in the living area had been knocked down and whatever was on them strewn over the floor. The cupboard doors in the kitchen end of the room were open and their contents broken and spilled across the counters. Between the stove and the bed, which was ripped to pieces, Willard Trachey lay sprawled on his stomach under a section of the broken table. The back of his pale blue shirt was black with blood.

"Anybody in there?" Katherine called.

She was coming across the sandy yard with Minna and Jesse in tow. Harry got out the porch door as fast as he could.

"Turn around and take the kids back to the car."

"Is Daddy in there?" Jesse asked.

"No, Jesse," Harry answered, looking at Katherine as he spoke, willing her to listen.

She hesitated for a moment, then turned and marched them to the car and put them into the back seat. By then they were both crying, but she rolled down the window, slammed the door, and backed the car into the shade of a big gumbo limbo. Then she got a couple of candy bars out of the trunk of the car and a can of warm Pepsi. The crying died down. While she did all that, Harry tried without much success to figure out how much to tell her. He was suddenly having trouble thinking.

"OK," she demanded, striding back to him. "He in there drunk? With a woman? What?"

He began to speak and faltered. Suddenly, the woman in front of him was no longer Katherine but Agnes Stone, holding open the kitchen door, her children crowding around her.

"What is it?" Katherine said. "You look like you've seen a ghost."

"It is . . . nothing. I'm sorry," he said when he could speak. "I thought for a minute . . ."

He shook his head, sweat sliding down his sides, and struggled to focus his thoughts. This has to be done, he told himself. Do it.

"Willard's dead," he said. "I'm sorry."

"Lord Jesus." She snapped her head around to look at the cabin.

"Can you drive back to my place?" he asked.

He knew it was a callous question, but he wanted her and the children out of there. They must not see what he had seen.

"Yes," she said, her unguarded face stiff with what Harry took to be fear. "But what are we going to do?"

"Call the Sheriff's Office, and we can't do it from here."

"What happened? How did he . . . ?"

"Not now," he said.

She looked at the cabin again. In a bitter voice stained with rage she said, "The bastard's run out on me again."

Chapter 2

Harry made the 911 call and gave the dispatcher the information she asked for. When he finished, Katherine was still sitting on the couch where she had dropped after coming into the house, dry-eyed, her face an expressionless mask. Minna and Jesse had found an old jigsaw puzzle on the bottom shelf of a bookcase and were quietly spreading the pieces on the floor.

"Do you want to call anybody?" he asked.

She shook her head.

"Can I call any of Willard's people for you?"

"Who would that be?"

"Family?"

"The few left alive are mostly in jail," she said.

He agreed without saying so that she was probably better off staying clear of her husband's relatives. An unmarked car drove into the yard. Harry recognized one of the two plain-clothes detectives who stepped out of it.

"Detectives from the Sheriff's Department," he said. She showed no interest in the car's arrival. "I'll take them to the cabin. Can you hang on here a little while by yourself?"

"If I have to."

He didn't think she ought to be left. He considered calling Tucker and rejected the idea. It occurred to him that there should be some woman he could call for help. But there wasn't.

"I'll be back as soon as I can," he said.

Katherine made no response.

"OK," he said. "I'm going."

"Go," she said, and he left.

"We met a while back on that cattle theft case in East Avola," the taller of the two policemen said in a deep drawl. "I'm Jim Snyder, Violent Crimes Division. This here's Detective David Herrera."

Jim Snyder was half a head taller than Harry, with big ears and a long face and cropped hair so pale he looked bald. David Herrera was shorter and heavier, with a shrewd intelligence in his dark eyes. Harry told the two men about Katherine Trachey and what he'd found at the cabin.

When Harry finished talking, Herrera asked, "Where is she?"

"Inside the house. But I think it's too soon to talk to her. Is there a woman on your team who could come?"

Snyder shook his head. "Everybody's tied up."

"You sure this guy's dead?" Herrera asked.

"Fairly sure," Harry said as he climbed into the Rover.

Harry stopped at the cabin door and let Snyder and Herrera go in. A moment later they were gasping and swearing and rushing through the cabin, shoving up windows and throwing open the back door to let the wind through.

"Looks like a twister touched down in there," Snyder said when the two men were back outside with Harry.

Herrera rubbed his hand across his face. "That much violence used to mean it was personal rather than professional. But now . . . who can tell?"

Harry nodded, his mind reverting to Katherine sitting in his living room, staring into despair. While the two detectives worked, he studied the wreckage as closely as he could without compromising the scene. All he garnered from his effort was more evidence that whoever killed Trachey had surely wanted him dead and had put a lot of work into wrecking the cabin. Why?

"He was down before they wrecked the place," Herrera said with a grimace when he and Snyder finished their preliminary examination.

"The table was on top of the body," Harry said.

Herrera nodded.

"For all the mayhem, there's not much besides the dead man to tell us anything useful. Maybe the forensics people in the Crime Scene Unit can ferret out something."

Snyder scowled. "And I don't think they're going to find much either."

"What was a young guy like Trachey doing living in this godforsaken place?" Herrera asked, pulling off his surgical gloves.

"He worked for Orville Boone," Harry answered.

"The developer doing the Avola Gold project that's causing all the stink?" Snyder asked.

"That's him," Harry said. "Trachey moved here about three years ago."

"Boone own this place?" Snyder asked.

"Boone owns most of Bartram's Hammock," Harry replied. "I lease from Boone. I tried to buy the place, but he's not selling."

"What was Trachey's job?" Herrera asked.

"I'm not sure. Caretaker? Someone Boone could call on to run an errand, deliver a message without attracting attention to himself?"

Herrera nodded and said, "He's developed everything else he's got his hands on, why not this place?"

"He'd like to, but that's all Stickpen Preserve." Harry pointed back at the cypress swamp. "And Tucker

LaBeau won't sell to Boone."

"Who's he?" Snyder inquired.

"We passed his farm on the way in here. You might have seen him working on his hen house."

"Oh, yeah. The old guy," Herrera replied. "Why won't he sell? He looks poorer than a church mouse."

"It's his home. And he doesn't like Boone or the way he makes his living," Harry replied.

"You, the old farmer, and Trachey the only people living out here?"

Harry said they were. Herrera nodded and said with a grin, "The three hermits." Then he asked, "What else can you tell us about Trachey?"

Harry bridled a little at being called a hermit. "He was seriously bent, but I don't know anything about him that would justify putting three bullets in his back and blowing half his head off. I didn't like Trachey, but I like less what was done to him. And I'd find it damned satisfying to . . ." With a bite of regret, he reminded himself, it wasn't his job to find Trachey's killer.

Snyder went to the car to call in their report, and Herrera and Harry walked down to the boat landing. Wind off the Gulf was bending the tops of the pond cypresses, scattering flakes of sunlight over the wet ground and the dark water.

Herrera took out his note pad and pointed to a deep V in the black mud. "Looks like a boat was launched here fairly recently. Might be how the shooter—or shooters—got away."

Harry studied the ground. "Only one set of tracks. But if there were others, they could have used the landing."

"Yeah," Herrera said, making notes. "The Crime Scene Unit will photograph all this, but I like to keep my own record."

He finished writing, closed his notebook, and turned away from the water and looked up at the soaring trees with a frown.

"This place is a jungle."

Harry tried seeing the Hammock through Herrera's eyes. The wind moving through the swaying branches was like the slow breathing of a huge animal. It was a sound Harry found comforting, but he saw it had the opposite effect on Herrera.

"It's complicated, if that's what you mean."

Harry checked his watch and wondered how soon he could leave and get back to Katherine.

"You like living in this place?" Herrera asked.

"Yes," Harry said.

Herrera shook his head.

"Takes all kinds."

He walked quickly over the damp, spongy ground, making for the sunlight in front of the cabin. Harry followed, noting that Herrera didn't like the swamp either, and spoke in the Hammock's defense.

"This is a special place. Boone and his people could destroy it in a month. But it couldn't be restored in a hundred years, maybe never. The good news is a lot of people want this hammock kept just as it is. The Florida Wildlife Federation, the Corps of Army Engineers, the Tequesta County Audubon Society, and the South Florida Water Board are all working to stop it from being developed."

Herrera showed interest. "Isn't that guy Luis Mendoza heading an anti-development group?"

"That's right. As president of The Preservation League, he's a major player, maybe the major player, along with the groups I just mentioned."

Snyder advanced on them through the bright sunlight with long, slow strides. He was sweating, and the heat had turned his ears a bright pink.

He stepped into the shade and wiped his face with a freshly ironed red and white checked handkerchief.

"What did you find out?" Herrera asked.

"Trachey has a charge sheet longer than Leviticus." Snyder carefully refolded his handkerchief.

"Anything in it to suggest why he was killed?" Herrera inquired.

"No. He hasn't served any time. There's a bunch of charges for possession of a controlled substance, DUIs, a couple of assaults and batteries, some bad debts, but he wiggled out of all of them. Looks like he's got a friend with a lot of reach."

"He's got a lot of bad acquaintances." Harry nodded toward the swamp. "Mostly, they get in here after dark, by boat. Draw your own conclusions."

"See any one person more than others?" Herrera asked.

"A guy about Trachey's age drives in two or three times a month. Rides a black Trans Am with custom painted yellow and red flames on the hood and the sides."

"Got a name?"

"No. But he sports a Florida Panther tag."

Herrera made another entry in his notebook and turned toward the swamp.

"What does the water out there hook to?"

"Puc Puggy Creek. You saw it at my place and crossed it getting onto the Hammock. A few miles west of the county road it feeds into the Seminole River. The river runs southwest past Avola and out through Oyster Pass into the Gulf. It's navigable by small boats all the way to here and through the Stickpen."

"Do you think boats come in here carrying drugs?" Snyder asked.

"What else?" Herrera snapped.

Snyder consulted his notes, and his drawl grew a little more pronounced. "Let's just see. There's poaching, illegal possession of wild animals, birds, reptiles, and snails. What would he be doing with snails?"

"*Liguus,*" Herrera said before Harry could. "There was some stuff in the department about them a while back. Colored tree snails. Threatened species. Eradicated in some areas. Their shells differ from one tree island to another. Some people will pay a lot of money for them." Harry was impressed.

"What about the other things?" Snyder demanded.

Herrera looked at Harry.

"Snyder says you were a game warden. Was Trachey a poacher?"

"Probably, but I don't have any proof."

Snyder shook his head.

"I could see skins and snakes and so on, but drugs?"

"The Stickpen borders I-75 about nine or ten miles northeast of here," Harry began. "It's an easy run for a boat."

A white Cadillac sedan swayed into the clearing and bobbed to a stop behind the detectives' car. Harry swore silently. More delay. He wanted to get back to Katherine. The man who got out of the Cadillac looked to be in his early fifties. He was taller than Snyder, broad shouldered, and heavy. His belly flowed over his belt, but he strode toward them with the assurance of a powerful man.

Harry recognized the outfit before he did the face. The western style straw hat, western boots, tan pants, and a brightly colored shirt were his trademark. Today it was a blue, short-sleeved shirt with cream colored dolphins leaping all over it. It was a rare day Orville Boone's picture wasn't in

35

The Avola Banner. Or on the local TV news. By the time he reached the three men, his broad face was glistening with sweat.

"I'm Orville Boone," he said when he stepped into the shade. I got a message from Sheriff Fisher saying Cousin Philmore's boy Willard has been shot. I'm hoping Bob was wrong, but I suspect that's not the case. Where is he? How bad is it?"

Smooth and effective, Harry thought. Without making a point of it, Boone had let the detectives know their boss Sheriff Robert Fisher made Boone a personal call, that he and the Sheriff were on a first name basis, and that Trachey was family, establishing his reason for being out here.

"I'm sorry, Mr. Boone, but Mr. Trachey is dead," Herrera said. "He's been shot, but we don't yet know if that was the cause of death. The body is still in the cabin. I'm afraid you won't be able to go inside."

Boone puffed out his cheeks with a fleeting look of annoyance and shook his head. Harry guessed the developer did not like being told what he could and couldn't do.

"Lord, that's a shame," he answered, quickly restoring his geniality. "I took him on for Cousin Philmore's sake. Not that Philly would know anything about it. He's been dead for about as long as young Will's been alive. I hardly knew the boy, but I believe he's been associated with a certain amount of trouble?"

"Hold on," he said, cutting himself off, the accent thickening. "I forgot myself. Let me shake hands with you all and get your names."

As Herrera made the introductions, Harry studied the developer. His reputation said he was a ruthless son-of-a-bitch. But Harry had other reasons to dislike him. When a piece of Boone's land was developed, it was drained, bulldozed, and covered with condos, strip malls, and asphalt.

The massive Avola Gold project he was launching with open houses, cocktail parties, and double-page advertising in the *Banner* was only his latest, and most ambitious and controversial, development scheme. From what Harry heard, Commissioner Emile Thibedeau was his chief cheerleader on the Tequesta County Board of Commissioners, the agency that issued all the County's development permits.

Trying to be fair, he reminded himself that he leased his house from Boone and had never had an unpleasant moment in the relationship. Of course his only contact with his landlord had been through Boone's law firm. Nevertheless, when the developer grasped Harry's hand, he asked if Harry was still enjoying the house. Slick, Harry thought.

"I considered living out here myself," Boone said. "But it was too far from town."

When he reached Snyder, he paused a moment, lifted his hat to scratch his head, and asked if he was related to a Eugene Snyder from Tallahassee. Snyder's long face split in a pleased grin.

"He's my great uncle Orion's grandson," Snyder said happily.

Boone said he had done business with Eugene and thought highly of him. Then he and Snyder explored a little further to see if they had any relatives in common. Herrera listened with a puzzled frown. Odd, Harry thought. Why, at a time like this, would Boone be talking kinfolk?

When the subject was exhausted, Boone grew more serious and said with a pained expression, "God damn, Will was a little wild, but why would anyone want to murder the boy?"

"We hope to find that out, Mr. Boone," Snyder said. "Could you help at all?"

Boone shook his head. "No, the truth is, I hardly knew him."

Herrera cut off Snyder's follow-up question. "Trachey worked for you, isn't that right, Mr. Boone?"

"That's right."

A little testy, Harry thought.

"Kept an eye on things out here for me." Boone looked away and spoke to Snyder. "But he was pretty much free to come and go as he wanted."

"Then I'm probably wrong to think you're the one who's been keeping him out of jail," Herrera said.

Right through the bullshit, Harry thought. Snyder's eyes widened in shocked alarm. Boone's eyes narrowed briefly, but he smiled his way into a quick recovery.

"Some of my people might have helped him out," he replied. "I don't always get told. Sometimes not near enough. I had no idea things were that bad. Saying that reminds me there's a wife and kids somewhere."

"They're at my house," Harry said. He made a mental note of Boone's evasion of Herrera's question.

Boone frowned at Harry. "I hope they didn't walk in on him."

The calculated drama of the statement irritated Harry.

"Mr. Brock found the body," Snyder said. "He kept Mrs. Trachey and the children away from the murder scene."

"Much obliged for your help, gentlemen," Boone said abruptly. "I'll be going, and if it's all right with you, Mr. Brock, I'll stop in and see if there's anything I can do to help Willard's family. It is surely a shame."

It wasn't all right with Harry, but he didn't see an acceptable way to say so. Boone shook hands all around again, and Harry thought he saw Herrera flinch when Boone grasped his hand.

"Touching," Herrera said. He stood flexing his fingers as they watched Boone's car disappear into the green tangle of shrubs and vines. "But what was he really after?"

Snyder responded sharply. "You heard him. Will was his cousin Philmore's son."

"What do you think, Brock?" Herrera asked.

"I'm not sure, but I'm betting he knew the answer to every question he asked before he asked it, including whether or not Katherine Trachey had seen her husband's body, and, possibly, that Carol June Boone was Sergeant Snyder's great aunt."

Snyder protested loudly, but Herrera laughed.

"I think Brock's right." He was still flexing his hand.

"That Boone's doing?" Harry asked him.

The detective forced out a hard grin.

"*El Jefe* was reminding me where the beef is," he said.

Chapter 3

Harry swung around the ancient live oak on the corner of his lawn, shut off the engine, and let the Rover roll to a stop. To his disgust, Boone's Cadillac was still in the yard. He sat for a while, letting the silence settle around him, swearing to himself.

He found Katherine and Boone in the kitchen. Katherine was making the kids lunch. Boone was leaning comfortably against the sideboard with his arms folded. Looming against the window, his bulk dominated the room. Harry felt the hair on the back of his neck prickle and wondered if his sense of menace was coming from Boone's physical presence or something in the man's cold gaze that belied his moon-faced smile.

Katherine was taking a ham and a loaf of wheat bread out of the refrigerator and paused to tell Harry she had made him a salad and a ham and cheese sandwich. "They're in here," she said.

Minna and Jesse were pitching into cucumber and egg salads. Harry noticed that her voice was stronger and her face had regained some color. Without knowing why, he found her going about her work as if she belonged there disconcerting.

"That salad is good," Boone said with a loud laugh. "This young lady knows her way around a kitchen. I long for one of those ham sandwiches, too, but I'm having to be careful."

Boone's fake bonhomie irritated him, and he turned away from the man.

"I'll eat later," he said.

Katherine put the bread and the ham on the cutting board, wiped her hands on the dishcloth, and with Boone giving her smiling encouragement, said, "Mr. Boone is going to have the cabin fixed up for me and the kids, and he's going to give me a job."

Harry knew he should say what good news that was, but he was so disgusted by what she was telling him, he managed only a tardy, "Great." By then, she had turned back to the sideboard and was slicing the sandwiches as if she was killing snakes.

His disapproval, which he regretted not hiding from Katherine, hung in the air like a bad smell. Boone's smile slipped. While a part of his mind was warning him that what she did was none of his business, the rest of his mind went right on insisting that whatever Boone did for her would put her in his debt. And he wanted to ask Katherine what Boone's benevolence was going to cost her. If he was right, the final price would be very high.

Boone snatched his hat off the counter and as he passed her dropped a big hand on her shoulder. "You just come along to my office when you get finished here. I'll have everything arranged."

He paused in the door and looked at Harry. "Just don't let this Yankee tree-hugger put any foolish ideas in your head. Y'all take care now."

Harry was not fooled by the bantering tone. Boone's stare was granite hard. Katherine followed Boone onto the lanai, then came back looking as if she'd walked her last mile. She pulled her braid over her right shoulder and stood holding it and staring miserably out the window. Harry lost all desire to criticize her for accepting Boone's offer.

"Can we talk about something in the other room?" he asked.

She turned and stared as if surprised by his presence, then nodded and carried the sandwiches to the table.

When they reached the living room, she dropped onto the couch. "Are the police finished up there?"

"No. They're just getting started." He sat down beside her. "The two homicide detectives are with Willard and the County Medical Examiner soon will be. When she finishes her work, he'll be moved to the County morgue. Later today or tomorrow, the police may ask you to make a formal identification."

"Would you go with me if that happens?"

"Yes." He was surprised by her request. "If you want, I'll go for you. And you're welcome to stay here until the cabin's ready."

To make the offer, he'd had to stifle the voice telling him to get her out of his life.

"Mr. Boone's making arrangements for me to stay in town," she told him. "I'll be starting work as soon as I can find someone to look after Jesse and Minna."

Katherine sat with her hands clasped tightly in her lap.

When Harry didn't respond, she said, "Why don't you say what you've wanted to say ever since I told you Mr. Boone is giving us the cabin? You think it's a bad idea."

Harry tried unsuccessfully to think of something to say that wasn't a lie and wouldn't hurt her feelings more than he had damaged them already.

"OK," she said angrily into his silence. "It's none of your business, but maybe it will help you understand what you're dealing with here. After Jesse and Minna came along, Willard Trachey began knocking me around. He kept me without money, ignored the kids, except when he was yelling at them, and then one day while I was at work, he left with the car and the cookie jar. I've been on my own ever since."

She paused, took a deep breath and launched herself again, her voice growing more brittle as she spoke. Harry forced himself to sit still and listen. But it was an effort. He wanted to tell her Orville Boone was so crooked the snakes wouldn't have him, and that if he was giving, he was taking.

"With two kids and no money, I had to go on welfare," she continued. "That was so goddamned humiliating, I began working again at any job I could get. My last employment was a highly skilled job in a converted garage. I worked nine hours a day stitching logos on T-shirts, but I could keep Minna with me. Half of what I earned went to day care for Jesse. Then the garage burned down, and I decided to come on down here and try to work things out with Willard."

She stopped and after a struggle began again, her voice shaking.

"When you told me Willard was dead, I was just about ready to stick the Chevy's tailpipe in my mouth. We've been living in the car for a week. My money's gone. There was nothing to go back to and nothing to go forward to. Then here comes Mr. Boone and he gives me a place to live and the offer of a paying job."

She paused and Harry decided she was making sure she had his attention.

"I'm listening."

He had been listening so hard, in fact, he had forgotten about issuing warnings. Instead, he kept asking himself what kind of glue had held her together this long?

"Good," she snapped, "because I'm saying this just once. I know what you're thinking. And I'm telling you that whatever he wants from me, he can have it, every day of the week if that's what it comes to. If that's what it takes."

Her eyes filled with tears, and with a choked cry she covered her face with her hands, fell against the couch, and began to cry as if every sob was tearing her flesh. Harry got his arm around her and held her. He didn't try to comfort her with words. What the hell good would they do?

Her tears, he thought, had been a long time coming. Maybe years. He did not notice he no longer wanted to step back from her pain. If this was my daughter . . . , he thought, his heart giving a lurch. And in that moment, a wall that Harry had been building between himself and the world for the past dozen years crumbled as suddenly as if Joshua's people had walked around it with rams' horns blaring.

Then Jesse pitched into him, fists flying.

"You leave my mother alone," the boy shouted, punching and kicking Harry as hard as he could.

"It's all right, Jesse," Katherine cried, pulling away from Harry and reaching for the child. "It's all right. Mr. Brock's not hurting me."

"You're crying! You're crying!" the boy shouted, his face wet with tears.

Minna ran into the room, yelling and crying and tried to scramble over Harry and the still battling Jesse in an effort to reach her mother. After a struggle, Harry got Jesse off him and into his mother's arms. Then he passed Minna to Katherine. Katherine pulled both children to her and held them, rocking them, quietly talking them down.

Harry, feeling as if a small tornado had hit him, brought her a box of tissues from the kitchen, and she wiped Minna and Jesse's faces and blew her own nose.

"Thanks," she said to Harry with something that might have been an attempt at a smile as she released them. "I'm sorry about Jesse."

"No need to apologize. He was worried about you. He's a brave boy."

He didn't say that the child must have seen her being hurt a lot to become that protective.

When Katherine had the children settled again with their lunches, she faced Harry across the table. "Look, about what happened in there. I'm sorry. You didn't have to hear all that . . ."

"Forget it," he said. Something in him was scrambling over the pile of rubble, trying to put the wall back up. Making an effort, he asked, "Do you feel any better?"

"Yes," she said, "I think I do, a little."

"Good." He was relieved, but he still thought her deal with Orville Boone stank of brimstone, and he prayed without much hope of being heard that Boone would not have occasion to call in his chip.

Then Snyder and Herrera returned. They talked with Katherine on the lanai while Harry sat reluctantly with Minna and Jesse, feeling all the time he should be with her, making sure the two detectives didn't take advantage of her. He knew all too well that in murders, the closest members of the family were the most likely suspects.

When she came back to the kitchen, he asked her how the questioning had gone.

"It went," she said. Stone-faced, she began to clear the table.

Harry said he'd do that later, but she ignored him. She seemed determined to get herself and the children out of the house as fast as possible. When the table was cleared and the dishes washed, she herded the kids out of the room and marched them across the yard to the car.

Closing the car door, Harry passed her a piece of paper with his phone number. He suddenly felt embarrassed and self-conscious.

"If you need any help or just want to talk, call me."

"OK," she said. She relented enough to give him a quizzical glance before starting the car.

"You know how to get where you're going?" He thought it was a foolish question but wanted to say something. And he didn't want her to go.

"I'd better." Harry took her answer to be an effort at humor. But she didn't smile and neither did he. She reversed the car. "So long," she said.

"Take care." He stepped back and watched her leave, dragging a funnel of dust.

As it blew away across Puc Puggy Creek, Harry became increasingly disgusted with himself because, instead of feeling relief, which was what he had been expecting, he felt seriously let down and, worse still, lonely.

Chapter 4

Three days after the murder, two of Boone's trucks, piled with tools and equipment, lurched and rattled down the Hammock road past Harry's house, stirring up clouds of dust. A dozen Latinos in long-sleeved white shirts, chinos, and straw hats sat perched on the loads wherever they could find space. They returned Harry's wave as they rocked past.

Harry told himself he was glad Katherine had not called him. It meant that things were going so well with her he no longer needed to be concerned. Also, being by himself for three days gave Fortress Brock time to partially resurrect itself. It was a shaky structure, but he did not let himself dwell on that or what had flattened his defenses in the first place.

Later in the day, Herrera and Snyder knocked on his door. Harry was working on his painting. He had given up on the egret, scraped it and the water away, and started over. It was too hot to paint on the lanai, and he had retreated to his second floor studio. He took the two detectives up to the room so that he could clean his brushes while they talked.

"That looks pretty good," Snyder said, planting himself in front of the painting, his gangling frame canted to one side, eyes squinted. "The cypress look a little peaked, but I like the seagull."

"It's a heron," Harry said, screwing the top onto his turp jar.

Herrera opened his notepad. "The water's too green. But I guess you can paint it any color you want."

Snyder drew down the corners of his mouth. "Water's supposed to be blue."

"The Gulf's more green than blue, especially in the summer. It's the lime dissolved out of the coral that does it."

Harry started to say it was Puc Puggy Creek and not the Gulf, but Snyder made his long face longer and straightened up to his full height. "In a painting, water's supposed to be blue. Our old creek was brown ten months of the year, and the other two it didn't run at all. You can't go around painting a creek brown or with no water at all in it. What would that look like?"

Snyder's ears were getting red when Harry broke in and asked what had brought them out here.

"We've got to take a statement," Herrera said. "I know it's a little late, but we got busy, and the time drained away. Just like the water in Snyder's creek."

Snyder bridled. "Don't go passing remarks on that creek. One spring my daddy took a channel cat out of it that weighed twelve pounds. Lord, it was good eating."

Harry put away the last of his brushes and interrupted Herrera trying to put in his stick. "Let's go where we can sit down. I'll get us some coffee."

When they were settled in the living room, Herrera said, "This is mostly about time. Specific time."

Harry thought for a moment. "Katherine Trachey got here a little before eight. I was painting on the lanai."

When Harry had given the two detectives everything he could remember, Snyder leaned back in his chair and scratched his head. "There's something that doesn't fit. She told you she'd just driven down here from Tallahassee?"

"I don't think she said where she'd come from," Harry answered. "She did say she and the kids had been sleeping in the car for a while."

Herrera checked his notes. "She came here from Talla-hassee. She'd been here a week before Trachey got hit. She and those two kids were sleeping in the car in Henderson's twenty-four-hour truck stop off I-75 and eating out of the Winn Dixie."

"She say why?" Harry was troubled by what he saw coming and wanted to say something in her defense, forgetting he wasn't supposed to be concerned any longer about her, but found himself stuck for a helpful comment.

Herrera grinned. "She said it was none of our fucking business where she slept."

Snyder shook his head. "Those children were right there when she said it too. Oh, there's something else. The crime scene people found five guns in the cabin. Under a trap door in the floor. Three hand guns and a couple of Chinese auto-matic rifles. Probably takes care of where the murder weapon came from. What in the world was he doing with all that hard-ware?"

"Protecting his home?" Harry asked.

Herrera laughed.

"Has the Medical Examiner got a time of death?" Harry inquired.

"She's saying he'd been dead four days. She could do a quick estimate by checking the maggots and the development of the blow fly eggs." He paused. "You know Maria Bene-dict?"

Harry thought Herrera looked uneasy asking the question and wondered why. But he nodded and let it go.

Snyder screwed up his face. "I'm glad we didn't turn him over."

"Is Katherine a suspect?" Harry had been waiting for them to tell him without being asked and had run out of patience.

"Everybody who has means, opportunity, and motive is a

suspect." Herrera snapped shut his notebook and got to his feet.

"I could have walked down to that cabin and back in under an hour," Harry said.

Snyder sighed. "We know. But the motive isn't too good. Of course you're pretty strong on the conservation thing. And Mr. Boone's been making you people pretty mad."

"He's been making Luis Mendoza mad, that's for sure," Herrera added. "Whacking Trachey might have been a way to send Boone a warning."

"And, of course, Katherine Trachey's motive is plain as a bear's bathroom habits," Harry said.

He did not like being thought a suspect, but he found he liked the idea of Katherine being one even less, although he knew her name would be high on the Sheriff's list.

Herrera chuckled. "You got that right. Her and you."

Harry saw them out the door. "I'll be here painting the Gulf a little too green in case you want to Miranda me."

"Let us know if you plan on leaving town," Snyder replied.

Herrera turned back. "The guy in the black Trans Am? Slade Hatfield, more generally known as Splinter. On account, so we're told, of that thin bladed knife he carries."

After they left, Harry was tempted to call Katherine. But just as quickly he suppressed the impulse. What was there to tell her? That she was a suspect? She would find that out soon enough, if she didn't know already. It was not his business, a familiar voice told him. Leave it alone.

Four days later, Harry got a late afternoon call from Luis Mendoza. He knew Mendoza only slightly through the Preservation League, but the call was still a pleasant surprise. Mendoza was a hydrologist, and from what Harry knew of his work, a good one. As most people did, Harry associated

Mendoza with aggressive opposition to the wholesale development of Tequesta County, which had already turned parts of Avola into the poured concrete and stucco horror of Florida's east coast.

"Harry," Mendoza said in his cultured voice after giving his name, "forgive me for troubling you, but I've got a problem."

"I'll help if I can, Luis." Harry expected to be asked to serve on a Preservation League committee or organize a call-in.

"Thank you," Mendoza said. "Let me tell you why I may need it. I have become a suspect in Willard Trachey's murder."

"Have you been charged?" Harry asked in surprise. The Sheriff's Department had moved unusually fast.

"Not yet, but I've been warned to keep myself available and not to leave Avola. Detectives Herrera and Snyder were very polite, but I am not deceived." Harry wondered if they'd had a similar talk with Katherine. "Trachey's boat was found hidden in a clump of leather ferns on a wooded part of my river frontage. Naturally, the police want to know how it got there. I told them I had no idea. It appears there was a handgun in the boat. I suppose it will prove to be the murder weapon."

Harry recalled that Mendoza lived in River Run, a tony suburb five miles north of Avola. The Seminole River formed the east boundary of the community, providing Mendoza a direct link to Trachey's cabin.

"There are things connected with this situation I would like to talk over with you. Things I don't want to discuss on the telephone. Can you get away?"

"Sure," he said. "Where?"

"The Avola Country Club. The one on 41."

"OK, but let's hope it's not Bikers' Night."

Mendoza seemed not to hear the comment or, Harry thought with some amusement, didn't know what he meant.

"Is forty-five minutes satisfactory?"

"I'll be there."

Driving to the club, Harry felt a stirring of interest. It was possible the boat had been left where it was found to implicate Mendoza in the murder. But what interested Harry more was the risk the person had taken. River Run was a gated enclave with its own security system, manned gates, and patrol cars doing twenty-four-hour surveillance. At any hour the person walking away from that boat and out of River Run, unless he was a resident of the place, would almost certainly have been stopped.

Harry did not think that Mendoza had killed Trachey. And after a little reflection he concluded there was not enough evidence to indict the engineer. Unless, of course, the police knew something he didn't.

With growing interest, he moved on to wonder why Mendoza had chosen a roadhouse as rough as the Avola Country Club for a meeting. Grinning, Harry decided Mendoza probably had never been in the club.

As he and Harry slid into a booth, Mendoza looked around with a worried expression. He had to raise his voice to be heard over the heavy metal roar of the jukebox. "It's going to be a little hard to talk."

He was a small, trim man approaching sixty, with a receding hairline and a scrupulously trimmed mustache. He was dressed in impeccably creased fawn-colored trousers, polished brown loafers, and a maroon Ralph Lauren shirt. Harry thought no one would mistake him for a regular patron of the Avola Country Club.

Scarred wooden booths lined both sides of the no-fly zone

that subbed as a dance floor. A long oak bar, backed by a mirrored wall and tiers of shelves stacked with bottles, made up the inside wall of the Club. In front of the bar and spilling out onto the dance floor, a shouting crowd of bearded men and tank-topped women, who had ridden in on bikes or pickups with dual exhaust pipes, were getting the evening under way with rebel yells and hog calls that rattled the windows.

Their waitress was way too big for both ends of her orange uniform, but neither that nor a missing front tooth had dampened her spirits. "It's roast shoat night," she boomed. "The name's Lisa. You want any of that pig, you better get it now." She pulled her pencil out of her big, yellow hair and laughed loudly. "The way this crowd is sucking down the booze, in another half hour there ain't going to be nothing left but the curl in its tail. It's good, too. I already had some."

She returned with glasses, plates, a heaping platter of pork, a giant pitcher of beer, red sauce, and a stack of paper napkins. Harry noticed she had taken a shine to Luis, and, when she put down his plate, she leaned way over and gave him a big smile and extra napkins. Then she straightened up, winked at Luis, and hurried off, leaving him with his face shining like an exit sign.

"You've got an admirer, Luis."

"I am flattered." Mendoza pulled his eyes back to the table. He pushed the plate of pork toward Harry. "Somebody's trying to set me up and I'm worried. The police don't seem very sympathetic to the suggestion. Perhaps I shouldn't be surprised."

He went on talking, laying out the situation as he saw it. Harry listened carefully while he ate, resorting to the beer whenever the sauce blurred his vision. After Luis stopped speaking, Harry fell back from the platter, wiped his mouth, and doused the fire in his stomach with more beer.

"They don't have much incentive to be sympathetic. The police, with some exceptions, tend to support the developers. Increased budgets, raises, new jobs, and promotions come from building homes and businesses, not from preserving swamps. Nevertheless, I think you've got a friend in Corporal Herrera."

"I noticed his interest," Mendoza said. "But Detective Snyder was pressing me pretty hard."

"Why?"

Mendoza shoved himself against the back of the booth and scowled uneasily. "Because during the time when Trachey is supposed to have been killed, I was at home working on a hydrology report for Glastonbury and Frick."

"Where was your family?"

"That afternoon my wife was in Boca giving a speech. Our daughter was at school. We were together for dinner. Then Isabel and Constanza went to a school play. I stayed home, working."

"A lot of time alone."

Mendoza shrugged. "The question is, who's doing this to me? You knew Trachey pretty well. It's got to be someone connected to him."

"You're right about one thing. That boat may have been pulled onto your land by someone who doesn't know you from a hole in the ground."

The barbecue and beer may have slowed Harry's reaction time a little, but he was sharp enough to see Luis didn't have much of a case for believing he was being framed.

"Ever hear of a Slade Hatfield?" he asked. "Herrera and Snyder say he goes by the name of Splinter."

Mendoza showed no interest. "He works for Emile Thibedeau. He runs Sampson's Marina, Thibedeau's dock and boat storage place on the east side of the river south of the bridge. What's he got to do with this?"

Harry was surprised by the information.

"Probably nothing. His name came up. Look, whoever popped Will probably did get away in the boat. He might even have gone in by boat. That doesn't mean there's no case against you, Luis. But if the gun comes up clean, it should all go away."

"It's not going away, Harry. Too many people want me silenced. Orville Boone has posted a ten-thousand-dollar reward for information leading to the conviction of his nephew's killer." Harry whistled. "Nephew!" Mendoza snorted. "If Trachey was his nephew, I'm his uncle. But the money's real. He would spend a lot of it to have me out of his hair."

Harry agreed. Luis and his Preservation League had filed for a restraining order to halt Orville's Avola Gold project, and despite repeated challenges, the courts, to everyone's surprise, had refused to throw out the League's suit.

Harry thought about Mendoza's story. "Boone's got deep pockets."

"I hear he's hurting for cash," Luis said. "He needs that Avola Gold project."

More interesting news. Harry was still exploring it when Luis spoke again, his voice deepened by the intensity of his feelings.

"I want your help with this thing. I'll give you salary, expenses, whatever you need. I'm scared, Harry. I don't frighten easily, but this scares me. Will you do it?"

Harry had not seen it coming, and the offer gave him a rush of pleasure. Will Trachey's murder had put some hooks in him. And he respected Luis Mendoza. If anything was going to save southwest Florida from committing suicide with a cement mixer, it was men like Mendoza. And there was something else. During their conversation Harry had felt a growing connection to Mendoza. And now he knew what the connection was. He had once stood in Mendoza's shoes and been unjustly accused of murder. Of course, he had actually killed a man, but he had done it in self defense. Nevertheless, he knew what Mendoza was facing. Sympathy for the man moved strongly in him.

"I'll work for you, Luis," he said, "but there's something you've got to understand. If I find anything significant that links you to Trachey's murder, they get it."

Mendoza stared at him for a moment then nodded and put out his hand. "Agreed."

Harry gripped it with satisfaction. To his surprise he found himself, for the first time in a long, long while, wishing there was someone besides Tucker to share the news with. Then he thought, trying to make a joke of it, Maybe I'll tell Katherine Trachey.

Chapter 5

When Harry got home, there was a message on his answering machine from Katherine Trachey. His day was suddenly brighter. He dialed her number.

She answered and went straight to what was troubling her without any small talk. "They never asked me to identify Willard. And nobody's told me what's happened to him. Not that I care."

Of course she cared. But he knew her well enough to know how hard she would find it to say so.

"Boone probably identified Willard. They're understaffed and just didn't bother to tell you. The Medical Examiner will call you when all the tests they're running are back from the state labs."

She seemed stuck.

"How are things going?" he asked.

She laughed, but Harry didn't hear any amusement in it.

"Well, we're sleeping in beds and I'm working. Jesse and Minna are in day care."

"Tell me about your job."

"Why?"

"Because I'm interested."

"Oh." There was a short pause. "Well, I don't have any title yet, but I'm learning to use the computer. I'm typing letters, answering the phone, and filling in wherever Helen Bradley needs me."

By the time she finished speaking, some enthusiasm

had crept into her voice.

"Do you like her?"

"Bradley? Why? Do you know her?" She sounded angry again.

Coping with her, Harry thought, was like trying to pick up a wet cat. "Yes, I know her. We've met at some Audubon events."

"She's OK. Are you and her . . . ?"

"No!" His answer was a lot more abrupt than he had meant it to be.

"Jesus, Brock, lighten up."

"Sorry. Aside from the work, how are you?"

"OK, I guess. I don't know. I feel weird, and sometimes I just start bawling. Like I did at your place. It makes me mad, but I can't help it."

"If you want to cry, you probably ought to." Harry winced. Was that all he could say?

"You licensed?" she asked.

"To do what?"

"Give advice to the recently bereaved."

"Sharp," he said. "Very sharp. Actually, I shouldn't advise a rabbit on its personal life. What I'm licensed to do is spy on cheating wives and husbands, find out if people are filing fraudulent insurance claims, and locate rustled cattle."

She laughed a full, rich laugh he hadn't heard before. Harry found himself smiling at the phone and quickly stopped. He had some news he wished he didn't have to give her.

"Luis Mendoza is probably going to be charged in your husband's death, and he has hired me to try to prove he didn't kill Willard. You're going to find out, and I want you to hear it first from me."

"Why should I care?"

58

"Well, my helping Luis could increase police scrutiny of you."

"Are you saying you think I killed Will?"

"No. No. Absolutely not. But if I can prove Luis couldn't have killed him, the rest of the people on their list are going to be looked at a lot more closely."

"That's all right. I didn't kill him. Although I had reasons enough to do it."

"Don't say that to anyone else." He felt a jump of fear for her. "For what it's worth, I don't think either you or Luis Mendoza shot Willard. But for political reasons, he's a target. You're a target because you're the person closest to him."

He expected her to be upset. She wasn't. She was sharper than he thought.

"For my own reasons, I want very much to find out who did kill your husband."

She let that pass. "From what I hear at work, Orville would like to see Mendoza cut up and fed to the pigs. Why is that?"

"Because Mendoza is trying to stop Boone from completing the Avola Gold project."

"OK. I know about that. Why do you care who killed Will?"

He answered carefully. "First, I care because whatever his failures, Willard didn't deserve to die the way he did. Second, I owe you, myself, and everyone else, and the Hammock in particular, my best shot at finding out who killed Willard Trachey."

"The Hammock?"

"Yes." After groping a little he found the rest of the words he wanted. "The Hammock is a special place to me, and in some way I'm not sure I can explain, Willard's murder has disrupted its harmony. Finding out who killed your husband would go a long way toward repairing the damage."

"OK, I guess I can understand that." She went on speaking in a stronger voice. "Look, I called to thank you for taking us in the way you did, offering us a place to stay and all. I know you didn't have to do it, and I want to say for me and the kids that I'm real glad you were there."

It sounded to Harry like a rehearsed speech. She had probably been so long without help that she had almost forgotten how to say thank you.

"No thanks necessary. I mean, I'm just glad I was there. And, by the way, the bill's in the mail."

"Smart ass."

"Look, if you and the kids want a change from the city life while you're waiting for the cabin to be repaired, give me a call. We could have a picnic and take the boat out onto the river."

"Thanks for the offer." She seemed to be stuck and finally said thanks again.

"You're welcome," Harry said. He was still smiling when he hung up.

The next morning Harry began thinking seriously about how he should begin looking for Willard Trachey's killer. After several false starts he decided to talk with Tucker LaBeau. Tucker was a walking library of Tequesta County history, and it was background that Harry felt he needed. Context, he told himself, was all.

He found Tucker picking caterpillars off his waist-high tomato plants. Harry approached Tucker's garden thinking he could be looking at the cover of a seed catalogue. At the same time, he felt, as he always did, that he was entering a different and better world than the one surrounding it. Tucker thought Harry's view highly romantic and said so.

Sanchez, Tucker's big blue-tick hound, was lying in the shade of a tall, umbrella-shaped oleander at the corner of the garden. Harry was surprised not to see Oh-Brother!, his friend's black mule. Harry doubted that Tucker had ever been a big man, but age had shrunk him to a thin strip of sun-dried leather with half a halo of white hair drifting over his ears and a pair of sparkling blue eyes. He had a prominent nose, thin as an axe blade. Marching down the row with his blue shirt and conspicuously patched overalls flapping around his wiry frame, Tucker looked to Harry like a runaway scarecrow.

"Where's Oh-Brother!?" Harry asked.

"Patrolling the perimeter." He gave a cheerful laugh as he shook hands.

"Are we talking about a mule here or a person?"

Tucker wasn't phased by the question. "He's trying to get a lead on what Bonnie and Clyde are planning next. They got us pretty good this last time. Sanchez still hasn't recovered."

Hearing his name, the dog raised his big, lumpy head without turning it and barked once. Then he dropped it back onto the grass and thumped his tail a few times on the ground.

Tucker scowled. "Never own a Spanish speaking dog who picked up English as a second language. Makes 'em too temperamental." Then, recovering his grin, he asked Harry what had pried him out of bed so early.

"I need to talk to you."

"Got time to look at the hen house roof first?"

"Sure." Harry was eager to hear about the raid.

He had reluctantly come to see the foxes' raids as having some of the mythic qualities of the best of Uncle Remus. As they crossed the shaded yard, Tucker gave an enthusiastic account of Bonnie and Clyde's latest raid. In Tucker's story the two foxes had, in addition to their mythic elements, all the color and dash of the Hole-in-The-Wall gang.

Tucker stopped by the hen run, where a dozen gray-and-black-barred Plymouth Rock hens scratched energetically in the dirt. They clucked companionably to one another under the watchful gaze of a huge, red-wattled rooster with a scored and scabbed bare spot on his back as wide as Harry's hand.

Tucker regarded his rooster with a doleful shake of his head. "It was a close call for Beauregard. The way I see it, Bonnie broke into the hen house while Clyde was trying to steal Sanchez's big hog bone off the back stoop. Sanchez was asleep, and Clyde managed to pick up the bone, but it was too heavy for him to carry, and he dropped it. That woke Sanchez, and set him roaring."

Harry liked to think he took Tucker's dog and fox stories with a very large grain of salt, but he was already caught up in the narrative and had gladly suspended his disbelief.

"Meanwhile, Bonnie was tangling with Beauregard when she heard Sanchez bellow." Tucker pulled out his orange handkerchief with a theatrical flourish and blew his nose. "Beauregard was taking more killing than she'd anticipated, and realizing Clyde had tripped the alarm, she grabbed a pullet, so as not to leave empty handed, and jumped back out the hole she'd made in the roof."

"Well, it looks strong enough now," Harry said, squinting against the sun at the foot thick covering of green palm fronds and the hairnet of wire stretched tightly over the new thatch.

"I've double braced the posts and buried the bottom of the fence two feet in the ground. But where Bonnie and Clyde are concerned, nothing's final. Just when you think you're driving them, they're coming up behind you. Let's go get some tea."

"What can you tell me about Orville Boone?" Tucker had settled them on his back stoop.

Sanchez came trailing around the house. He climbed the stairs slowly, slouched into the stoop's deep shade, and collapsed with a thump onto the floor as if he'd been shot.

Just then, Oh-Brother! came around the house from the other direction wearing his straw hat. Tucker had cut holes in the hat's brim for the mule's ears. Harry waved to the big animal without thinking there was anything odd in his action. Oh-Brother! waggled his ears at Harry. That didn't surprise Harry either.

Oh-Brother! walked along the stoop and gave the sleeping hound a push with his nose. Sanchez lifted his head and glared at the mule. But Oh-Brother! persisted, and after a moment Sanchez groaned and struggled onto his feet. After some further silent communication, the hound and the mule went off around the house together.

"Oh-Brother!'s got something he wants to show Sanchez," Tucker said. "I'll hear about it later. That was a bad thing about Will Trachey. Herrera and Snyder stopped for a talk. But I couldn't tell them much. I want your take on what happened down there, but first, what's your interest in Orville Boone?"

"I'm curious about his connection with Willard Trachey."

"Kin of some kind," Tucker answered. He took a long swallow of tea and sighed contentedly. Harry eyed his tea suspiciously. It was the color of mangrove water and strong enough to walk on.

"Orville's got kinfolk all over this country and clear up to eastern Tennessee," Tucker added. "That's where all the Boones around here came from at the turn of the century. Drifted down here and began living off the country. Did a little farming. A lot of hunting. Some trapping and fishing.

Nothing too tiring. Raised corn enough for meal, seed, and whiskey."

Harry crossed his ankles and leaned farther back in his chair. He wanted the information but was more interested in just listening to the old man talk. He remembered very clearly that when he had first come to live on the Hammock, it was Tucker who had more or less put him back together. And the farmer accomplished that by making him weed the garden, then sit on this back stoop, drink his dire tea, and listen to stories about the early settlers of Tequesta County. Gradually, the terrible images and memories that made Harry's own thoughts a hell were exorcised by Tucker's voice and the quiet labor of tending to living things. Harry was profoundly grateful to his unassuming friend.

"You've come to a good place," Tucker had told him when the worst of the nightmares were purged. "Just don't let it turn you into a hermit the way it has me."

Harry had thought at the time, and not seen any reason since then to change his mind, that Bartram's Hammock and Tucker LaBeau had saved his life. Harry had laughed at the idea of his becoming a hermit. There was no chance of that happening to him.

"I doubt Orville had a pair of shoes until he was most grown," Tucker continued.

"Are you saying Boone's family lived off the land, or that his people way back did?" Harry asked.

"Both. Orville never had any schooling to speak of. By the time he was twelve or thereabouts, he had turned full time hide hunter. Alligators mostly. Made some money and joined the Army. Then, in the seventies, when he came back, he bought a boat and started gill netting.

"He got tired of fishing, bought a thirty-foot launch, and rode it to the east coast, where he began picking up marijuana from freighters offshore and running it into Fort Pierce and other places. When he'd put together enough cash, he came back here and started buying land. Then he started a construction company. He could just about sign his name. But look where he is now."

Harry thought for a while about what Tucker had said and then asked him if Boone had stayed straight since those days. Tucker drained his mug and wiped his mouth with the back of his hand.

"I guess he stopped running drugs, but clawing his way up made him flexible, if you take my meaning. And turning into a developer gave him a lot more space to be flexible in."

"I think Trachey was floating drugs through the swamp to I-75," Harry said. "You figure Boone had a piece of that?"

"He might have, but I didn't hear the police say anything about finding drugs in the cabin."

"Neither did I." Harry moved on. "You hear any shooting the afternoon or evening Trachey was killed?"

"No. Being inside the way they was . . . As you say, there's been a lot of stuff going on up there. But, hell, you know that. Slade Hatfield called a lot. All hours of the day and night."

"I've seen him." Harry shifted ground. "I'm still finding it hard to understand why Boone was so interested in Will. Or why he's rebuilding the place and putting Will's wife and kids in the cabin. You got any thoughts about that?"

"Orville's a little cracked on the subject of family," Tucker said thoughtfully. "He don't really fit in with that crowd he's running with. All them moneyed people. He spent most of his young life alone in a swamp, poling a john boat, shooting and skinning alligators. Then he got shipped halfway round the world, given a rifle, put in a jungle, and told to shoot whatever moved. My guess is his adjustment to civilized life is damned fragile. His parents are dead. His marriage is busted.

He's got no kids. He just might be trying to convince himself he really does have a family."

Harry nodded. That could be it. Maybe.

After leaving Tucker, Harry made some calls and drove to the Goodnight Complex in Avola. The Complex was an office and shopping mall development off the East Trail. He had a ten o'clock appointment with Maria Benedict, the Tequesta County Medical Examiner, in the County's new morgue. As one of the County's public information people told him proudly when he called for directions, "It was either build a bigger morgue or buy a hell of a big freezer."

The comment, Harry knew, wasn't much of an exaggeration. Tequesta County was growing by twelve thousand residents a year, and visitors in several multiples of that number were spending the winter months there. As a consequence, a lot more people were leaving again by way of the morgue.

"This is a nice surprise, Harry." Maria Benedict led him into her office. "What brings you way over here?"

She was short and trim with straight, black hair and equally dark eyes. She wore a white lab coat over a maroon blouse and navy skirt. Harry felt a familiar tug of pleasure as he greeted her. They worked together now and then on fundraisers for the Audubon Society and other conservation groups. And once again he wondered why they hadn't become better friends.

"I need some help."

"Sit down." She motioned him toward a chair.

He had reached her office down a white-tiled corridor cold enough to raise goose bumps on his arms, but the temperature in her office was comfortable, and a pleasant smell of furniture polish replaced the faint stench of formaldehyde permeating the rest of the building.

"What do you need to know?" She returned to her desk chair.

"I want to know when Willard Trachey was killed."

Harry liked her office. She had hung colorful pastel prints of garden corners, boats, and cockatoos on the oyster white walls. In a blue vase on her mahogany desk, she had arranged branches of flame-colored bougainvillea.

"Life in the midst of death," she said, noting his interest and speaking with surprising seriousness.

"Speaking of life in the midst of . . ." He looked out a window at the adjacent office tower with a faint stirring of resentment. "It's hard to believe that just a few years ago this area was all woods and had a substantial deer herd."

"I suppose pictures are a poor substitute for the deer." She spoke a little stiffly. "Now, why are you asking about the time of Will Trachey's death?"

"It's not your fault the land was developed. Luis Mendoza hired me to prove to the police he didn't kill Trachey."

Maria listened to him intently.

"Are you qualified to be doing this?" she asked.

"I'm licensed. I'm not sure I'm qualified."

She regarded him closely and not, he sensed, with full approval.

"Harry Brock. A private investigator." She leaned back in her chair, increasing the distance between them. "Well, well."

"What?"

Her shoulders rose and fell. He took a card out of his wallet and laid it on the desk in front of her. She regarded it with apparent distaste.

"You knew I was a game warden. Once upon a time."

"Yes. Now you're a painter and an environmentalist."

"And a private investigator."

"I know Luis Mendoza. I respect what he's doing, has done. Does he really need this kind of help?"

"He thinks he does." Harry thought he was beginning to understand her hostility.

"That's not a straight answer, Harry."

"He does."

Harry knew very well that Luis Mendoza was one of the Hispanic community's leading figures. Harry also knew the strains that existed between the Anglo and Hispanic communities in Tequesta County. Maria's prickliness reminded him just how sensitive the situation was.

"I don't believe he killed Trachey," Harry said. "But it may take me a while to prove it."

"Forgive me, Harry." She came around the desk and dropped into the chair beside him. "I'm shooting the messenger."

"It's OK. I found Trachey on May fifth. Sergeant Herrera told me you are giving the first as the date he was shot. Is that right?" She nodded. "Did he die from the bullet wounds?" She nodded again. "Can you tell me when on the first he died?"

"That is not so easy, but I would say he died on May first, between three and eleven p.m."

"Could you support that in court?"

She sat a little straighter, a slight frown clouding her face.

"Of course. Otherwise I wouldn't have said it."

"I know that. It's just that the time of death may become a major hinge in deciding who could have and who couldn't have killed him."

"Such wretched business."

Harry assumed she was thinking about Luis's involvement and said he agreed.

"Did your autopsy turn up anything else I might find interesting?"

"I don't think so. There were traces of cocaine use, but I suspect that was not unusual. He was a healthy young man, carrying a little too much fat, perhaps. He had been smoking for a number of years. That had, of course, affected his lungs."

"But the police found no drugs in the cabin."

"Strange."

"Very." Harry stood.

Perhaps Snyder and Herrera hadn't been as forthcoming as he'd thought. If not, why not?

"Thanks for the help," he said.

"You're welcome." She walked him to the door. "I hope it helps Luis."

"So do I," he answered.

When Harry got home the phone was ringing.

"You want a picnic?" Katherine Trachey asked.

"I asked first," he answered.

"No boats."

"OK, but you can't swim in the creek. There's too many snakes."

"Have you turned comedian?"

"Sorry. What have you got in mind?"

"No swimming, no boating, no alligators. This one is limited to lemonade, egg salad and ham salad sandwiches, cucumbers and tomatoes, potato chips, and brownies, and the brilliant company of me and two bratty kids."

Harry suddenly felt about twenty years younger.

"It's not the kids who are bratty. Where do you want to go?"

"Your lanai in an hour, and watch your mouth. Then I want to see how the work is going on my cabin."

"Fine." He grasped that Katherine was paying him back

for helping her and the kids through the day she came looking for Willard.

"You got any ice?"

"Enough for the lemonade."

"I'm on my way."

She hung up. In the ensuing silence, his years came back, but her voice left him with a distinct lightness of spirit.

After they finished eating, he and Katherine carried the dishes and what remained of the food into the kitchen. They had eaten under one of the big oaks and accumulated a variety of ants, lacy-winged katydids, and a variety of small creatures, including a pair of Anole lizards that found the tablecloth a rich hunting ground for flies. Minna had insisted they carefully put all of the ants and the other bugs back on the ground.

"What a pest," Katherine said, pretending to be annoyed, but Harry wasn't fooled.

Katherine had vetoed again Harry's suggestion they go out in the boat. And after the children had tried playing in the yard but given up because the sun was too hot, she put them in the living room with their new electronic games and Minna's new dolls. Then she and Harry carried their coffee onto the lanai.

Katherine folded herself into a lounge chair. "Things are going pretty good. My job is OK. The kids are signed up for the school they'll be in this fall. Orville even got a new transmission put in my old junker, and I feel safe driving it again."

"I'm glad things are working out for you." He tried to sound upbeat.

He was pleased to see her feeling more in control of her life, but he was not happy she was involved with Boone. So he forced himself away from that subject and risked having an ear chewed off by asking why she had been living out by the Winn Dixie for a week before showing up on the Hammock.

"The police have been talking to me. I expect you know what about."

"They want to know why you were living in your car."

She gave him a frowning look of appraisal and nodded.

"That and whether I came in here the night of May one and shot Will. I told them I swam up the creek out there with a gun in my teeth and blew the bastard away. They didn't think it was very funny. Do you?"

The edge was back in her voice.

"I guess I'm more interested in why you'd tell Herrera and Snyder something like that." Harry tried to keep his face straight, but kept imagining the look on Snyder's face when he heard her answer.

"Ask a dumb question, get a dumb answer," she replied.

"Why did it take you so long to come looking for Willard?"

Jesse exploded out of the house with Minna tearing after him.

"Snake's after the redbird!" he shouted. "Can we go see?"

Harry looked at Katherine.

"If Mr. Brock will take you."

Harry turned to Katherine. "Want to come?"

"You go along. Just don't let them get bitten."

"Safe as houses." He shepherded the jumping kids out the door.

As the children skipped ahead of him toward the sea grapes where the cardinals were nesting, Harry thought what a miracle sleeping in a bed and eating proper food had worked on them.

The cardinals, chipping loudly, flew out of the sea grapes at their approach. Harry knelt on the soft ground and slowly parted the branches. A gleaming four-foot yellow rat snake was twisting his tawny length up through the sea grapes, black tongue darting in and out, testing the air for the smell of a warm nest and its eggs.

"See it?" Harry asked.

The children were so absorbed in the twining snake they barely nodded.

"Hold the branches for me, Jesse," he said.

Then he reached slowly into the bush and grasped the snake behind its head and carefully unwound it from the branches. Once clear of the bush, it convulsed into loops and curls in its efforts to escape. The two children drew back but were too fascinated to be very frightened. A moment later, the snake grew quiet. Harry looped the snake around his arm and held it toward the wide-eyed children.

"Touch it. It's warm and silky and dry. Go ahead. It won't mind. You won't hurt it."

"Is it poisonous?" Jesse asked.

"No," Harry said. "It's a constrictor. It kills its food by squeezing it to death."

They inched forward and put out their hands. A moment later, they were leaning against Harry, talking to the snake and gently stroking it. Harry watched them with a tangle of feeling he made no effort to unscramble.

"Now we'll let it go," Harry said, not wanting the moment to end but guessing the snake had enough stress for one day. "It won't hurt us. Are you ready?"

He lowered it to the ground. Minna and Jesse caught their breath as the snake lay for a moment in the thin grass, glowing like a golden rope, slowly unlooping its length. And then it released itself like a spring and raced away across the grass toward the trees. Minna hopped across the grass in its wake.

"My father's not coming back, is he?" Jesse asked. He

stared bleakly after the snake and his sister.

The question caught Harry short. "What does your mother say about that?"

"She just said he's gone away. But he's not coming back, is he?"

"Do you remember him at all?" Harry stalled, trying to decide how to answer the boy.

"A little. I saw him at the truck stop. He and Ma talked. Then he drove away in the red car we saw at the cabin. Why did he go away without his car?"

"Are you sure it was your father?" Harry was startled by what the boy had told him.

"Sure. Ma said it was. How did he go away without his car?"

"I don't know, Jesse. You'll have to ask your mother about that." Harry decided it was Katherine's choice what the boy should be told, but he still felt bad about lying to him. He felt even worse hearing that Katherine had been talking with Willard at Henderson's Truck Stop.

Minna trailed back to them, beginning to miss the snake.

"Will it come back?" she asked.

"I wouldn't," Jesse said sadly. "Not if I'd been caught like that."

Harry wondered if Jesse was commenting on his father's disappearance but saw no way to respond.

"It lives here," Harry said. "We'll probably see it again."

They walked back toward the porch door, Minna and Jesse holding Harry's hands. Minna was full of ideas about the snake, but Jesse was silent, lost in his own thoughts. Harry worried about what the boy was thinking but told himself again the issues surrounding his father's death were between Jesse and his mother. Katherine, standing in the door, watched them approach with an expression on her face

Harry couldn't read.

She shaded her eyes with a hand. "Looks like you did all right."

"Hard to miss with a snake show," he replied. His cheerfulness was forced, but Katherine didn't seem to notice. Showing the kids the snake, talking with them, and holding their hands had produced in Harry a tangle of emotions. Memories of his own children at Minna and Jesse's ages came flooding back, trailing pleasure and pain in their wake.

Minna had the last word on the snake.

"I 'spect it's a prince," she said with satisfaction. "He's much taller than me."

The kids wanted a ride in the Rover, so Katherine agreed to let Harry drive them to the cabin. Repairs on the building were going forward slowly. But as Harry walked around inside the cabin, with all its window frames out and sections of walls and roof removed, the sharp, clean smell of new wood did not rid the place for him of the stain of death.

"I'm not going to be moving this week." Katherine climbed morosely into the Rover.

Harry turned into the narrow track and bumped out to the road. "Are you sure you want to be out here at all?" He was thinking about the fact Katherine had lied to him. She had lied to the police, and if it hadn't come down to quoting Jesse against her, he would have straight out asked why.

Katherine slumped in the seat. "It goes to what I told you before. My big three choices were welfare, a high place, or Will. It took me a while to decide which one I'd choose."

The kids were bouncing on the seats, playing some kind of guessing game.

"The police will think about your choice and see the possibility that he turned down your request for help, and you shot him." Harry knew he was being harsh, but he hoped by being tough on her she might tell him about talking to Will.

"Where would I get the gun?" she asked. "Where were Minna and Jesse?"

"He had a damned arsenal out there. I don't know about the kids. Left them in the car?"

"I guess you don't know about me either," she said. "Not if you think I could have done that."

"I'm only telling you what the police are probably thinking. What they're paid to think."

She flashed him an angry look. "Their sticking that on me would make things easier on Mendoza."

"The odds that he killed Willard are about the same as those that say you did. I'm trying to make sure he doesn't get blamed for something he didn't do. If he did kill Will and I find out before the police, I'll turn him in."

"Is that supposed to make me feel better?"

Harry braked for a foot-long gopher tortoise that broke out of the ferns on the left side of the road and clumped single-mindedly across the sandy road in front of the Rover.

"Turtle! Turtle!" Jesse and Minna shouted.

"One nature lesson a day is all I can stand," Katherine protested. "Christ, I don't know if there's room enough out here for us. The goddamned place is stuffed full of animals."

Harry tried to make himself heard above the racket. "It's a gopher tortoise. Turtles live in the water. Tortoises live on land."

Minna and Jesse began chanting, "Tortoise, tortoise." The name had struck them as funny. They collapsed in laughter.

Katherine spun around on the seat to face him, her green eyes blazing. "I'm not asking myself if I want to live out here. I'm here because the place isn't costing me anything, not even the utilities. In comparison to where we were living, this cabin is going to be a palace."

"Has he told you what he's got in mind?" Harry asked.

"What do you mean?" she demanded.

"Boone's got a dozen places he could have put you. Why out here?"

Doubt clouded her face and was just as quickly replaced by a flush of anger.

"He didn't say, and I didn't ask."

Harry was not sure he believed her. "You're going to have to explain to Jesse pretty soon what happened to his father."

He started to tell her what Jesse had asked him while they were looking at the rat snake, but Katherine interrupted him. Pale with anger, she swung around on the seat and shouted, "Mind your own fucking business."

Chapter 6

Harry drove them back to his place in silence, Katherine glaring through the windshield and the kids whispering to one another in the back seat. If she had slapped his face, it wouldn't have cleared his mind any quicker. His I-told-you-so voice was piling abuse on him and on her with indiscriminate glee.

As soon as the Rover stopped, the kids jumped out of the car. "We're looking for the rat snake," Jesse called over his shoulder as he and his sister left at a run for the rear of the house.

They both sat staring through the windshield as if they were cemented to their seats. And while he sat, Harry managed to wrestle his anger and insulted pride down far enough to hear himself think. And the first non-angry thought he had was that finding Trachey, telling her he was dead, and going through with her what had followed had forced them into an intimacy they weren't ready for.

"I'm real sorry about what I said back there," she said. Her voice was hoarse with strain. "I'd like to take it back."

"Sure," he said. "Not your fault anyway. What you tell or don't tell Jesse is not my business."

He said it and almost believed it. But what he was saying had only part of his attention. He was remembering the completely deserved abuse his wife had heaped on him after the shooting, and he knew that, deserved or not, he never wanted to go through it again. Not with anybody or for any reason.

"It's no excuse, but I guess I'm still not right as I should be," she continued. "And Orville did say what he wanted from me. Or some of it anyway. He told me he needs someone out here to keep an eye on things."

She paused long enough to give him a quick look. She must have been satisfied with what she saw because she went on speaking.

"Don't ask me what things I'm supposed to be looking after." She still sat rigid as a statue. "Maybe it's you or old LaBeau or the goddamned gopher tortoise." She cut him another glance. "Until you asked, I thought he'd said that to make it easier for me to take the place." She gave a short, harsh laugh. "Fat chance I was going to say no."

"Maybe he wants the place lived in," Harry said, forcing himself to accept the olive branch she was offering him.

"Sure." Her voice rose. "He rebuilds the place just so he can move me in there to give it the lived-in look. How smart does that sound to you?"

"Forget I asked," Harry said, making sure he didn't sound dismissive. "What can Boone expect you to do? Really, let it go."

In fact he had no idea what Boone wanted from her, and, at the moment, he was even ready to believe Tucker might be right, that Boone was doing it because he needed to believe she was a part of his family. And less romantically, it might be he needed for legal reasons to have the property lived in while he maneuvered for permits to develop the Hammock.

"OK." She relaxed a little and took a deep breath.

Harry tried to get beyond the fact she had lied to him. "Thanks for the picnic."

"Thanks for showing them the snake." She managed a smile.

She's ten years older than my daughter, Harry thought suddenly, regarding her with admiration. When she sheaths her sword, she's flat-out beautiful, and aside from her looks, she's got moxie enough for an army.

"What is it?" she asked.

He scrambled out of the truck. "Nothing," he said.

They walked to the house and gathered up her picnic basket and the kids' gear from the kitchen and the living room and carried them back to her car. She called to Jesse and Minna.

"Come back soon," he said as he put her things in the car. "We'll do some bird watching."

She herded the kids into the back seat and turned to grin at him. "How will I stand the excitement?"

When they were out of sight, Harry went back to the house and began painting. He told himself he was not going to think about Katherine or Will's murder. It didn't work that way. She and the two children and the day mingled with the paint, the colors, and the way the light fell on the canvas. He painted swiftly until he was too tired to concentrate any longer.

As he cleaned his brushes and put away the paint, he asked himself again if he believed Katherine's assertion that it had taken her a long time to decide to see Trachey. Was she actually capable of killing anyone? He dismissed the second question. No one knew what another person would do, pushed hard enough. He felt marginally better sticking with Herrera's trinity—motive, means, and opportunity.

Still telling himself he was being objective, he admitted there was plenty of motive. As for means, there were guns in the cabin. The one used to kill Trachey could have been lying on the table. Opportunity? Sure. She could have shot Trachey, and driven out. Her appearing at Harry's door four days later could have been staged to give herself cover.

Harry was almost certain Jesse had not seen the cabin

before the morning he found Trachey dead. Could she have left the kids at the truck stop? Sure she could. Trashed the cabin? Possibly. But what about the boat?

Harry saw no way she could have committed the murder using the boat. Unless she had an accomplice. But who? No. He dropped the idea with relief. Rules one through five: stick with the simplest solution until it proves inadequate. Besides, he told himself, shouldering aside his objectivity, Katherine Trachey did not kill her husband.

Whoever shot Willard used the boat. The killer escaped from the cabin in the boat and left it and the gun behind Luis Mendoza's house. That was the simplest explanation. So far as Harry could see, the only problem with the theory was getting the shooter to the cabin, which was solved if the killer had ridden to the cabin with Trachey. And that meant he knew the person who shot him, probably knew him well.

Harry had unplugged the phone while he painted, and now he went into the living room to plug it in again and found the message light blinking. He punched a button and heard Herrera's voice.

"Give me a call."

The dispatcher patched him through to the detective.

"What are you doing in the office?" Harry asked. "Shouldn't you be out fighting crime?"

"Paperwork. Snyder's here too. Look, I want to ask you how come I have to hear from office gossip that you're working for Luis Mendoza? Is it true?"

"It is."

"Why?"

"Why not?"

"You're not off the hook on this Trachey murder, you know."

"I know, but I have the feeling your people are a lot closer to tagging Luis than me. Am I right?"

"Maybe. Are you still cooperating with us?"

"Of course."

"OK, let's run a test. What has Katherine Trachey told you that we ought to know?"

"She didn't kill her husband."

"How do you know?"

"Because if the gun you found in Trachey's boat is the murder weapon, there's no way she could have shot him."

"We haven't heard from ballistics yet."

"And this is another freebie." Harry was enjoying himself. "If the gun is the murder weapon, Luis couldn't be the killer either."

"Because he wouldn't be idiot enough to leave the gun in the boat. Not with a river to throw it into." Herrera recited the words as if they came from a song.

"Right."

"Unless that was what he wanted everybody to think."

"Maybe," Harry admitted. "But would you do it? With a river at your feet?"

Herrera ignored Harry's question. "Tell me about Katherine Trachey."

"She says she was at the truck stop because she couldn't afford to stay anywhere else. As for why she waited so long to see Trachey, she says she couldn't make up her mind whether or not to do it. I'm inclined to believe her."

"Maybe it's the truth," Herrera said. "But just before she and Trachey broke up, she threatened him with a gun. Seems she chased him out of the house with it and took a couple of pops at the car while he was making his getaway. Neighbors called the police. The judge gave her a warning and dismissed the charges."

"Where did she get the gun?" Harry asked. He found he

was more pleased than alarmed by the story.

"It belonged to Trachey. He had a license for it. If you can believe it, he was working for Wells Fargo at the time."

"I believe it." Harry considered telling Herrera what Jesse had said about seeing his mother and father talking at the truck stop and decided he would tell them when he had to.

"When do you expect to hear from ballistics about the gun in the boat?" he asked.

"I don't know. They're backed up."

"I'd like to know the results when you do get them."

"You will. But you may not like it."

The next day Harry decided to talk to Slade Hatfield. His talk with Herrera had left him uneasy. And the more he thought about it, the more curious he had become about the connection between Hatfield and Commissioner Emile Thibedeau. Perhaps Hatfield really was, despite his unsavory reputation, a skilled marine engine mechanic, a breed scarcer than hens' teeth. But the answer didn't satisfy Harry.

He found Hatfield in the small second-floor office of Sampson's Marina and Boat Storage. The rickety wooden building leaned precariously over the river on oyster- and algae-caked pilings. The office was an unpainted plank construction suspended among rows of stored boats swung on cables from the building's roof beams. The stairs to the office swayed and creaked so much under his weight Harry was tempted to think, a little weirdly, he was on an old windjammer.

"What do you want?" Hatfield turned away from the window when Harry rapped on the half open door and stepped into the office.

Hatfield was tall, three or four inches taller than Harry, thirty-five or so, lean, with a thin nose, pale blue eyes, and nondescript brown hair hanging on his shoulders. He stood beside a beaten-up wooden desk with a can of Miller's in one hand. The other hung by its thumb from the waistband of his jeans, which were greasy enough to stand alone. The room was empty except for a battered refrigerator, a couple of aged spool chairs, and an ancient swivel chair.

Harry gave Hatfield his name and wondered if it was worth trying to find a good way of approaching the sullen shit glowering at him.

"Trachey and I were neighbors." He showed Hatfield his identification. Hatfield ignored it. "I'd like five minutes of your time," Harry continued. "And I'm sorry about what happened to your pal."

"Who says he was my pal?" Hatfield slouched around the desk.

Harry took a moment to look through the grimy window behind Hatfield at the jumble of shop and marina roofs along the ramshackle waterfront. He took in the view while he made up his mind about something.

Over the years, Harry had run into a lot of Slade Hatfields. He usually encountered them in the woods where they were trapping illegally, meat hunting deer and moose, dynamiting trout pools in brooks, or in a dozen other ways indulging their greed, stupidity, and penchant for destruction. And they were usually armed with weapons a lot more dangerous than the knife this jillpoke was supposed to be carrying.

"I don't give a fuck whether you were his pal or not, Hatfield," Harry said evenly. "I'm just trying to find out who killed him. You want to help me or not?"

Hatfield set the beer on the desk, rocked up onto his toes, tipped his head back in a yawn, and ran his hands through his hair.

"You a detective?" He dropped back onto his heels, kicked

a straight backed chair toward Harry, and dropped into the swivel chair behind the bare desk.

"Private investigator."

"You're working for that prick Mendoza."

"You know anyone who might have a reason for killing Trachey? His cabin was just about torn down from the inside out. It was so bad it looked personal."

Hatfield suddenly showed interest, started to say something, then changed his mind.

"Yeah. That greaser Mendoza."

He laughed with his mouth wide open at the joke. His teeth, Harry noticed, were as good as Katherine's. He thought he would like to put a foot into them.

"Aside from Mendoza."

Hatfield stopped laughing and pulled his ear. The silence stretched far enough to persuade Harry the young man was thinking. Judging by the puzzled frown on his face, it was hard work.

"Will and I done some things together." Hatfield paused to drink from the can and set it back on the desk. "He was all right. We had some good times."

He leaned forward and put his elbows on his knees and looked at Harry from under his brows.

"Will was in business. You know what I'm saying? Some mean dudes used to show up at his place. I don't scare easy, but those fuckers . . . Man."

Words failed him and he sat shaking his head.

"You mean the ones who came in by boat?"

"You seen them?"

Harry nodded.

"This is just between us. I ain't going to remember nothing about them or this conversation if it comes to the law. You understand?"

"I hear you," Harry said. "Why was Trachey working for Orville Boone?"

"Well, hell, he was a relative, wasn't he? But he just about never did see old Orville," Hatfield said with another open-mouthed laugh. "I couldn't figure why the man had him out there. Shit. That Hammock didn't need no looking after." He paused and snickered. "Maybe Will was the one needed looking after."

"What do you mean?"

"Old Will had a lot of sides. Mr. Thibedeau thought Orville was making a mistake keeping Will out there on the Hammock."

"The Commissioner have any particular reason for thinking that?" Harry asked.

"Mr. Thibedeau plays his cards close. But he didn't like Will. That's for damn sure."

"How well did he know Trachey?"

Hatfield stood up.

"Don't know. Don't care. I got work to do."

Harry nodded, decided not to press him, guessing Hatfield had caught himself talking too much. He could find him if he needed him. He thanked him for his help and got as far as the door when Hatfield stopped him.

Hatfield frowned. "There's a lot of people saying Mendoza killed Will. He's in a bad place. It might be a damn good time for him to disappear."

"He got anything in particular to be concerned about?" Harry realized Hatfield was giving what he thought was good advice.

"Shit happens, man," he said seriously.

"To the just and the unjust," Harry replied. The faces of Luis Mendoza and Willard Trachey flickered in his head.

Chapter 7

Some of Harry's most hopeful moments occurred when he was standing in front of a primed, empty canvas, his brush raised to make the first stroke. After that, it was more often than not a struggle between him and the sinister force that cramped his hand, muddied his browns, and transformed the glory of his vision into linoleum. But, in compensation, the labor usually cleared his mind. Not today, however, and after an hour of barren struggle, he fell back in disgust, totally blocked.

Frustrated, he decided to take a look at the pair of barred owls nesting in a big cypress a mile beyond Willard's camp. He tried to encourage himself by saying that on his way to the nest he would go over his conversation with Slade Hatfield. There was something about that interview that had left him unsatisfied. Maybe walking and thinking he would decide why.

He was just leaving the house and pulling on the disgraceful piece of once-white canvas he called his hat when Herrera turned into the driveway in a Sheriff's Department pickup, trailing an aluminum boat with a fifteen-horse Johnson on its stern.

"Oh, shit," Harry said.

Herrera got out of the truck. "Where are you going?"

"For a walk." Harry shook hands with the detective. "What's all this?"

"How about taking a ride with me instead? What are you grinning about?"

Herrera had traded his pants and jacket for denims, topsiders, and a green T-shirt. The cotton Floppy he had on his head was not a complete success.

"You working undercover?" Harry asked.

"Cut the shit." Herrera's face bloomed. "You want to go or not?"

"Where?"

Herrera jerked his thumb over his shoulder toward the creek.

"We put the boat in at Trachey's place. Then we time ourselves down to Mendoza's. I'm not too keen about doing this on my own, and Snyder got dragged into a murder/suicide over in East Avola."

"Sure."

"Snyder should be free in another couple of hours. If he's not, the dispatcher will send somebody to pick us up."

With Mendoza exposed as he was, Harry had planned to do what Herrera was suggesting. Of course, it might put a rope around his client's neck. Harry tossed his shoulder sack into the cab and climbed in after it. Herrera looked relieved.

When they reached the cabin, Boone's crew saw Herrera in the pickup and began cheering.

"Friends of yours?" Harry asked.

"Very funny."

The men scrambled down from the roof and called the rest of the crew out of the cabin to help launch the boat. The ground behind the cabin was too wet to support the pickup or its boat trailer, but the ten men easily picked up the boat, carried it to the water, and launched it bow first with another cheer.

Harry saw Herrera hanging back. "Sit up front, unless you'd rather run the motor."

"No." Herrera continued to look worried.

As the men called on him to hurry, the detective stepped gingerly into the rocking boat and, to their delight, made his way to the bow in a bent-over crawl. Harry's Spanish was limited, but he understood the enthusiastic warnings the men were giving Herrera about the size of the alligators in Puc Puggy Creek. And the six-foot water moccasins. Then in a ragged chorus came mention of the hundred-pound gars waiting to grab him if he trailed a hand in the water or fell out of the boat.

Herrera was too worried about getting to his seat to respond to the laughter and comments. He crawled onto his seat like a man clinging to a high beam. Harry got in, grinning in spite of himself, as the men added more encouraging commentary for Herrera about the gringo and the creek's inhabitants. Still laughing, they pushed the boat out onto the black water. Harry swung around on the seat to start the outboard and the boat tilted.

"Jesus!" Herrera shouted. He had a death grip on the gunwales.

"Si! Si!" the men called encouragingly from the shore. "No hay Jesu en la marisma."

Harry kicked the engine into life amid a ragged cheer. The prow lifted under the thrust of the propeller, and the boat slid smoothly through the trees and out into the channel. Herrera freed his left hand long enough to check his watch.

"Nine-ten," he said loudly.

Harry nodded and throttled the engine down to a low purr.

"Whoever killed Willard probably did it between three in the afternoon and eleven at night on May first," he said.

"You've been talking to Maria Benedict." Herrera tried to look at Harry over his shoulder.

Harry wondered why Herrera sounded offended.

"Turn around if you want to. It's safe. You know those guys back there?"

The detective inched around, scowling suspiciously at the water.

"No, never saw them before, but they're probably related to my wife."

Harry pretended he hadn't seen anything unusual in Herrera's sloth-like maneuver. "I'd bet a lot that whoever killed Trachey waited until it was dark to leave the cabin and come down the creek."

"Throttled way down," Herrera said. "By the way, this motor's a fifteen, same as the one on Willard's boat. Seemed odd to me."

"Didn't you ask for a motor with the same hp?"

"Sure I did, but why was Trachey running such a wimpy engine? Hell, some of the fishing boats have a hundred and fifty, two hundred horses hanging off them. What's he doing with a fifteen?"

"You need a small engine in here," Harry said. "It's shallow. There's no current to speak of, and you want to travel quietly, especially if you're taking the occasional low profile trip through the Stickpen to I-75. And there are places in there where it's so shallow you'd have to pole the boat or get out and pull it with the motor tipped up."

They had come out of the shade cast by the tall bald cypress and were slipping quietly through the smaller and more scattered pond cypress. In the ragged patches of saw-grass, red winged blackbirds were swaying on the tall stems and singing loudly. Water lilies made a dark green mat along the shoreline. The morning wind was sending small, dark ruffles across the water and rustling the cattails. Herrera, apparently relaxing a little, risked a look over the side of the boat at the dark water.

"This fresh water?"

"For another mile or so. Then it gets pretty brackish. You'll be able to tell. The cattails disappear and the mangroves take over."

"What a place. I wish I'd stayed in Miami."

"Why did you come over to this coast?"

Herrera shrugged. "My wife said she wanted some place better for the kids. Most of her family's in Avola."

"She come from Avola?"

"She was working in Miami when I met her. She hated the place. I thought she'd get used to it after we were married."

Harry was surprised by the sudden look of pain that froze Herrera's face.

"No luck?"

"Got worse. When our first kid was on the way, she started hollering about wanting to be where her mother could help her."

The water was deepening and Harry advanced the throttle slightly. "You find Avola boring?"

Another shrug. "It's OK, I guess. I miss the city life though. You ever live in a city?"

"For my sins I worked a couple of years for a detective agency in Boston."

Herrera gave a short bark of laughter.

"I got a brother up there. He's with Boston First. Likes the money but not the winters."

"Tell me about it."

They slid along quietly for a while. Herrera continued to grip his seat as if expecting the boat to pitch him suddenly into the river.

"It's OK," Harry said, trying to ease his mind.

"Thanks for nothing," Herrera replied, but gradually he loosened his hold on the seat and even leaned to one side or the other to look into the water. Harry named the birds they encountered and explained why the water was coffee colored instead of clear. For a while, Herrera responded as if he was interested, then finally fell quiet.

He had been watching the water slip past, apparently lost in his own thoughts, when suddenly he grabbed the seat and yelled, "Jesus!"

Harry had been thinking about Katherine Trachey while pretending not to, and Herrera's shout almost jumped him onto his feet. He cut the motor.

"What is it?" Herrera shouted.

They had overtaken a brown shark, half as long as the boat, swimming slowly downstream, its back wrinkling the surface of the water. A thick, black remora was riding its side.

"It's a sand shark," Harry said. "I wouldn't grab him, if that's what you were thinking of doing, but the thing's not particularly dangerous."

"Why is it up here?"

"See that remora on him? He's up here in the fresh water trying to get rid of it. He might have to stay here in the fresh water for a couple of days before the thing drops off."

"Sharks belong in the sea," Herrera said emphatically, and for the rest of the long ride, he gripped the seat and did not look over the side.

When the boat finally bumped softly against the grassy bank behind Mendoza's house, Herrera checked his watch. "Two hours and fifteen minutes."

Harry did some arithmetic and swore silently in disappointment.

"Mendoza's still got a problem," he admitted as they dragged the boat onto the bank.

Herrera pulled off his hat and wiped his face with it. "Maria puts the time of death between three and eleven p.m.

Mendoza's covered by his wife and daughter from four-thirty to six-thirty. They all agree she and the daughter came back from the school play between ten-thirty and eleven. That leaves . . ."

"Four hours," Harry said.

"Lots of time to get out there and back, even if he returned by boat." Herrera made no effort to hide the satisfaction in his voice.

"We've got to move it," a tall deputy said, pushing through the bushes behind them. "Lieutenant Snyder needs you over in the Gate."

The deputy drove Herrera and Harry back to the Hammock.

"Thanks for the help," Herrera said.

"Helped me too," Harry replied.

When he went into the house, the message light was blinking on his answering machine. He ignored it. Messages were from the past. Nothing good came from the past.

He got a beer from the kitchen, hoping to improve his state of mind, and then sat down with his back to the blinking telephone light, telling himself it could wait a few more minutes. He faced the fact that if Maria Benedict was right about the time of death, Luis Mendoza had plenty of time to kill Trachey. He also had access to the gun and plenty of motivation. It was not good news. But how did he get out to the cabin? Walk? Not likely. Ride with Willard? Also not likely. Had he driven to the cabin, shot Trachey, and then after taking the boat down the river hitch-hike back for his car? No jury would believe it.

That should have made Harry feel better, but it didn't. If the gun in the boat was the murder weapon, it would weigh heavily against Luis. With means and motive locked up, the Assistant State Attorney might seek an indictment despite the difficulty in placing Mendoza at the scene.

He was saved from being completely dispirited by recalling Herrera's low key comment that tougher drug interdiction on the east coast was shifting some of the traffic west of the Keys. He did not doubt Trachey had been dealing drugs, and he also thought Hatfield could be right in thinking that Trachey had fallen out with his connections and gotten himself killed.

The question was how to prove it. And it would take a lot of proof to lift Luis off the hook. Harry wondered briefly if Trachey had been running an independent operation or whether Boone was bankrolling him. Getting nowhere with that thought, he sighed and pushed out of his chair. The damned red light was still blinking. It was a message from Jim Snyder.

The gun in the boat was the murder weapon.

"They're coming, Luis," Harry said as he punched the erase button.

Chapter 8

The following morning Harry walked through the pearl glow brightening the eastern sky to get his paper. Listening to the dawn chorus slowly rising around him and watching the dawn light gradually turn from gray to pale yellow, he was suddenly grateful for being an early riser.

When he reached Puc Puggy Creek, he stopped on the bridge just as an immense slice of red sun edged into view. He was still haunted by the distressing certainty that Luis would be arrested and charged with Trachey's murder, but he put the concern aside to watch the sunrise spectacular unfolding before him.

When the trumpets of the east had become a little less brazen, he crossed the bridge and pulled *The Avola Banner* out of his mailbox. Returning to the bridge, he unfolded the paper in the growing light and swore. The item had front page billing: SUIT FILED AGAINST COMMISSIONER THIBEDEAU.

He lifted the paper into the sun and read.

Local hydrologist and conservation activist Luis Mendoza has filed a breach of ethics suit against County Commissioner Emile Thibedeau with the Florida Ethics Commission. The suit alleges that Commissioner Thibedeau's uncritical support of Mr. Orville Boone's Avola Gold project and his voting record regarding the project constitute a breach of public trust and an abuse of his office, warranting his removal from the Tequesta County Board of Commissioners.

If the Ethics Commission calls for an investigation, it will be conducted by State Attorney Sean Fergus of the 21st Judicial District. A source close to the Sheriff's Office has told the *Banner* that Mr. Mendoza is being questioned by the police in connection with the death of Mr. Willard Trachey.

"Shit," Harry said as the news wrecked his sunrise.

Mendoza's Southwest Engineering, Inc. headquarters consisted of two rooms in the Great Northern Bank building in Minsky Plaza in a section of Avola called Old Town. By two o'clock that afternoon, Harry was sitting in Luis Mendoza's office, listening to his secretary clicking her keyboard in the outer office while her boss finished signing some letters. Harry studied the two photographs of Mendoza's wife and their daughter. There was a third picture of his wife and daughter standing with a cream-colored poodle between them. Lucky man, Harry thought. Even the dog looked good. Then he checked himself. Luis was going to be charged with murder. Not so lucky.

Mendoza capped his pen, briskly gathered the finished work, and carried the signed papers out to his secretary. He quickly returned and closed the door.

"Sorry," he said. "We drown in paper."

Harry nodded.

"The gun the police found in Willard's boat was the one that killed him." Harry decided to save his comments about the suit against Thibedeau until later and get the bad news over as quickly as possible. "It was a trash gun. No serial number. There were no prints on the weapon either. It can't be linked to you. That's the good news. The bad news is that Herrera and I timed a boat run from Willard's camp to your back yard. You could have gotten out there and back in the time you say you were home alone."

Herrera sighed and nodded wearily. Harry was surprised Luis wasn't more upset.

"Sergeants Herrera and Snyder were here this morning," Herrera said. "I keep being dragged over the same ground. I suppose they hope I'll eventually say something to contradict what I've told them. And I probably will. I'm getting so sick of the story I'm tempted to change it out of boredom."

"Don't," Harry said sternly. "And don't forget, everything they've got is circumstantial. So just keep telling the truth. By the way, I talked with Hatfield."

"Who?"

"Slade Hatfield. He works for Emile Thibedeau in Sampson's Marina."

Mendoza had fidgeted impatiently through Harry's warning. His inattention troubled Harry. The man had no idea of the extent to which being arrested and charged with murder would shatter his life.

"I'd forgotten about him. Learn anything helpful?"

"Not much. He thinks his boss had some kind of beef with Willard. Do you know anything about that?"

Mendoza shrugged without apparent interest. "No. It doesn't seem likely the two would even know one another. What interest would Thibedeau have in Willard Trachey?"

"I have no idea. Hatfield might have been trying to sound as if he knows more than he does. He knows some of the people who were calling on Willard. But beyond saying they scared him, he didn't tell me much else."

"What do you do now?"

"Try to shake something loose."

"How?" Mendoza shifted irritably in his chair.

Harry tried to sound upbeat. "It takes time. You're no worse off than you were before you hired me. Except for one thing."

Mendoza showed interest.

"The lawsuit you've filed against Thibedeau."

"What about it?" Mendoza demanded. "The man is a criminal. He should be taken off the Board of Commissioners and sent to jail."

"Maybe," Harry replied calmly, "but your timing stinks."

"This suit has nothing to do with Willard Trachey's murder. Or my being a suspect."

"I wish it didn't, but the *Banner*'s got your name on the front page, and you're already linked to the murder. Tonight, the local news will have your face all over south Florida."

Mendoza waved his hand as if brushing away a fly.

"I am often in the news."

"Not this way. The next time you see yourself on The Florida Hour, you'll be Mendoza the Murder Suspect. Your life will become transparent in a whole new and unpleasant way."

Mendoza's face darkened with anger, and he indulged in a spurt of Spanish too fast for Harry to follow.

"I am guilty of nothing!" he shouted.

"Maybe not, but now you're news. If I were you, I'd check with your daughter's school to see about security."

Harry drove home wondering if he'd been too tough on Mendoza. He thought he might have been, but the man needed waking up before the tsunami moving on him hit. He was vulnerable, and Boone and Thibedeau knew it. They would go for him. Luis, he told himself, shaking his head in quiet dismay, was not in any way prepared for what was coming.

Harry was almost certain that Eric Smith, the Assistant State Attorney, was going to convene a grand jury and charge Luis with murder. If that was true, he needed to do some serious thinking about how to keep his client out of jail. And the best way to do that was not to think about the problem for a while. He stopped at his house long enough to put his sketchbook, pencils, binoculars, compass, water bottle, and bug repellant in his blue canvas backpack, change into denims and a long-sleeved shirt, grab his hat, and drive to Trachey's cabin.

A much reduced crew was putting siding on the refurbished cabin. The roof gleamed with cedar shingles, and the fireplace chimney had been re-bricked and mortared. All ready for Katherine and the kids, Harry thought. He was pleased they were coming, but his pleasure was well salted with doubt as to what Boone was planning. He parked the Rover and set off on foot along the edge of the Stickpen.

The sound of the men's hammers faded quickly as he walked deeper into the Hammock. A mile beyond Willard's cabin he found a colony of *Liguus* tree snails, their brown, pink, and orange whorled shells glowing in the deep shade. He thought Willard had long since cleaned them out. Their presence suggested he must have found something that paid better than selling contraband snail shells. He carefully fixed their location and pushed on.

In his first blundering efforts to adjust to the alien world of the Hammock, Harry spent a lot of time sitting and watching its creatures go about their business. The watching grew into an ongoing study of the dense, interconnected, and deeply layered life of Bartram's Hammock. And he still found a deep satisfaction in watching the Hammock's teeming life.

The owls' nest opening, as big as a honeydew melon, was located in a hollow of one of an ancient cypress's upright branches. The adult owls were sitting in nearby trees in characteristic stillness. The occasional swiveling of their heads was only slightly more noticeable than the flicker of the surrounding leaves.

They were large, gray, darkly barred birds, well suited to the mingled shadow and light of the canopy. A young, fully fledged owl scrambled awkwardly out of the nest cavity and hopped along a nearby limb. One of the adult birds slipped away through the trees and soon returned with a mouse in its beak. With thrashing wings, the young owl rushed forward and swallowed the mouse in a series of violent gulps. Harry drew rapidly.

When he had filled several sheets with sketches, he put down the pad to watch the owls. But instead he began thinking about Luis Mendoza. Harry knew Mendoza's suit against Thibedeau would provide his enemies with a platform for launching an all out campaign to discredit him and to build credibility into the charge that he had killed Trachey. Developer interest, where most of the hostility against Luis resided in Tequesta County, was a major force in the state's political life, if not the major force. Boone's colleagues would scramble to throw money Orville's way to support an attack on Luis, if they thought Mendoza's influence with the county and state agencies monitoring their activities could be destroyed.

If Harry could prove Luis was not Trachey's killer, the assault on him would melt away. But the more Harry considered the problem, the more he became aware that aside from doing what he could to insist that there was no convincing account of how Luis actually got to Trachey's cabin, he had no actual evidence that would exonerate his client. Feeling very frustrated, he gathered together his drawing equipment and the rest of his gear, stuffed them into his pack, and started for home.

Harry was jolted out of his gloomy thoughts by finding Slade Hatfield's Trans Am parked in the yard. He got out of the Rover just as Hatfield and Katherine Trachey came around the wisteria at the corner of the lanai. Seeing them together did not improve his day.

She ran forward to greet him. Despite his growing anger and concern, he found himself smiling. She was wearing new sandals, a new pair of blue shorts, and an orange top. She looked wonderful.

"Hey, Harry, great hat." She caught his hands and swung them cheerfully. Awash in smiles and her green eyes dancing with pleasure, she leaned forward and kissed him.

"You know Slade Hatfield," she said.

"Yes, but I'm surprised you do."

"Slade's been helping me catch up on Willard." She laughed. "Willard wasn't much of a letter writer."

"Find out anything interesting?" Harry was more interested in how these two had found each other.

"He was in over his boots," she said, frowning. "Not that the water needed to be very deep."

Hatfield came up to them in a sprawling walk.

"Brock," he said.

He was dressed in snakeskin boots, clean, stone-washed jeans, and a purple and black Harley Davidson singlet.

"Hello, Slade." Harry turned back to Katherine. "What brings you two out here?"

"Slade drove me out to see how the cabin's coming along," she answered. "We stopped to see if you were home. I wanted to say hello."

"How are Minna and Jesse doing?" Harry was growing

more and more uncomfortable.

"Oh, they're great. Minna's in pre-school. Jesse's in day camp." She laughed again. "I'm supposed to be working, but instead I'm playing hooky. Promise you won't tell, Harry."

"How did you two get to know each other?"

Hatfield appeared not to be listening and was looking around, chewing gum with his mouth open and showing every sign of being completely bored. But he stopped snapping his gum and pulled his head around at Harry's question.

"Orville introduced us." Katherine turned to Hatfield with a smile. "He said if I was going to be living out here, he wanted somebody he trusted to be looking in on me now and then."

She turned back to Harry, tilted her head, and smiled. "I told him I had you, but he said all you were interested in looking after were goddamned woodpeckers."

Hatfield laughed raucously.

"Orville has a sense of humor." Harry managed a skinny smile. "Look, if Slade would excuse us, could I have a word with you alone?"

"I guess."

Hatfield scowled, but Harry ignored it.

They stepped onto the lanai out of Hatfield's hearing. "This is none of my business, and you're free to say so, but Slade Hatfield has a rap sheet longer than Willard's."

She listened to him with what he read as amused indifference.

"And next you're going to say he's called Splinter because he's a knife fighter." She laid both hands on his chest and leaned toward him. "Harry, honey, I'm not going to marry the man."

She looked hard at him for a moment, her smile fading. Despite his anger and general sense of approaching calamity,

Harry thought how easy it would be to get lost in those eyes.

"But thanks for caring," she added. She gave a short sigh and turned away. "Got to go," she said in a much louder voice. "See you later. Bye."

She paused at the door, looked back, smiled, and spoke in a lower voice. "I meant it when I said thanks, Harry. I really did."

She let the screen door slam behind her, and ran toward Hatfield's car, her long braid flying in the sun. Harry watched them drive away, scattering sand and gravel. His mouth tasted of the grave. He had no quick answer as to what Boone was plotting in bringing them together. But he was sure that if he knew, he wouldn't feel one bit better. He was turning to go into the house when it occurred to him with a jolt of dismay that she might be one of those women with a talent for choosing men who hurt them.

He thought with a stab of pain how much he liked her. Stopping to look back at the deserted yard, he asked himself suddenly why he was so angry and upset. It's because Hatfield's such bad news, and it's certainly not because I'm jealous. He strode into the house and slammed the door behind him.

Chapter 9

On the following Wednesday, having exhausted his other leads, Harry began interviewing Mendoza's neighbors in River Run Estates whose property backed on the Seminole River. He would have had a warmer welcome at the hives of killer bees. His identification finally got him through the security gate, but not before the scowling guard, who regarded the Rover as if it was The Flying Dutchman, telephoned his supervisor for clearance.

The man who answered the door at the house closest to Mendoza's claimed not to recognize the name. He kept the door on its chain, and told Harry neither he nor any of his family had been in Avola on May fifth. He refused to answer any questions and told Harry to get off the property or he'd be facing a suit for trespass and harassment. Harry left.

A slim, perfectly groomed blonde woman in her fifties answered the chimes at the next house. It was nearly ten-thirty, but she was still in slippers and a flowered wrapper.

She returned his card and swung open the door. "I'm Abigail Blakeley. I'm having a cup of coffee and listening to Glenn Gould."

Nice way to spend the morning, Harry thought just before being enveloped in a gust of very expensive perfume.

"Come in, Harry Brock," she said in the same friendly voice. "We can talk in the morning room."

The morning room, done in white and rose and polished

glass, was the size of Harry's living room. On the table there was a huge bouquet of fresh white carnations and cream roses in a crystal pitcher. Beads of water glittered on the blossoms. Tempted, he bent over the roses and breathed in their fragrance.

"Are you surprised?" she asked.

"Very. Do you grow them?"

"Yes." She waved him toward a white wicker chair. "They're antique roses, and in this climate devilishly hard to raise." She laughed. "The gardener does most of the work. But I do my share. I love it."

Harry sat down in the brightly cushioned chair with the very odd feeling of having found something he'd been looking for. The *Goldberg Variations* were playing softly somewhere in the house. He couldn't see any speakers, but the music surrounded him. He wondered for a moment if there was a Mr. Blakeley but warned himself not to ask.

With an effort he dragged his mind back to business. "Mrs. Blakeley, I'm doing some investigative work connected with Willard Trachey's murder. Have you heard the name?"

"I don't think so." She passed him coffee in a gold-rimmed cup so thin he dreaded lifting it out of its saucer. "Is there any reason I should?"

"I don't suppose so, but it's been in the paper."

"The local mullet wrapper?" She pulled out a chair and sat down facing him. "I never read it. And I don't watch the Avola stations. My god, they're a persecution."

There was no rancor in what she said, only an amused dismissal.

"He was shot on May fifth." Harry was bemused by her response. Was there a connection between her world and Willard Trachey's? He abandoned the speculation. "The murder weapon was found in a boat pulled up on Luis

Mendoza's property less than half a mile from here."

He pointed up the river, visible from the windows.

"Ah, the Latino family. I know Mr. Mendoza to speak to. I think he's a hydrologist."

"That's right." Harry was impressed. Most people, if they knew Mendoza at all, knew him as an environmentalist. "Did you hear or see anything unusual on that night, such as someone walking along the edge of the river?"

He nodded toward the windows and the expanse of manicured lawn stretching down to the water. She adjusted her cushions and settled herself more comfortably. Then, without haste, she picked up her coffee cup and with a half smile seemed to drift away with the music. Harry wondered if he should repeat the question and, at the same time, wondered if the question had any importance. Wouldn't it, he asked himself, admitting after some resistance that he found this woman very attractive, be better just to sit here, listen to Glenn Gould work his miracles, and talk with her about growing roses? He tasted the coffee. It was delicious.

"Have I lost you, Mr. Brock?" He brought his gaze back from the window.

"Do you know the story of Odysseus and Calypso?" Harry asked.

"Oh, yes." She smiled warmly. "Is that what you were thinking of? How very interesting."

"It's not important." He had embarrassed himself and was trying to get his mind off her perfume and the slithery whisper of silk as she crossed her legs. "Can you recall anything at all unusual from that night?"

"Nothing." She set down her cup and looked at him earnestly. "You can be sure, if I had seen strangers on my lawn, I would have called security. There have been several robberies in the area over the past year."

She straightened her back, leaned forward slightly, and turned her hands palms up in a graceful movement. Her movements lifted her breasts, and he was alarmed to find himself staring at them. Rallying, he forced himself to raise his eyes. He was relieved to find that if she had noticed his gaffe, she gave no hint of it.

"People are so careless," she continued. "They forget to switch on their alarm system. Or don't bother. What can they expect? Of course, everyone is insured. But it's such a nuisance."

For the second time since sitting down Harry felt his perspective being violently altered. In her world it was, apparently, in the nature of things to be robbed. In the view of this very lovely woman, there was no reason to be upset or angry or overly concerned about it. She really was very attractive. If one did not turn on the alarm, one could expect to be robbed. He shook his head to turn off her voice.

"Nothing you can tell me?" He forced himself to his feet.

"I'm sorry, but no. Must you go? I would so like to know what the Homer reference was all about."

Oh, Calypso, he thought and said truthfully that he regretted having to leave, but, unfortunately, he had other people in River Run to talk to. She smiled and led him to the door.

She shook his hand and smiled. "Goodbye, Mr. Brock. Good luck. I hope you find what you're looking for."

He walked down the winding brick path and thought, *I'm going the wrong way.* At the gate he turned and looked back at the house. She was still standing in the door. She waved to him. Something about the way she was standing reminded him of Katherine. He did not welcome the comparison and quickly suppressed it. Then he waved back and went on his way feeling unaccountably better about the world. At the

same time, to his annoyance, he felt slightly guilty about
feeling so good.

On Friday afternoon he exhausted the possibilities in
River Run. No one had seen anything. Or if they had, they
were not admitting it. What he had learned was that the men
and women who answered the doors of their immense houses
did not want to be asked questions or to answer them. With
varying degrees of coldness and in several unpleasant ways,
they or their minions told him to go away and stay away. A
few expressed annoyed astonishment that he had been
allowed into River Run at all. Frustrated, he finally asked one
man if he felt any responsibility at all to help bring a murderer
to justice.

"Are you some kind of nut?" the man replied. "Get out of
here."

That's it, Harry told himself. He drove to Luis Mendoza's
house.

"Do you know any of these people?" Harry asked
Mendoza.

They were sitting beside Mendoza's pool under a table
umbrella. Harry was drinking cold beer. Mendoza was fid-
dling with a glass of lemonade he clearly didn't want and
looking at the list of names. He shook his head.

"Most of them are away more than they're here," he said.
"Only a few of us are year-rounders."

Year-rounders. A subspecies of . . . what? Harry decided
he was suffering from interview lag.

"What about the Blakeleys?"

"Mostly one Blakeley. She takes walks. Sometimes I see
her passing the house. We wave. Or if we're close enough, we
speak. Why?"

"She lives in that huge place alone?"

"There's a husband, but he is very seldom here. She has beautiful gardens. In this climate they must be a burden."

"She has a gardener." Harry remembered the roses.

Mendoza gave him a blank look, as if he'd said, She breathes.

"Tell me what else you've been doing," he said.

Harry had little to report. "Have you heard anything more from Boone?"

"No, but I received this."

Mendoza opened the folder lying on the table in front of him. He took out a letter and passed it across the table. It was an unsigned note written on high quality, dusty rose paper.

Mr. Louis Mendoza:
I am concerned for you and your family. You may be in great danger. Please be careful.

Harry read the sentences three times.

"Have the police seen this?" He dropped the letter on the table.

"No. They would never take such a thing seriously."

Harry leaned forward. "Luis, believe me. They'd take it seriously."

"But it's a warning, not a threat. Besides, a woman wrote it." Mendoza waved a hand in dismissal.

"You don't know who wrote it, Luis. You could be right. It may be only a warning. And I admit it's a little weird, but let me take it to Herrera."

Mendoza shrugged. "If you wish. But I think he will say what I've said."

Harry leaned back and blew out his cheeks. The letter was a puzzler.

"Do you have the envelope?" he asked.

Mendoza opened the folder again and after sorting through some papers, found the envelope.

"Same paper," Harry said. "Same script for the address."

"There is a trace of perfume," Mendoza said.

Harry raised the envelope to his nose and sniffed. He couldn't believe it. He sniffed again. No doubt about it. It was Abigail Blakeley's perfume. A graceful, smiling figure formed in his mind. Abigail was saying something that he found amusing, a piano was playing . . .

"Harry?"

"Sorry," Harry said. He dragged himself out of the fantasy and took a swig of beer.

A month had passed since Willard Trachey was murdered, and beyond identifying the gun used in the shooting, the police had made no progress with the case. Neither had Harry. But as he carried his paper through the pale but hopeful morning light, he could find no reason to change his growing certainty that within a few days Luis Mendoza would be arrested and charged in the killing. A grand jury had been convened and dismissed. The Assistant State Attorney almost certainly had his charge.

There was no new evidence against Mendoza and no development of the existing evidence. What they had was Trachey's boat, the gun found in the boat, and the return of the ballistics report proving the gun was the weapon used in the crime. They could also demonstrate some motive, access to the means, but not much opportunity.

Harry doubted it was enough for a conviction, but in the possibility that Mendoza was a murderer, the media had found a story with legs. Boone and the other developers were in full-throated pursuit of him. Emile Thibedeau was using the *Banner* and the bully pulpit of his Commissioner's position to urge calm and deplore negative ethnic stereotyping while insisting the guilty be punished. And he had taken to ending his pieces with the reminder that, in Florida, sheriffs are elected.

When Harry finished breakfast, he decided to call on Tucker LaBeau. He was stuck. It was time for a talk. Oh-Brother! was grazing on the patch of grass behind the garden, so Harry knew he'd find Tucker in the small barn beyond the hen house cleaning out the mule's stall. Oh-Brother! was tall and rangy with slim ankles, the legs of a ballet dancer, a belly like a barrel, and dark-lashed, cynical eyes. He raised his head when Harry approached and stopped chewing long enough to wigwag his ears in greeting. According to Tucker, Oh-Brother! got his name early in life because of the trouble he caused.

"Actually," Tucker said, "when he was a colt, he had me saying, 'Oh-Shit!' a dozen times a day. But when I named him, I had to take his feelings into consideration. So I called him Oh-Brother!."

Sanchez stepped out of the barn, gave a deep whoof, and trotted forward to take Harry to Tucker. The dog, his tail stiffly erect, and a loud chorus of locusts in the live oaks ushered him into the barn. Harry felt like arriving royalty and was pleased to see that Sanchez had recovered some of his *joie de vie*.

Tucker had spread clean straw in Oh-Brother!'s stall and was now turning over the manure pile outside the back door, to keep it from heating too much and burning at the center. Oh-Brother!'s manure pile was the epicenter of Tucker's composting project. Rotted straw and manure were the engine that drove his remarkable garden, and he took pains to keep it running smoothly.

"What are you doing up so early?" Tucker asked with a grin when he saw Harry.

"If you can spare the time, I want to talk with you," Harry said.

"Good. Let's have some tea," Tucker said. "Sanchez, fetch Oh-Brother!."

The dog came back with the mule. Oh-Brother! had his ears pricked in interest, but they flopped back when Tucker told him to go into the stall.

"Don't complain," Tucker said. "There's bran in your feed box, and there's a fresh pail of water. And I'll leave the gate open."

Harry found the exchange amusing because except at night Tucker never closed Oh-Brother!'s stall door. The mule and Sanchez wandered wherever they wanted.

"The bran keep him regular?" They were walking toward the house, and Harry was pleased with his joke.

"That's it." Tucker either missing the humor or was just giving it another spin. "He's getting on, like me. Bowel movements are no longer a subject of merriment. Besides, he likes bran. So I give him some now and then. When he stays out of the garden."

"You couldn't see him," Harry said. "How do you know he didn't grab a bite while you were cleaning out his stall?"

"Sanchez would have told me."

Harry let it go.

"There's a problem," Harry said. They were seated at Tucker's kitchen table with mugs of tea in front of them and a plate of ginger snaps on the table.

Tucker grinned. "There always is."

The windows and door were open, and the gingham curtains lifted and rippled in the occasional puff of wind blowing through the room. There was a freshly ironed red and white cotton cloth covering the table, and the hard pine floor under their feet glowed from years of scrubbing.

"Katherine Trachey lied to me," Harry said. Saying it made him feel angry and generally wretched. "And I found out she'd lied only because of something her boy said without knowing he was giving his mother away. I'm troubled by it. Especially now because I'm almost certain Luis Mendoza is going to be charged in Will's killing."

Harry was interrupted by a thumping behind him. He turned to see Sanchez trying to drag his big beef bone into the house. He had jammed it between the screen door and the sill.

"We've already had this discussion, Sanchez," Tucker said in a patient but firm voice. "You can come in if you want, but the bone stays on the stoop." The dog looked at Tucker, and Tucker looked back and shook his head. "Nope, it stays outside."

The dog shouldered the screen open and dragged the bone away. The door slammed shut.

Tucker turned back to Harry. "He knows better than to let that door slam, but he's a little mad." He paused briefly to blow on his tea and went on. "The big political contributors calling in their chips?"

Harry nodded.

"And you can't decide what to do with the information."

"That's about it."

"How much more can you tell me?"

"Most of it." Harry repeated what Jesse had told him about seeing his mother and father together at Henderson's Truck Stop. Then he went on to say what she had told the police.

"How much does that change things?" Harry was dealing very slowly with the tea. It was so strong it took both hands to stir it. He wondered if Tucker had boiled it all night.

"Maybe not at all," he said. "And Katherine might have lied for good reasons. I lied to Jesse about his father coming back."

Tucker nodded. "But there's the possibility it makes a lot of difference," he said. "For instance, if she killed him, which, I assume, you don't think she did."

"No, but what if it's something else? What if she and Willard were planning something, and it was connected to his death?"

"There's that possibility," Tucker agreed. "And something else. If he ran away from her in the first place, what was he doing driving out to Henderson's to talk to her? From what I know of Willard, I'd expect him to avoid her like a fire ant nest."

"Maybe they'd been in touch for while," Harry said.

"Or maybe there was something he wanted or needed to give her."

"I'm not likely to find out, unless she tells me. Which I don't think she will."

"Could be she told Boone," he said. "By the way, I've seen her with Hatfield a couple of times. That's not good news."

"Tell me about it," Harry said. "What made you bring up Boone's name?"

"He showed up awful quick after the shooting."

"I thought the same thing and assumed he's in pretty tight with the Sheriff."

Tucker leaned back in his chair and laughed. The breeze from the door floated the fringe of white hair over his ears like dandelion fluff.

"I expect I've got it all wrong, but my guess is that sooner or later anything involving Will Trachey, Slade Hatfield, and those connected with them will connect up with Orville."

"Well, we'll see," Harry said, "but even if you're right, I'm still stuck with information I don't know what to do with."

"The boy and his mother." Tucker scowled.

"If I say anything to her, she's going to know I found out from Jesse." Harry risked another swallow of tea. It hit him like a shot of adrenaline. "If I don't, I'll be suppressing what might be significant information. And more than that, I'm damned curious about what she and Will were discussing."

"Hell," Tucker said, "the boy's too young to know he was passing along family secrets. Go talk to her and ask if it's true. Could be the boy just wanted to believe he'd seen his father."

"The same thought occurred to me." He had been avoiding saying something. Now he decided to say it. "I think you might be in some danger."

Tucker got up and hobbled to the stove for a refill, swearing about old knees. He came back moving more easily. Harry remarked on that, and Tucker said his knees were a lot like Oh-Brother!, hard to start but easier to keep going.

He spooned brown sugar into his cup. "I'd rather have molasses, but I forgot to buy a jug the last time I was in town. Oh-Brother! eats it about as fast as I can bring it in here."

"Tucker."

"All right. How do you figure I'm at risk?"

"How does he eat it?" Harry demanded. A mule eating molasses?

"In an ice cream cone when he can get it. When he can't, he likes it on his bran."

Harry put up both hands. "I'm not going to pursue it." He was already pretty far down the rabbit hole with this man and his animals. "I'm going to remind you that whoever shot Trachey may have seen you standing in your garden as he and Willard drove by. He may not know whether you saw him or not. If you're dead, he doesn't have to ask the question."

"You got the preacher hired?" Tucker's blue eyes danced with amusement.

"This isn't funny, Tucker. A funeral is what I'm trying to avoid."

"All right. Let's say you're right. What am I supposed to do about it?"

"Keep your shotgun handy. Don't answer the door until you know who's calling. Draw the shades at night and never, ever stand between a light and the window."

Tucker smiled calmly. "The biggest risk I'm running around here is from Bonnie and Clyde. They've got me worrying big time. They haven't been around for a while. I think the struggle has entered a new phase. Psychological terrorism. You saw what happened with Sanchez trying to drag his bone into the house. Keeping us hanging. Weakening morale." He scowled. "Beauregard didn't crow this morning. Bad sign. Wouldn't surprise me if the hens stopped laying." He sighed and ran his hand over his bald head. "Well, we'll just have to wait them out."

"I guess so," Harry said. He got up feeling as if he was full of electricity and might never sleep again. "You think about what I've said."

Sanchez might have been mad about his bone, but he led the way to the Rover. Oh-Brother! joined them as they passed the barn. Harry couldn't help laughing. "I feel as if I was in a parade."

"You are." Tucker clapped a hand warmly on Harry's shoulder. "But think how impoverished life would be without ceremony."

Chapter 10

Harry finally made up his mind to talk to Katherine about what Jesse had told him. He called her at work and asked her if she would like to have lunch, telling himself he owed it to her to cushion the confrontation as much as possible. She ran out of the Boone Construction building to the Rover and jumped in beside Harry, bubbling with excitement. "This is my first lunch date from the office," she cried. Then she leaned over and kissed his cheek.

"It won't be your last," he replied. He felt his face burning as he drove away from the curb. "You look beautiful."

She was dressed in a long-sleeved yellow blouse, a pleated green skirt, and green shoes. She looked very professional. Harry thought her hoop earrings were a little over the top, but she had wound up her braid and looked stunning.

She blushed, reached for her braid, which wasn't there, and laughed. "You're embarrassing me."

"Get used to it. You are going to get a lot of compliments."

"OK." She gave him a quick grin, then reached over and gave his arm a squeeze. "Now, come on. Where are you taking me."

"To Oppenheimer's. Where we can get the best oriental salad this side of Singapore."

"I'm not much into weird food," she said.

"This is not weird stuff," he protested. "This will free you from regret and inhibition. And they make a Key lime pie that once tasted will make you a sybarite forever."

"A what?"

"Someone who lives for pleasure."

"Just as long as I don't have to eat seaweed." She gave him a sidelong look that obliterated thoughts of the Key lime pie.

He took the shore drive to Oppenheimer's, and along with comments on the views, Katherine brought him up to date on Jessé and Minna. Both kids were thriving. Minna was already singing her alphabet song and demanding Golden Books like the ones the teacher read from. Jesse was having fewer nightmares and liked school.

Harry listened with much less pleasure to Katherine's account of her developing relationship with Slade Hatfield. In Harry's opinion the man was a loser, and it was only a question of time before he left her grabbing air and, if she wasn't damned careful, pregnant. The last possibility was so repellant he refused to think about it.

Oppenheimer's occupied a corner of a small, rectangular mall shaded by tall fig trees that cast a cooling shade over the open square. Ringed turtle doves were nesting in the trees, and their soft, melancholy calls drifted over the square in shimmering bubbles of sound.

Katherine chose to eat outside, and they were seated between the buttress roots of one of the giant figs at a round, black metal table with a maroon umbrella and white linen napkins.

"Jesus, Harry," Katherine said, "this is going to cost a fortune."

He opened a menu. "Fear not. My credit is good here."

She vetoed the oriental salad with chicken in favor of the Portobello mushroom, roasted pepper slices, and goat's cheese.

"You lied. You do eat weird food."

"I lie a lot." She had worked up the courage to try the wine.

It was the lead-in he needed, but he pushed it aside, unwilling to spoil the moment. Their food came and they ate and talked as if they had been coming to Oppenheimer's for lunch for years. Harry even had the Key lime pie, telling himself it was just to make Katherine feel comfortable about ordering dessert.

While they were waiting for their coffee, she said, "I'd like to believe you brought me here because you really like being with me, but I bet there's something else. Am I right?"

"You're right about my really liking your company," he said, discomfited by the accuracy of her comment and pinned by her question. "But I do have something to tell you and something to ask you. Both things could have been done over the phone. So let's say I used them as an excuse to invite you out for lunch. Can you buy that?"

"After the food and the wine and an hour in this place, Harry, you could sell me a bridge."

Her smile was still in place, but Harry saw with a stab of guilt that some of the pleasure had faded from her eyes. He hesitated. It wasn't too late to change his mind. But he fought off the temptation.

"The day you brought the kids out to my place for a picnic, Jesse told me Willard came out to Henderson's to talk to you. Is it true, or is it just something the boy would like to believe happened?"

Katherine looked down and for a moment or two smoothed the napkin that still covered her lap.

She raised her head and stared defiantly at him. "He was out there, but he didn't want to see the kids. He'd been drinking, and he was scared."

She stopped speaking and looked down again. Harry felt

like a felon doing this to her, but she was in trouble. And if he was going to help her, he had to know why Willard had come looking for her. Then he had to persuade her to tell the police before they found out on their own that she had lied to them. Harry was damned sure Jesse wasn't the only person who had seen Katherine and Willard together at the truck stop.

"How did he know where to find you?" Harry asked the question as gently as he could.

When she looked up, her eyes were brimming with tears, but she pushed out her chin and kept on talking. "Because I called him and told him." She said this a little too loudly for the comfort of their fellow lunchers. "There's no law says a wife can't call her husband, even if the worthless son-of-a-bitch has run off and left her."

"You're right," Harry ignored the stares. "The difficulty begins when the husband gets himself killed, and the wife tells the police she hasn't seen him since riding into town."

She propped her forearms on the table and clenched her hands as if she was strangling something. "He was in trouble. I don't know what it was, but it was bad, and I didn't want to get dragged into it. He bragged about being right on the edge of making a whole lot of money. Nothing new there. Then he gave me a letter and told me to keep it for him and not to tell anybody."

The check came, interrupting the conversation, and he didn't pick it up again until they were driving out of the parking lot. "Did you read the letter?"

"Sure."

"What does it say?"

"Something about some construction and who was going to be paid for doing what. I couldn't see anything important in it."

"Why did he give it to you?"

"He said he had to put it somewhere where it would be safe."

"And you agreed to keep it for him."

"Yes, because he said it was worth a lot of money. It could have been the booze talking, but I don't think so. I think he believed what he was telling me."

"And you've still got the letter."

She shook her head.

"Where is it?" Harry tried not let his concern show.

"I don't know. It was in my pocketbook, but it must have fallen out because it's gone."

"Probably just as well." He pulled up to the Boone building and made a major effort not to let her see he was lying through his teeth.

"Should I tell Herrera about the letter?" she asked. They were standing on the sidewalk.

"Probably, but let me think about it. OK?"

"I don't care if I never tell them." She gave him a quick kiss and hesitated.

"Thanks for lunch, Harry. Look, I know it's bad to say, but I don't really think Willard was playing with a full deck. I wouldn't sweat that letter. He might have found it in the street." She forced herself to smile. "Next time we have lunch, leave out the business."

"It's a promise." He wanted to say how much he'd enjoyed her company, but something stopped him.

She started to leave then stopped and came back to stand close to him. "Harry, you don't like my being with Slade Hatfield, do you?"

"No."

"Is that why you took so long to call me?"

The question angered Harry. She had no right . . . he caught himself.

"No."

She looked at him quizzically, waiting for him to say something more. When he didn't, she sighed. "Do you mind if I call you?"

"Anytime," he said. Then he found his tongue, disregarding the warning flags that shot up when he started to speak. "Truthfully, would you like to do this again?"

She gave him a smile that made his face burn. "Of course I would, but don't wait too long. My date book's filling up fast."

She gave him another kiss and ran up the steps into the building.

Harry drove away with his emotions trying to run in opposite directions. He felt good about how well she was adjusting to her new life. The fact she wanted to see him almost had him singing. But her being with Slade Hatfield made him want to break things. Telling himself sternly he had no claim on her affections and didn't want one only made him feel worse. Possibly her story about why she and Willard had been together at Henderson's Truck Stop was true. He wanted to believe it. But a miserable doubt persisted.

He also knew that Katherine and Willard might have been teamed up in some kind of scam that crashed when he was killed. There was even the possibility, as he had suggested to Tucker, that Willard was killed because of whatever the two of them were doing. If that was so, Katherine was in great danger. Whatever the truth was, he suspected she was a much different person from the one he thought she was, or wanted her to be.

Trying to get a little more speed out of the Rover, Harry set aside the problem to do something about the letter Luis Mendoza had received, warning him to be careful. Luis was still refusing to take it seriously. It hadn't helped that David

Herrera didn't think it had any weight either. Harry was not satisfied, and he went to see Abigail Blakeley.

Once again, the guard at the River Run security gate checked by phone before letting him in. To his considerable disappointment, instead of a chiffon vision in beige and gold, a tall, heavy-set man with steel-gray hair and a jaw like a bulldozer blade answered his ring. He scowled at Harry. "Yeah?"

"I'm Harry Brock. Is Mrs. Blakeley in?"

"What do you want with her?" The man blocked the door like a jammed refrigerator.

Without waiting for an answer, he started to close the door. A woman's voice called, asking who he was talking to.

"It's Harry Brock," Harry shouted.

"Homer!" she cried. "Let him in, Joe. I'll be there in a minute."

Joe glowered instead, and they waited in a kind of Mexican stand-off until Mrs. Blakeley arrived.

When Harry was through the door, she said, "Mr. Brock, this is my husband, Joe Speroni."

Today she had her hair pulled back in a severe knot, pierced with a gold pin with a couple of red stones in it that flashed like dragonflies as she turned her head. In place of the gown, she wore a severely tailored light tan suit and mid height heels. Harry approved.

"You the P.I. I been hearing about?" Speroni asked. He spoke in a gravelly voice and accent that could have been a joke. "What do you need a P.I. for, Abby? You having me tailed?"

His black-jawed scowl collapsed into a horrid parody of a grin.

"This man is a New York stockbroker and an expert on eighteenth-century American clocks," Mrs. Blakeley said to Harry with an unruffled smile, "but he likes to pretend he's an enforcer for the mob. Go away, Joe, I want to talk to Mr. Brock."

"Harry."

"Harry it is," she agreed. Smiling, she led him into the morning room as her husband had retreated deeper into the house. "And you may as well call me Abby. I was named Abigail after my maternal grandmother. My mother had a quaint sense of humor."

"And the Blakeley?" Harry took the wicker chair he had occupied the last time he was there.

She disappeared into an adjoining room without answering, and returned with an ultramarine blue coffee pot and bright orange mugs.

"Abigail Speroni doesn't chime for me. How about you?" She asked the question with a straight face. "Besides, you can't just go on changing your name every time you change husbands. It gets too confusing."

Harry laughed and wondered while she poured the coffee how many changes there had been. Whatever the number, she showed very little wear. Of course it could have been artifice, but he doubted it. She had, he thought with admiration, a quiet beauty that usually came with a mind at ease with itself. Of course, he conceded, the skillfully applied make-up didn't detract from the total effect. He wondered without either envy or resentment if she was one of those fortunate people who float through life apparently immune to the knocks and scrapes that lame and scar the rest of mankind.

"I'm delighted you're here," she said. Passing Harry one of the mugs, she folded elegantly into a chair. "But what brings you?"

"Luis Mendoza received a letter."

She set her mug carefully on the glass table. Then, very deliberately, she drew her knees together, straightened her back, and folded her hands in her lap, her pleasant expression showing neither surprise nor alarm.

Charm, beauty, intelligence, and experience, he thought. Too many guns for a butterfly. And she's giving herself time to think. She probably did the same thing when the sorority selection committee asked her a potentially damaging question. It occurred to him it might always have been possible to ask her a potentially damaging question. He found that possibility very appealing and immensely to her credit.

"Harry, my husband is here for only another day or two," she replied, equally quietly, "and, to be honest, there are things I have to do with him. Could we have this conversation another time?"

He got up. "We should have it soon."

"I'll call you."

When they stepped into the hall, Harry saw Joe Speroni dodge into a room to their right, moving with remarkable agility for a man of his size. If Abigail noticed, she gave no indication.

Chapter 11

About midmorning on June eleventh, Katherine moved into the cabin. A faded black truck, with no front bumper and a fender flapping like an injured wing, swayed and banged past the house just as Harry was putting away his painting gear. The truck looked as if it had been on the road ever since Tom Joad drove it to California. Harry went out the lanai door for a better look. Its splintered plywood body bore the name BRAZO in hand painted letters of varying heights and shades of blue.

"Hey, Harry!" Katherine popped the top half of her body out the rider's window in Hatfield's car and waved enthusiastically at him over the roof as they trailed Brazo's truck deeper into the Hammock.

Harry waved back. The kids waved and grinned at him through the back window. Slade Hatfield didn't wave. Harry had no trouble controlling his disappointment.

The parade had just passed out of Harry's sight when Sanchez appeared out of the blowing dust, followed by Oh-Brother!, pulling a cart loaded with black muck that was draining tar-colored water. The mule was wearing a new straw hat with a bright red band. Tucker walked beside the cart carrying Oh-Brother!'s slack reins in one hand.

"New neighbors," Tucker called. He pulled off his straw hat and wiped his forehead on his shirt sleeve. "Don't it seem to you the heat's a little heavier this year?"

Harry walked out to the road. "Could be. You met

Katherine Trachey yet?"

Sanchez woofed at him in a neighborly way and then ambled off to lie in the shade. Oh-Brother! was looking at something over by the creek that had caught his eye. The load of muck simmered in the sun and stank like a dead eel.

"We've said hello. I like her and her kids. They've got good manners. More than I can say for Slade Hatfield. I told them about Bonnie and Clyde. They told me about the rat snake. The little one figures it's a prince."

"Luis Mendoza's been arrested," Harry said. He needed to get beyond having to think of Katherine living in the cabin with Slade Hatfield.

"I heard that. Too bad. Can they make it stick?"

Where Tucker got his information was an ongoing mystery to Harry.

"I don't see how, but Herrera tells me they've got probable cause. They've sent the affidavit to Eric Smith in the State Attorney's office."

"I hear they're going for murder one."

"Meanwhile, the County can hold Luis in jail for thirty or forty days and probably longer if they can find a judge to extend the confinement on a fear of flight concern."

Tucker shook his head. "Giving the police time to come up with more evidence, and while they're looking, everybody else can drag Mendoza around in the mud and do him a hell of a lot of damage and sound righteous."

"That's it." Harry regarded the wagon and its fetid cargo with distaste. "What are you doing with this muck? It makes a rotten egg smell like perfume."

"Black gold." Tucker swept off his hat again as if he was going to make a speech. "Stick a seed into that and jump back. But it does stink, don't it? I'll let it dry a little, mix in some compost and a couple of shovelfuls of lime, fork it over a few times, and turn that into the best dirt you ever hoed. Grow tomatoes as big as a pumpkin. Mind if we get out of this sun?"

"Pull in under the oaks," Harry said. "We can all have a drink."

While Tucker got the wagon out of the road and Oh-Brother! unhitched, Harry went into the house and brought out a gallon jug of lemonade for him and Tucker and a pail of water for the animals. Tucker was sitting on the grass near Sanchez, and the mule was grazing close by on the Bermuda grass.

"Did you put that hat on Oh-Brother! for a joke?" Harry asked, pouring lemonade for Tucker.

He had not admitted how angry seeing Katherine and Hatfield going together to the cabin made him feel, or how badly distracted he was, and his comment about the mule's hat had come out uncensored. Oh-Brother! lifted his head and looked at him, but Harry thought it was a coincidence. Tucker didn't. He gave Harry a long, sharp look.

He scrambled up and led Harry out of the mule's hearing. "That was a mistake. Oh-Brother!'s sensitive about his appearance. He'll probably sulk. You got any cube sugar?"

Harry was in no mood to indulge what he wanted to think was Tucker's damned foolishness about his talking animals, but he managed not to say so. It was less threatening to his pride to be irritated by Tucker than by Katherine. Nevertheless, he hated it that every time he got around Tucker and his animals, he found himself losing his grip on reality.

"Sure."

"Then go get a handful and we'll give it to him and talk about how good his hat looks. It might not work, but it's worth a try. Then I've got something I want to ask you."

Feeling like an idiot, Harry got the sugar, and the two men

took it over to Oh-Brother! and gave it to him. The mule waggled his ears and ate it, while Tucker and Harry said how good he looked in the hat and how sensible it was to wear it in this heat. Then they went back to the jug of lemonade and sat down.

"What do you want to ask me?" Harry was glad not to be talking to a mule.

It wasn't that he didn't like Oh-Brother! because he did. And he reluctantly admitted he was afraid he was coming to believe the mule understood what was said to him and actually thought about it. Scary.

"It's not my business, but I'm going to ask anyway," Tucker said. "What are your feelings regarding Katherine Trachey?"

Harry was caught off guard. He had no idea he'd given Tucker reason to think he felt any particular way about her. There certainly wasn't anything between them. But he could feel his face burning.

He put a humorous spin on his answer, hoping to duck the question. "I like her a lot better than I did when we first met. Why are you asking?" Tucker didn't laugh.

"Because that cabin belongs to Orville Boone, and she's working for him. That's what led me to ask the question. I hope you don't take it amiss."

"Of course not," Harry said.

"It's a bad business."

His comment startled Harry. "What's happened? Is she in some kind of trouble?"

"Not yet. At least not so far as I know, but there's booze, drugs, and easy women drifting through Boone's crowd like birds through the trees. She's bound to see things, hear things, get to know things she can't blink at and stay straight."

That was a very long speech for Tucker, and it laid out

what Harry had been trying not to think about. It was also clear Tucker thought Harry should do something about it.

Harry shifted uncomfortably. "Tucker, there's a problem. Katherine and Hatfield are sleeping together. There's not much I can do."

Tucker didn't cut Harry any slack. "I'm an old man who ought to be minding his own business, but was I you, I'd find some way to talk to her before it's too late. Thanks for the lemonade. I'll be on my way."

Harry helped Tucker hitch Oh-Brother! to the wagon and said goodbye to Sanchez and the mule. Oh-Brother! avoided looking at him and didn't waggle his ears.

Tucker looked at Harry and shook his head. Then he gave the reins a little shake. "Walk on," he said.

Harry watched them go off down the dusty road and, to his disgust, found himself worrying that he really might have offended Oh-Brother! with his comment about the mule's hat. He turned and set himself a stiff pace back to the house. Of all the damned foolishness.

Harry made himself lunch and while he ate it thought about Katherine and what Tucker had said. But he refused to think about how he felt about her. He was in no position, he told himself harshly, to think any way at all about her. As for Tucker's thinking she was in danger, well, it was obvious that her contacts with Boone carried some risk.

Looking to extricate himself from the issue altogether, he persuaded himself that if he did say something to her about Boone, she would probably hand him back his head, shaved and on a platter. For once, he was relieved when the phone rang. It was Abigail Blakeley. His relief turned to pleasure.

"Hello, Harry," she said. "Do you have any time this afternoon to talk with me?"

"At your house?"

"No. Can we meet at the Jetty? Say an hour from now?" The line was crackling and buzzing.

"We can, but why the Jetty? Do you have a problem with your telephone or is it mine?"

"I'm calling from my cell phone. I'm in a mall. There must be interference. Goodbye."

The Jetty was Avola's premier logo. It occupied a central place in all the promotion the city produced to fuel the tourist trade. For all the hype, it was just a big, wooden fishing pier, mounted on pilings. It was a dozen or so feet wide with seats and fish cleaning stations mounted at intervals along its length. It poked out into the Gulf of Mexico about a hundred yards. At its western-most end it widened into a square with a roofed-in center measuring thirty feet on each side.

Harry found Abigail sitting on the square on one of the stained wooden benches. She was wearing a robin's egg blue sundress and white sandals. She held a pale yellow parasol with a silver handle folded and propped against her thigh. Her wrap-around sunglasses protected her eyes against the glare from the water, and a straw hat with a low crown and rolled brim kept her hair from blowing.

"Harry!" she said over the sound of the wind and the hard rock and country music blaring from scattered radios. She reached out her hand to him as he approached. "What an extraordinary place. Do you know this is the first time I've ever been here? I just saw that man over there with that wicked looking knife on his belt pull in a black tipped shark almost as big as he is. It was very exciting."

And very illegal. The man she was describing wore a bushy beard, long sun-streaked hair, aged sandals, and frayed rainbow-colored shorts, glinting with fish scales. He was chewing on a cigar and looked as if he wrestled alligators. The two sun-blackened women with him, barefoot and wearing thongs and little else, were fishing with hand lines and carrying on a harsh, rapid fire conversation, broken by frequent laughter, in a language Harry didn't recognize. The man ignored them.

The rest of the men and women, hanging over the rails in various stages of undress, were shifting their attention between their fishing and Abigail. Most of them were smoking, drinking from brown paper bags, taking snuff, and shouting obscenities at the pelicans waddling around the deck, pooping copiously, and trying to steal fish out of the bait buckets. Abigail, apparently unaware of or undisturbed by the attention she was getting, appeared to be completely at ease. Harry thought with amused astonishment that she wouldn't have looked any more out of place in an igloo.

"What did they do with the shark?" he asked.

"Subdued it after a spirited struggle by knocking it on the head, filleted it, and pitched what was left into the water. I never saw anything disappear so fast. Two small, dark men gave our buccaneer some money, packed the fillets in two sacks with some cracked ice, and rushed away like Mayan messengers. I wouldn't have missed it for the world."

Her recital had attracted some additional attention, and Harry quickly sat down beside her and said quietly, "It's against the law to catch sharks from the pier. Better not say any more about it."

"Is it a sensible law?"

"Yes. It has widespread support among the sharks. Now, why are we out here?"

"So that you can walk me back to my car, and we can talk without fear of being overheard."

"I thought your husband had gone back to New York," Harry said. They got up and she handed him the parasol.

"Do you want me to carry it?"

"No, Dear. I want you to open it for me." He opened it.

"Thank you. He has left, but, distressing as it is to face, I think Joe has installed a surveillance system in the house. I'm no longer comfortable using the phones. I'm not quite sure what to do about it."

If Harry hadn't seen Joe Speroni sprinting around a corner in his own house, he would have asked her what she'd been smoking.

"How upset are you?" Harry asked.

"Manageably. He has some peculiar friends. My guess is he wants a record of their calls. But I do not wish to have my conversations recorded."

"Get someone in to run a check on the lines," Harry said. "If you don't know who to call, I'll give you some names."

They made their way slowly past the people fishing and through those who had wandered up from the beach to watch them fish. "Could I hire you to do it?" she asked.

"Better get a specialist."

"All right."

"Why did you send that letter to Luis Mendoza?"

She smiled at him from under her parasol. "Because I believed him to be in danger. I was almost relieved when I learned he had been arrested. Have you been remiss in some way, Harry, in allowing that to happen? Luis must be very disappointed."

That was a sore spot.

"It's worse than remiss," Harry admitted. "I totally failed to come up with anything to move him out of the Sheriff's Department's line of fire. I've tried to tell him his lawyer is going to have him on the street within a week and that there's zero chance of his being convicted, even if the case ever comes to trial. But Florida prisons do not foster optimism."

"No, I should think not," she replied. "Such a gentleman. He must be finding it very difficult."

They were off the pier, and the crowd thinned as they crossed the narrow strip of sand into the welcome shade of the gumbo limbo trees lining the street where her car was parked. She handed him her parasol.

"Tell me why you think Luis is at risk," Harry said.

She took off her hat and sunglasses and shook out her hair with a sigh of relief.

Harry felt very good to be walking with her. He knew it was foolish, but, to make it easier to go on feeling good, he told himself truthfully that she looked as if she had just stepped off the cover of *A*, Avola's upscale fashion publication.

"My husband has business dealings with a developer by the name of Orville Boone. Do you know the name?"

"I know him." Harry tried not to sound surprised.

"He and another man came to see my husband on the evening of the day you interviewed me. Do you remember the date?"

Harry took his notebook out of a back pocket and thumbed through some pages.

"May twenty-eighth," he said.

She nodded.

"They came about nine o'clock. Joe took them into his study, and they stayed over an hour. There was a lot of shouting. Mr. Boone, in particular, was very angry."

"Who was the third man?" Harry asked.

"Someone I had never seen before. Joe introduced us. I think the name was Tibbs or Trudeau. Something like that."

"Thibedeau?"

"Yes. That's the name. Unusual."

"Could you hear what they were talking about?" He was

both startled and excited by what she was saying.

"Only when they were shouting. Luis Mendoza's name kept coming up whenever the Avola Gold project was mentioned. Mr. Boone was particularly incensed with Luis and threatened all sorts of dire things. I seldom heard Mr. Thibedeau's voice, but when I did he was swearing about Luis."

She relieved Harry of the parasol, thanked him for being so gallant, and then sighed again. She was too polished, he thought, to show all of her feelings, but he guessed she had heard things that seriously upset her.

They had reached her white Jaguar. It was, Harry noted, a Vanden Plas with leather interior, walnut trim, and all the gold bells, silver whistles, and platinum spark plugs the company offered.

"Is your husband interested in the Avola Gold project?" Harry tried to sound as if the answer was not particularly important.

"Oh, yes. He handled the IPO of the stock in Avola Gold. He has sold a great deal of it. I believe that despite the problems the project has encountered getting permitted, the stock has done very well."

"And there were threats made against Luis Mendoza's life at that meeting?"

"Oh, perhaps nothing that direct, but, Harry, I admit what I heard frightened me. They were so abusive. And Joe's response later when I asked him about the meeting was intense, to say the least. You know he can be very intimidating. I decided to write anonymously to Luis. I was afraid something might happen to him."

"Did any other names come up?"

"Mr. Thibedeau referred to someone named Hatfield several times. He kept referring to him as that . . . I would prefer not to be more specific."

While she gave him the information, her voice and facial expression remained calm and unambiguous. Harry wondered if she had ever been on the stage and looked without success for laughter in her lovely blue eyes.

"I understand." He kept his own face straight. "Can you remember anything else?"

"No, except to insist I felt Mr. Mendoza was in danger."

Something else occurred to Harry.

"Do you and your husband see a lot of Orville Boone?"

"He and my husband have a close business association. He is sometimes at the house for social events. I have decided to reserve my judgment about Mr. Boone." She smiled sweetly.

"You may be right about Luis being in danger," Harry said. He did not want to frighten her, but he wanted to be clear about the risks she was running. "Promise me you won't send any more letters. You could get yourself into some very serious trouble."

She protested that she was only trying to help.

"I know, but it's easy to misunderstand an unsigned letter like that. The police have it, and I'm almost certain they're not going to do anything with it. I'm not going to say anything about it, and I hope you'll be smart enough not to."

She tilted her head and smiled at him, her eyes dancing.

"How masterful, Harry." She tapped him on the shoulder with the parasol. "You are a very interesting mix of a number of things. Thank you for indulging me this afternoon and for your advice. I am truly grateful. Now I must hurry. I will get the phones swept, and when I know they're clean, I'll call you. Goodbye."

More than one of us is a mix of a number of things, Harry thought, returning her wave as the Jaguar silently stole her away.

Chapter 12

When Harry had absorbed what Abigail had told him, he knew he was going to have to share at least some of it with Herrera and Snyder. He called Herrera and arranged to meet the detectives at nine Thursday morning at the North Avola Sheriff's Station.

"I hope you're not going to waste our time complaining because we arrested your client," the detective said in an abrasive voice when Harry said he wanted the meeting.

"I wasn't going to mention it because I didn't want to embarrass you," Harry replied. "But since you brought it up, does the decision to charge Luis have anything to do with Sheriff Fisher's re-election campaign and his standing with the One Hundred Committee? The last time I looked, the OHC was a PAC made up of Orville Boone and a bunch of other developers, big land owners, and their lawyers. Or doesn't it matter in which campaign basket that elephant drops its load?"

"You know what, Brock?" Herrera said. "Go to hell."

After he had hung up, Harry reminded himself with a flicker of remorse, instantly overshadowed by glee, that responding in kind or extending and intensifying an unpleasantness was wrong.

On the way to meet Herrera, Harry stopped at the county jail to talk to Luis. He wanted to see how he was weathering his ordeal and to run past him some of what Abigail had said.

A guard led Harry into a small, windowless, cement block

room to meet Luis. The walls and the floor, Harry noticed, hadn't been painted in the year since he'd last seen them and had moldered into the sinister color of algae growing on the ponds around the County's water treatment plants. The ominous click of the one-way lock as the guard closed the door behind them and stepped into his observation cubicle reminded Harry this was not summer camp.

It took Harry's mind off the room's paint job and the one-way lock to see how poorly Luis was adjusting to prison life. His baggy orange coveralls and one-size-fits-all cap gave him a forlorn, Chaplinesque look without the comedic charm. Luis told Harry he had not found his colleagues to be good conversationalists, and the challenge and excitement of mopping the corridor floors had petered out as soon as he had wrung out the mop for the second time. Between the shouters and the TV he wasn't getting much sleep. Worst of all, the food wasn't agreeing with him. Harry could see that without being told. There were dark circles under Luis's eyes, and his olive complexion was washed down to the color of old putty.

They were seated on opposite sides of the severely wounded metal table in the interview room. "What does Smolkin tell you?" Harry asked.

"He tells me to be patient. That he is working on it. I think that means I'm stuck here. Do you have any good news, Harry? I could use some. Theresa and Gisela come in often, but this is no place for them. They cry. I am almost glad when they leave."

He stopped speaking and sat hunched in a miserable silence. Harry knew he wasn't feeling sorry for himself. It was just that he had nothing meaningful to do, and it was wearing him down.

Harry tried to sound optimistic. "Jeff is good. If there's a way to get you out of here, he'll do it. But nothing moves quickly through the courts. You know that."

He did not add that most of the power brokers in Tequesta County were cheering his incarceration. Luis nodded, sighed, and made an effort to look as if he was interested when Harry began speaking.

"Someone I talked to yesterday told me Joe Speroni is hooked up with Emile Thibedeau and Orville Boone. Do you know anything about Speroni?"

"A little. He is Abigail Blakeley's husband. You talked to Mrs. Blakeley. Do you remember?"

"I remember," Harry said he did, but kept the enthusiasm with which he remembered out of his voice. "I've been told Speroni is a New York stock broker. He pushed the IPO when the Avola Gold project went public. My information is that the stock's doing well."

"For now," Luis said. "Outing Thibedeau over his misuse of his Commissioner's position could lead to a major public outcry about influence pedaling. That might cause people to start dumping the stock, especially if the project itself is held up."

"Is Boone a player?"

"Almost certainly. A lot of very important people invested heavily in the stock."

"Might that be why Boone and Thibedeau are having night meetings with Speroni? From what I was told, the three of them were doing a lot of swearing. Your name came up several times."

"Are you surprised?" His voice betrayed his impatience with the news.

"No. But I was surprised to hear Thibedeau was also calling Slade Hatfield names. Can you make anything of that?"

Luis leaned back wearily in his chair and rubbed a hand over his face.

"I don't think so. Unless . . ." He sat forward with a sudden show of energy. "Is there any possibility they and Hatfield might have been involved in some way with Will Trachey's murder?" His shoulders sagged. "No. Of course there isn't. I'm grasping at straws. What reason would they have for killing Willard Trachey? God, if I stay in here much longer, I will lose the ability to reason at all."

Harry didn't take Mendoza's theory very seriously, but he didn't want to dismiss it. "The idea may not be all that ridiculous. Just because you can't find a motive for them wanting him dead doesn't mean there isn't one."

He pushed back from the table.

"You hang tough, Luis. I'm not quitting on this. And if nothing else, I've now got a reason to talk to Thibedeau. I'll rattle his cage. See what shakes loose."

Brave talk, Harry thought. He watched sadly as Luis was led away.

On Thursday morning, Harry talked to Herrera and Snyder. The North Avola Sheriff's Office was a low, tan stucco building with wide eaves and an oversized parking lot. The building was set in a dense clump of cabbage palms, live oaks, and white oleanders. Harry stepped out of the Rover into an orchestra-sized buzz of locusts in the oaks loud enough to muffle the traffic noise on the road. It was a busy, good-natured racket that cheered him considerably.

"Officers Snyder and Herrera are not here." The dispatcher glowered at him from behind her glass barrier. "Sit down, and I'll see what I can find out."

Sheriff's Department deputies were all required to wear uniforms a minimum of one size too small and greet the public as if everyone was on probation. The dispatcher was no exception. She came back to her station scowling darkly.

"Sergeants Herrera and Snyder will see you," she barked. She did not explain why she had said they weren't in. She pointed to the right. "I'm going to buzz you through that door. Proceed straight down the corridor until you are intercepted by someone. If you reach the end of the corridor without seeing anyone, turn and come back to the chairs. Sit down and wait."

Running over all the clever, witty remarks he might have made to the dispatcher but had the good sense not to make, Harry waited in front of the gray door until it finally growled at him and pulled it open.

"Hello, Harry." Snyder was waiting for him in the corridor.

They shook hands and Snyder led him into a cramped gray office with a gray tile floor and two black metal desks shoved against the left and the right walls. Herrera was seated behind the desk to Harry's right, studying a charge sheet. Except for dead flies, the walls were undecorated and flooded with icy light from the recessed fluorescent tubes in the ceiling. The room, Harry thought in disgust, was even less inviting than the one in which he had talked to Luis Mendoza.

"Nice place," he said.

"Furnished from The World's End Shop." Herrera looked up from his charge sheet. "What do you want?"

"Whoa," Jim Snyder said. He dropped a hand on Harry's shoulder. "Hold on. You've got to excuse my partner here. Dave got out of the wrong side of his bed this morning and forgot to pick up his manners before he left the house. He's sour as old mash." His long face broke into a grin.

"How are you Harry?" he asked. "I hear Trachey's cabin is occupied again. Katherine Trachey and her kids in there now?"

Harry took the folding chair Snyder pushed toward him. "They've moved in." He did not say that Hatfield was also there most of the time. "Why do you guys think Boone put her there?"

"She needed a place to live," Snyder said.

"Who gives a shit?" Herrera inquired.

Harry grinned. Snyder lifted his head and stared at the ceiling as if seeking guidance.

"I'm not going to reveal my source," Harry said, getting to the purpose of his visit, "but there's something I need to tell you. It involves Orville Boone."

"Go ahead," Snyder said, squeezing behind his desk and awkwardly folding himself into his chair.

Herrera had already flipped open his notebook and cocked his pen.

"A few nights ago, Orville Boone, Emile Thibedeau, and Joseph Speroni met at Speroni's house in River Run and had a long, loud, angry conversation which was overheard," Harry began. "Luis Mendoza's name kept coming up. Boone cursed him and made unspecified threats against him. Based on what was said, my informant expressed the fear Mendoza's life was in danger."

"That it?" Herrera asked.

"Two more things." Harry was determined not to start up with Herrera. "They seemed to be focusing on the Avola Gold project. At least its name came up a lot. They also talked about Slade Hatfield. Thibedeau in particular swore a lot about him, although my informant couldn't say why. And I've got a line on a letter Will Trachey had in his possession just before he was killed."

"What letter is that?" Snyder demanded. He was bent over his notebook scribbling diligently.

"A letter he may have been using to blackmail somebody,"

Harry responded. "It's fragile, but it may have something to do with why he was killed."

Herrera finished writing and dropped his pen on the desk with a clatter and looked up.

"You got this letter?" he asked.

"No," Harry said. "It seems to have gone missing."

Herrera made a snorting noise and leaned back in his chair. He had stopped scowling, but Harry could see that whatever was bothering the detective had not let up.

"Too bad the letter's been lost," Snyder said. "Does it have any connection with the meeting?"

"Maybe. But first," Harry said, "I think the fact you haven't asked me who Joe Speroni is means that you know who he is. I think you've seen him and Boone together often enough so that you aren't surprised that Boone and his broker are meeting secretly at night with a County Commissioner to shout and swear at one another about two people as apparently unconnected as Luis Mendoza and Slade Hatfield. Finally, I think it's reasonable to assume this meeting might be connected with Will Trachey's murder."

Herrera had turned back to watch Harry until he was finished speaking and then looked at his watch without any change of expression.

"One: I'd say you've got nothing," the detective said. "Two: businessmen meet all the time. They even swear at one another and third parties. But since you think it's important, I'll give it some more thought, but right now Snyder and I have work to do."

He got up.

"Gentlemen," Harry said in a friendly voice but very firmly, staying planted in his chair, "you're making a mistake. Give me five more minutes."

Herrera made a lot of work out of picking up his notebook

and his pen and pushing his chair back. It was clear to Harry he did not want to talk about this, and all his body language said so.

"When you decide to tell me who's peddling this garbage, I might be willing to listen. But not before," Herrera said.

He pointed at the door.

"After you, Harry."

Snyder started to say something, then changed his mind. He got slowly to his feet, avoiding Harry's eyes. Something, Harry thought, is seriously wrong here.

"I'm not going to tell you that, Herrera," he said. "You know I don't have to. At least at this point."

He had stayed seated.

"Let's go, Harry," Herrera said sharply.

Harry saw he was not going to be listened to. He got to his feet.

"And what I told both of you is privileged information. Are we in agreement on that?"

That got Herrera's attention.

"What do you mean?" he demanded, the color climbing up his neck.

"I mean I don't want anything I've said to you leaking back to Boone."

"Will you get the hell out of here, Harry?" Herrera said in a loud voice.

Harry glanced at Snyder, but the detective only shook his head.

"Have a nice day," Harry said and left.

Chapter 13

The following morning Harry decided to talk to Thibedeau. He also decided to stop trying to figure out why Herrera had become so hostile during their meeting yesterday afternoon when Harry talked about Boone, Thibedeau, and Speroni, and the letter that Mendoza had received. Snyder's puzzled response to his partner's behavior added to Harry's concern, but for the moment there was nothing he could do about it.

It was too early to call on Thibedeau, and Harry was tired of the house. He pulled on his hat and set off to find out what Tucker had to say about the South Avola Commissioner. The road lay before him, and he walked to Tucker's to stretch his legs, feel the sun on his back, and listen to the mockingbirds. He came upon an indigo snake, sunning in the road. It was nearly four feet long and glittering black; Harry was almost on the snake before the creature discovered it had company. It lifted the first two feet of its length into a graceful S, regarded Harry briefly with an onyx-eyed stare, and then, with a liquid ripple of muscles, slipped haughtily into the coffee bushes lining the road. Harry allowed himself to feel a little put out by the snake's departure because usually indigo snakes were remarkably tolerant of humans.

Tucker met Harry at the door with his news fairly bursting out of him and waved Harry into the house. "They've struck again," he said.

They, Harry knew, had to mean Bonnie and Clyde. He crossed the porch, eager to hear the details of the bandits' raid. Sanchez woofed him through the door and rushed ahead of them into the kitchen, his tail erect. There was something odd about the way he moved, but before Harry got a good look at him, he was out the door again.

"It's got him pretty worked up," Tucker said in a whisper.

Harry sat down at the kitchen table. "What have they done?"

Tucker brought the tea. "They decided to tunnel into the hen house." He poured the tea and pushed a plate of sugar cookies toward Harry.

"That fence is buried two feet deep," Harry said in surprise.

"They'd been planning this for a good while," Tucker said. "And if it hadn't been for Oh-Brother!, they might have carried off the whole flock."

At this point Sanchez barked his agreement through the screen door.

"The short version," Tucker said, "is that the two villains started their tunnel in the middle of that saw palmetto tangle just north of the hen run. With the entrance hidden under the palmetto fronds, they could take their time with their digging."

"How did Oh-Brother! find out what was going on?" Harry was caught up in Tucker's narrative and had forgotten to be skeptical.

"He fell into the tunnel with both front feet." Tucker slapped his leg in his excitement. "It was the sandy ground that beat 'em. I was working in the garden, and Oh-Brother! left off watching me and went to tell Sanchez something. He was walking around the north end of the hen run when all at once the ground gave way, and there he was up to his chin in the dirt."

Harry turned around to see Sanchez grinning at him

through the screen. Harry grinned back and then caught himself.

"The tunnel collapsed?" he asked.

"That's it. Sanchez came along and found Oh-Brother! in the hole with his hat over his eyes and started laughing at him. Well, if there's anything a mule don't like, it's being laughed at."

Sanchez limped off the stoop, and went around the house.

"He's been hurt," Harry said, watching him go.

Tucker nodded.

"He doesn't want to talk about it, but Oh-Brother! kicked him."

"For laughing at him?"

"Oh-Brother! feels bad about it." Tucker was struggling to keep his face straight. "But a mule is sensitive and has been so put upon by life, it's easy for him to get carried away by his emotions. That's what happened. While I was digging away the dirt so Oh-Brother! could climb out of the hole he'd fallen into, Sanchez kept grinning and passing remarks. I told him to cut it out. He didn't listen, and when Oh-Brother! got out of the hole, he let Sanchez have it."

Tucker couldn't control himself any longer and burst out laughing.

"Oh-Brother! forgets how strong he is," Tucker said when he caught his breath, "and he kicked old Sanchez right into that clump of oleander. The poor soul sprained a leg getting out of the bush and he's been limping ever since. Of course, he limps a lot worse when he's where Oh-Brother! can see him."

Harry found himself laughing right along with Tucker and took a good belt of the cast iron tea to get hold of himself.

"Those devils were within four feet of going under the wire." Tucker wiped his eyes with a big red handkerchief.

146

"One more night and it would have been goodbye, chickens and farewell, Beauregard."

"I'm surprised Sanchez didn't catch on to what was happening out there." Harry tried and failed to free himself from the animal drama unfolding all around him.

"Well, he's become so afraid of losing his bone, he carries it with him on his rounds, and when he's got it in his mouth, he can't smell anything else. I imagine whichever of them gray Indians was on watch signaled the one down in the hole to stop digging when Sanchez came along. Oh, they had it all worked out."

"You'll have to start leaving Oh-Brother! out at night," Harry said before he could stop himself. "I expect he's got a score to settle with them."

"Can't do it." Tucker spoke in his most serious voice. "Oh-Brother! would trample them into hamburger. Smart as they are, they can't hold a candle to him, and he'd have one in his teeth and one under his feet before you could say Jack Robinson."

"I can see that." Harry was sobered by the picture of Oh-Brother! tearing into the two foxes. Then he caught himself thinking of Oh-Brother! as an avenging mule, and, making a major effort, broke out of the spell the story had cast on him.

"Tucker," he said, "I need your help. What can you tell me about Emile Thibedeau?"

"Let me heat that up." Tucker held the pot over Harry's cup. "Well, I know a little about Commissioner Thibedeau. What's your interest in him?"

Harry told him.

"Emile Thibedeau came from the Louisiana bayou country. Cajun stock, most likely."

"What brought him to Avola?"

"Smell of money would be my guess. Started as a tax lawyer. Then worked himself up or down, depending on your view of such things, into a small-time politician. He was on the city council for a while. He's always been linked with development projects. He's a big property rights man, not that he had much of it himself, up until recently. Property rights is the song he always sings when he's campaigning."

"Straight or crooked?"

Tucker grinned.

"He's been in half a dozen scrapes with the State Ethics Committee, but nothing ever sticks to him. The Avola Gold project is only the latest. He's been tight with Orville Boone for a while now. I'd say their relationship has paid off for him."

Tucker paused and then made a face. "Thibedeau has always sailed damned close to the wind and voted positions that benefited his companies and his partners' interests. The way I see it, in the Avola Gold thing he just got a little more arrogant and a lot more greedy."

"According to Luis Mendoza, millions more greedy," Harry said.

Tucker scratched his chin. "You know, in the last few years money has poured so fast into Tequesta County a lot of the natives have gone from being barefoot crackers to big operators. Only their brains haven't developed with their wardrobes. Most of them still have the mind-set of plume hunters, gill netters, and alligator poachers. On the other hand, they mostly want to forget what they came from. That's one of the less obvious reasons they're trying to cut down all the woods and drain the swamps."

"And Thibedeau's one of them. Is that what you're saying?" Harry pushed back his chair.

"More or less. You been down to see Katherine since she

moved in?" Tucker walked Harry to the door.

"No. Have you?"

He shook his head. "She's been over here a couple of times to borrow milk and once sugar. She seems pretty happy with how things have turned out for her. But I'm still worried about her."

"I'll see her one of these days," Harry said. He did not want to re-enter the discussion of what he should be doing about Katherine. "And don't you forget what I said about watching yourself. Whatever this mess is we're in here on the Hammock, it's not over yet."

Oh-Brother!, wearing his straw hat, came around the barn to see Harry off and waggled his ears at him in a friendly way. Right then Harry remembered laughing at Oh-Brother's hat and wished Tucker hadn't filled his head with thoughts of a killer mule. He said goodbye in a friendly way to the big animal but stayed clear of his heels.

Just before noon on Monday, Corporal Jim Snyder drove into Harry's yard. Harry was painting the front hall and put down his roller with a flicker of anxiety. For no good reason, he thought something had happened to Katherine. He had no reason for thinking such a thing. But as the tall, lanky man came up the path with his long, slow strides, carrying his hat in one hand and his jacket in the other, Harry couldn't get the worry out of his head.

"I got some bad news to deliver to Katherine Trachey," he said as Harry let him into the lanai. "I thought you might help me out."

Harry gestured toward a couple of chairs, and they sat down. Snyder's long face was drawn with concern. "Slade Hatfield's been killed." He leaned forward and dropped his elbows onto his knees.

Harry glanced at his watch. She would be at work. The kids at school. God, he thought, this is really going to hit her. Harry couldn't claim he had seen it coming. But now that it had happened, he found he wasn't surprised.

"What happened?" he asked.

Snyder leaned back and lifted his arms off his knees and dropped them on the arms of his chair. The movement did a wonderful job of conveying his frustration and anger.

"Somebody shot him. Christ Almighty, he must have half a dozen bullets in him. He looks like a sieve."

Harry remembered what Willard Trachey looked like and felt a chill pass over him. "Where was he killed?"

"At Sampson's Marina. Up in that weird office. You been up there?"

Harry nodded, recalling the stairs and the room that reminded him of a ship.

"Any idea when it happened?"

"I'm betting it was sometime this morning. One of the boat space renters called it in about ten-fifteen. Hatfield had been dead a while when Dave and I got to him."

"Leads?"

Snyder shoved his long legs out in front of him like a big kid and shook his head, pulled on an ear, and scowled out through the screens at the live oaks.

"The place looked clean to me," he said. "Of course the Crime Scene Unit might find something."

He didn't sound hopeful. While Harry was listening to Snyder, he was also searching for something that would tie Slade Hatfield's death to the Trachey killing and help him clear Luis Mendoza. He followed those thoughts until Snyder finally began shifting in his chair and shuffling his feet.

"Sorry," Harry said. "What were you saying?"

"The thing is, I'm the one stuck with the job."

He stalled.

". . . of telling Katherine, and you want me with you while you do it," Harry said.

Snyder scowled more ferociously and shook his head. For a moment, Harry couldn't figure out why he was shaking his head. Then he got it.

"You want me to tell her," he said.

"I'll be there." Snyder fixed Harry with his earnest blue eyes.

Harry suddenly remembered Tucker saying Snyder belonged in the woods somewhere running a still. Harry studied the young man. Snyder seemed far too thin-skinned for this job.

"Sure," he said. "I'll wash the roller, clean up a little, and we'll go."

While Snyder drove, Harry asked him if there was some particular way he was supposed to go about breaking this kind of news.

"We're not supposed to do it in front of a lot of other people," Snyder said, "but aside from that, we're pretty much on our own. Dave vanished like smoke up a chimney when the super showed up with the orders in his hand." He sounded shocked by Herrera's defection.

"OK," Harry said.

Harry gave the receptionist his name and asked her to call Helen Bradley and tell her he needed to speak with her in private. "She's Boone's office manager," he told Snyder. "I know her. She might be able to help us with this thing."

Snyder nodded. The receptionist made the call and sent them with a smile to the second floor conference room. Helen was waiting for them when they got off the elevator, a slim woman, with thick, honey-brown hair worn loose over her shoulders. The blue suit she was wearing matched her eyes.

"Hello, Harry," she said, shaking his hand warmly. "This is a long way from the Caloosa Trace."

"Hello, Helen," Harry said. "I wish I was there. This is Detective Sergeant James Snyder of the Sheriff's Department, Criminal Investigation Division."

"Harry and I swapped birding stories and sandwiches from our sack lunches some months ago on an Audubon field trip to the Trace," she told Snyder and shook his hand. "It's one of the few places outside the Everglades where it's still possible to see a snail kite. Are you a birder?"

Snyder's face turned crimson. "No, Ma'am," he said.

"Recruit him, Harry," she said, grabbing Harry by the arm and leading them into the conference room, talking over her shoulder to Snyder about the Trace. She closed the door and changed voices. "What's going on here?"

"Slade Hatfield, a friend of Katherine Trachey's, has been killed," Harry said. "Sergeant Snyder has to tell her. I'm here because she's my neighbor and because I know her."

Helen nodded.

"Were they living together?" she asked.

"I guess," Harry said reluctantly. "They were seeing a lot of one another."

"He was living with her, Ma'am," Snyder said.

Harry ground his teeth. Snyder didn't have to right out say it.

"The poor kid. She mentioned him a few times. I didn't much like what I heard, but she talks about you a lot more." She cocked an eyebrow at Harry. "Mostly it's been, 'Harry said this, and Harry said that.' There was a while I thought you were her therapist."

"Harry found her husband dead," Snyder put in. "Afterward, he looked after her and the kids until Orville Boone got her into an apartment."

"I remember," Helen said. "It was in the paper. You need a place to tell her where you won't be disturbed. Will this room do?"

Harry glanced at Snyder. The policeman nodded.

"All right," Helen said. "I'll get her."

While they waited for Helen to return with Katherine, Snyder, too nervous to stand still, occupied himself pulling out three of the chairs from the conference table and arranging and rearranging them in an open triangle. Harry watched him and brooded.

His anxiety for her suddenly erupted. "Katherine Trachey should begin looking four ways before crossing a street."

"You could be right," Snyder said.

Katherine burst into the room.

"Has something happened to one of the kids?"

Harry stepped forward and caught her hands. They were cold as spring water, and her face was dead white.

"They're OK, Katherine," he said. "It's not about them."

"Oh, God," she said in relief, dropping onto a chair, "I was sure . . ."

"Would you like me to stay?" Helen asked, holding the door open.

"Not on my account," Katherine said quickly, pulling herself together. She turned in her chair and added, "But I thank you for coming up here with me. I thought . . ."

She let the sentence trail away and turned her back to the door. Helen looked at Snyder and Harry. Snyder didn't respond to her question. That left it to Harry.

He decided Katherine would rather hear what they had to say in private, even if, as he knew, by tomorrow it would be on the front page of *The Avola Banner*.

"Thanks, Helen," he said. "We'll be OK."

"Thank you, Ma'am," Snyder said, finding his voice. "You've been very helpful."

Helen backed out of the room, giving Harry a quick, cross-fingered wave before pulling the door shut behind her.

"You remember Sergeant Snyder?" he asked Katherine, sitting down next to her.

Harry gave Snyder's jacket sleeve a twitch to get him off his feet.

"We talked a few times right after Will was killed," she said, keeping her eyes fixed on Harry.

"Katherine," Harry said, repeating himself as way of getting started. "Minna and Jesse are fine. But we've got some bad news."

"I guess you'd better go ahead and tell me," she said.

"It's about Slade Hatfield," Harry continued.

She gave me a short nod and looked down at her folded hands. Then she reached for her braid. Not finding it, she refolded her hands with a quick grab, like a person trying to catch her balance. He started to speak again, but she interrupted him.

"He's dead, isn't he?"

"Yes. I'm sorry, Katherine."

"I believe I've been expecting it," she said.

Her voice was flat and soft, and she seemed to be calm. But the moment she stopped speaking, she spun the chair around, threw her arms onto the table, dropped her head on them, and burst into tears, twisting her hands together and rocking her face back and forth on her arms, saying, "Oh, oh, oh, oh," over and over.

Harry put his arm around her shoulders and held her as tightly as he could without hurting her. What he wanted to do was lift her up from the table and get both arms around her, but decided not to. He thought Snyder might be going to bolt.

Feeling her body shake with her sobs, Harry made himself admit she'd probably found in Slade Hatfield someone who might love her. Now he'd gone the same way as Willard; the only good thing about the whole sorry business was that she was never going to have to find out what Hatfield really was.

When she finally sat up, she turned and pressed herself against Harry for a moment before easing out of his embrace.

"I'm so sorry, Katherine," he said.

"Thanks, Harry," she whispered.

Harry picked up her pocketbook from the floor and set it on the table beside her. After a moment, she pulled it front of her and took a tissue out of it and blew her nose. She sat again for a while, staring at the wall, then gave a shuddering sigh and pushed back from the table.

"How did it happen?" she asked, wiping her eyes.

"He was shot." Harry said. He felt there was no point in lying.

"Like Will," she responded as if all her roads had just run out. "Who did it?"

"We don't know." Snyder replied. "But we are surely going to find out."

"Perhaps you will." She spoke without much conviction. "Did he . . ."

"He would have been gone before he could feel anything," Snyder said.

She looked up at him briefly. "That was a mercy."

"It was," Snyder agreed.

"We'll take you home," Harry said. "If that's what you want. I'll talk to Helen. You won't have to do anything but walk out of here."

"No, Harry. I've got my car. I think more than anything else, I'd just like to be by myself for a while. After that, I'll decide what to do."

Snyder stepped closer to her. "Don't you think you might better have somebody with you?" he asked. "Maybe this is not a good time for you to be alone."

Harry held his breath, but Katherine managed something approaching a smile.

"I appreciate your thinking of it," she said. "But I'm good at being alone. I've had a lot of practice."

"We'll gladly sit with you."

She shook her head gently.

"Do you want to stay here?" Harry asked.

"I believe I will," she replied. "If I can."

"Nobody will bother you," he said. "I'll see to it. I'll give you a call later. If you need anything before then, I'll be home."

She nodded.

"I'm really sorry this has happened," Snyder said to her.

"Thank you." She spoke without turning her head. "I do appreciate your caring."

When he and Harry were hiking along the corridor toward the elevator, Snyder said in a voice tight with anger, "Sometimes, it does seem the Lord gets carried away with piling it on."

"That's a fact," Harry agreed. "But it's said what doesn't kill us strengthens us."

"You draw a lot of comfort from that?" Snyder inquired.

"No," Harry answered. They dropped silently toward the lobby.

Harry talked to Helen before he and Snyder left, and she agreed to look in on Katherine and take her some coffee.

"Nice seeing you, Harry," she said.

"Nice seeing you, Helen," he replied, "and thanks for your help."

Snyder was quiet driving back to the Hammock. But

Harry, despite being deeply absorbed in his concern for Katherine, could see the detective was chewing on something, and going over the bridge Harry asked, "Did anything Katherine told us make you stop and think at all?"

"That she's been expecting to hear Hatfield was dead?" Snyder suggested.

"That's it," Harry answered. "Could be she just said it to try to ease the blow."

"But you don't believe it."

"I'd like to."

"So would I." He paused for a moment and added, "But Herrera wouldn't."

"No," Harry agreed. "He would want to know why she'd been expecting it."

Snyder nodded, screwed up his face and said, "I suppose we'll be asking her that pretty soon."

"Speaking of Herrera," Harry replied, changing the subject, "when I was in your office yesterday, Herrera chewed half a dozen holes in me. What was that all about?"

"Don't take it personally." Snyder made another sour face. "For a while now, he's been meaner than a bear with a sore jaw. I don't know what's wrong with him."

"I thought it had to do with what I was telling the two of you."

"No," Snyder said. "It's something else. I don't know what." He made a stab at adjusting his hat. "Look, keep your eye on Katherine Trachey, will you? I don't like it that we'll be questioning her again and adding to her problems."

"I'll do that." Harry was surprised by Snyder's interest.

"I'm much obliged for your help," Snyder added, turning into Harry's driveway.

"Glad I could help." He got out of the car and stooped to speak in the window. "She's had a hard time, and I've got the feeling things are not going to get easier for her."

"No, and it does seem to me a damned shame," Snyder agreed. He spoke with more edge than he generally displayed.

"It does," Harry said. Unbidden, his memory suddenly reminding him of the lost letter Willard had given Katherine.

Chapter 14

An hour after Harry got home, he saw Katherine drive past, bent over the wheel of her car, trailing a plume of white dust. Almost before the dust had settled, she came racing back and swerved into his yard, dragging another cloud of dust after her. She jumped out of the car and ran toward the house, carrying what looked to Harry like a green canvas shopping sack.

He pushed open the lanai door and asked, "Are you OK?"

She marched past him into the house without answering. Puzzled, Harry followed her. She walked into the kitchen, thumped the bag down hard on the table and turned to face him.

"Harry," she said, "I'm feeling real bad."

"I'm sorry you had to hear about Slade from Snyder and me." Harry was already feeling guilty.

She interrupted him impatiently. "Oh, that's not it. I'm not talking about losing Slade."

Harry was surprised enough to wait for her to go on.

"It's that bag."

They both looked at the bulky sack sitting on the table with its worn handles drooping like a hound's ears. Harry made a guess.

"When I told you Slade was dead, you said you'd been expecting it. Does the bag have anything to do with that?"

"Maybe." She gave him what he read as a worried frown. "Before we moved into the cabin, Slade began getting real nervous. He wouldn't say what was bothering him. But the

159

night after we got there, he brought me this bag and said real serious, 'Should there be any trouble, you hide this.' "

Her voice faltered. She put her hands to her face and said, "Could I have a glass of water?"

Harry pulled out a chair and steered her toward it. "Sit down."

She slumped into it and rested her elbows on the table, still holding her face with her hands. When he brought her the water, he also brought a box of tissues. She took one and dabbed her eyes. Then he pulled out a second chair and sat down beside her.

"Thanks," she said. "This keeps happening. I hope I can stop crying before the kids come home."

"You should cry all you want to," Harry said. "If you need some time to yourself, I can pick them up from the bus and keep them with me for a while."

She drank some of the water.

"Thanks. No. I'll be all right. I guess crying must dry you out." She made an attempt to laugh and had to settle for rubbing the back of her hand across her eyes.

"You want to put off talking about whatever it is until later?" he asked. He started to put his arm around her then stopped himself.

She turned to face him. "I'd better tell it now," she said, "in case . . . or I'll get no peace. And maybe not even then. But I surely won't unless I do tell you, and I know it's not right for me to be troubling you this way, but . . ."

"Forget apologizing," Harry said. He put his hand over hers. "Anytime you want to talk, I'm ready to listen."

She said thanks and managed a watery smile. Harry wondered if she'd been going to say, . . . in case something happens to me, before she stopped herself.

"Well, as soon as Slade told me about the bag, he looked

real mean at me and said, 'Don't you go near this bag otherwise. You hear?' "

Katherine took in and released a long, shaky breath, closed her eyes, and sat still as a stone.

"I didn't like that, Harry," she said. "I'd seen that mean, closed down look enough times on Will's face. The person staring at me right then was not the Slade Hatfield I thought I knew. It passed across my mind that I might have made a mistake in hooking up with him."

Harry stifled his impulse to say she'd been right on target.

"But, you know," she continued, shaking off the memory, "afterward I couldn't stop thinking about that damned sack. I didn't look in it or ask about it. But it got so I couldn't be alone in the cabin without having it on my mind."

She paused and sighed again and drank some more water.

"Well, anyway, I guess I do believe that sack is somehow connected to what's happened to Slade. And I wouldn't be surprised if somebody came looking for it. I don't want it in the house. I'm maybe a little scared for myself, but I'm more scared for the kids."

"You sure you don't know what's in it?" Harry asked the question as if her answer wouldn't be particularly important.

He hated having to admit it, but although he didn't believe she had killed her husband, there was still the possibility she had been involved with him in whatever had caused his death. And now Hatfield was dead.

Unless Maria Benedict brought in a time of death that made it impossible for Katherine to have killed him, Herrera and Snyder would have to consider her a prime suspect in this second shooting. Her bringing the bag to him was itself a troubling development.

"No, and I don't want to," she fired back. "I just want it out of my house."

Harry knew well enough the police should have it, but he also knew he was not going to give it to them until he'd had a chance to look through it. Harry grabbed the bag off the table and carried it into the living room and dropped it on the floor behind the couch.

"I'll take care of it," he said when he came back to the kitchen. Then a bad thought hit him. "Either one of the kids hear Slade tell you what you just told me?"

"No. They were both asleep, and he put it up on the high shelf in the bedroom closet and never spoke of it again."

Harry nodded, relieved the kids weren't involved.

"Snyder and Herrera have Slade's case," he said. "Snyder said they were going to have to talk to you sometime soon. Will you tell them about the bag?"

"Should I?"

"I think so. I might have to give it to them. Is that going to be all right with you?"

"Yes, it's OK." She got up, looking drained of energy.

"Are you going to take off some time from work?"

"No, I'm going to keep just as busy as the Lord will let me." Her tears spilled over again.

"When the kids come home, bring them over here. I'll get us dinner. If you don't want to sit, you can help."

She wiped her eyes. "Thanks, Harry, but I think I need to be alone with them tonight. I've got to do it. I'll be OK."

"Sure you will." He sounded more convinced than he was. "Just remember, you can change your mind."

They crossed the lanai together. At the door she turned and rested her head on his shoulder. Harry put his arms around her and without thinking about whether or not it was appropriate, pressed his face against her hair and rocked her gently as he held her.

Instead of pulling away, as he'd expected, she slipped her

arms around him and clung to him for a long moment. When she finally stepped away, she said in a soft voice, "Thank you, Harry." Then she blew her nose and gave a self-conscious laugh. "God, I'm a mess," she said.

"No, you're not. You're just great. I don't know anyone braver."

As she started for the door with her head up and her back straight, she said in the voice Harry knew best, "I know you're just saying that, but I'm going to pretend I believe it."

Harry watched her drive away, feeling as if his emotions had been hit by a twister. Disturbed over being disturbed, he strode back into the house and carried the canvas bag into the kitchen. Here at least was something that didn't make him feel as if he wanted to climb mountains and swim alligator-infested rivers. It smelled of thrice-fried grease and mildew. With an uncomfortable mixture of repugnance, curiosity, and reluctance, he dumped its contents onto the table. A jumble of loose sheets of paper, spiral bound account books, and envelopes of varying sizes tumbled out and slid into a discouraging heap.

Harry sat down and began sorting through the jumble. The account books ran back for several years and contained a surprisingly thorough record of Hatfield's finances. In the envelopes were automobile and boat insurance policies, old and current payment books for his car, a boat, appliances, and a job offer from Emile Thibedeau, dated three years earlier. These envelopes were scattered through a jumble of unsorted notes, dunning letters, hunting knife brochures, pages from gun catalogues, pictures of automobiles, naked women, porn ads, and old reminder lists. It was, Harry thought sadly, the depressing flotsam from a wrecked life.

He forced himself to look at every piece of paper in the

bag. He found nothing of interest. He was about to throw the papers back into the bag when he noticed an envelope stuck with a bit of pink gum to the back of a letter from a collection agency. Inside the envelope was a letter with Avola Gold Association, Inc. embossed across its top. It was addressed to Commissioner Emile Thibedeau. Harry skipped to the bottom of the sheet and saw Orville Boone's name over the title President. Above the printed name, Boone's signature.

The first paragraph of the letter described the outcome of some drilling tests Boone's construction company had completed for the Avola Gold project. The second talked about street locations in the projected development. But the third paragraph gave Emile Thibedeau a six-hundred-and-fifty-thousand-dollar share in the Avola Gold Association and a lifetime, no-fee membership in the Gold Club.

After a little thought, Harry remembered the Gold Club was the name of the two eighteen-hole golf courses that were being built as part of the Avola Gold development project. There was nothing in the letter about what Thibedeau was bringing to the table in exchange for the gifts.

Harry checked the date of the letter. He was pretty sure the date was at least two months earlier than the controversial vote by the Tequesta County Commissioners that gave the Avola Gold Association a development incentive grant of six-hundred-and-fifty-thousand dollars. Harry whistled and leaned back in his chair.

This letter was the reason Hatfield told Katherine to hide the bag if some unspecified trouble caught up with him. It also explained why he had told her not to look at the contents of the bag. It was, almost certainly, the letter Trachey had given Katherine at Henderson's Truck Stop.

"Blackmail," Harry said out loud.

And the person or persons being blackmailed? Emile

Thibedeau or Orville Boone. Possibly both men. Harry tapped his finger on the letter. If this was the letter Katherine said she lost, there were two possible explanations as to how Hatfield came to have it. One: she had given it to Hatfield and lied about losing it. Two: Hatfield had stolen it out of her pocketbook. And if he had stolen it, it was either because he found it by accident when, for some other reason, he was going through her bag, or, what was more likely, he went into her bag looking for it.

Harry thought it was probable Hatfield knew what Trachey was up to. If that was so, after Willard's death he probably made a move on Katherine in order to find the letter, concluding from the way the cabin was wrecked that whoever killed Will had looked for the letter and hadn't found it.

Harry's mind braked to a jarring stop. How could Hatfield have known the cabin was wrecked? Then he remembered. The first time he talked to Hatfield, he had told him. He couldn't remember telling Katherine about the damage done in the cabin, but he might have mentioned it. Or Herrera and Snyder may have mentioned it. So Hatfield could have heard it from several people, including Thibedeau and Boone.

Once he had the letter, Hatfield probably used it in the same way Trachey had. And gotten himself killed for his trouble. What had Katherine said about Willard getting in over his boot tops? Poor, dumb bastards, Harry thought; they had stepped into water way over their heads. In all likelihood, they had tried to blackmail Boone. He was the man with the real money and probably had killed both of them.

That brought Harry back to Katherine and two questions that had dogged him since Trachey's death. Why had Katherine hung around Henderson's Truck Stop so long, and why did Boone want Katherine in the cabin? Now he thought he had the answers. Trachey probably told her about the letter and what he planned to do with it. She had wrestled with the choice of going in with him for a slice of the money or staying out and getting nothing. Which choice had she made? He let the question go unanswered. At the moment, there was no way to answer it.

Turning his mind back to Boone, he decided the developer would have figured out that Will had given her the letter, and his first thought would have been to put her where he could keep an eye on her and have access to her without it creating suspicion. Yes, Harry thought with an angry scowl, the job and the cabin. But he hadn't counted on Hatfield moving in with her.

After Hatfield made his move, Boone would probably have thought that she had given him the letter. She may or may not have understood its importance. That thought pushed Harry out of his chair and set him pacing around the kitchen. If he was right about what had happened, someone would be calling on her in the very near future.

He picked up the phone.

"I've got something to show you."

She came out of the cabin to meet him, and he noted with a lift of spirits that the color had come back to her face and she looked as if she had just redone her plait. She looked calm and in command of herself. He gave her the letter. When she finished reading it, she nodded.

"That's the one Will gave me," she said. Her flat delivery did not disguise the pain that furrowed her face. "Guess I didn't lose it after all."

"He could have been looking for cigarettes."

"Harry, even Slade would have noticed that I don't smoke."

He opened his mouth, shut it again, and said, "I'm sorry."

"Well, what can you expect?" She pulled herself up and spoke harshly as if she was talking about someone else. "A widow with two kids and no money and halfway over the hill. It figures."

"It doesn't figure at all," Harry told her with a lot more feeling than he had intended.

"What?" She came back from wherever she had gone to contemplate her general unworthiness.

"I said it doesn't figure at all. You're young, beautiful, and bright. You've got two wonderful children. It didn't have to be this way."

She frowned a little, as if she didn't know who he was talking about.

"Well, it's nice of you . . ." She stared at him, letting her voice trail off.

"Don't look so surprised," Harry said. "I'm telling you the truth."

The color rose a little in her face, and she nodded, still staring at him in silence, as if she was seeing something that took her by surprise.

"If anybody comes looking for this letter, you tell them you never saw him get any letters, but you gave me Hatfield's personal effects to turn over to the police," Harry said. He spoke hurriedly, embarrassed by her steady stare. "Don't hesitate. Don't even think about lying."

"Are you going to give that letter to the police?"

"Not yet, but I will, and my offer still holds. If you want to bring the kids over for dinner, I'm barbequing chicken."

She came to dinner with Minna and Jesse. The children now treated Harry's house like a second home and ran in and out happily. Katherine was subdued, but Harry thought she was at ease with herself. She helped him set the table and made the salad. He told her about Tucker, and Bonny and Clyde's latest raid in the hen house. He managed to make her laugh, and laughing made her cry. But she recovered quickly, and they sat down together to eat just as the sun was setting.

Minna, who had been watching intently as the saffron and gold light flooded the room, said quietly, "In *The Littlest Hill*, it says the sunset is God's coloring book."

"I guess that will do for a grace," Katherine said, looking at Harry as she spoke.

"It's beautiful, Minna," he said.

He saw them all sitting together. It was a good moment. He felt peace and something very like happiness running through him like a healing river. In the next moment, another woman and two different children were staring back at him. Terrified, he shut his eyes and slammed the door shut on the memory so hard he flinched.

"Harry!" Katherine cried. "What's wrong?"

"Nothing. Nothing," he said. "Nothing at all. Let's eat." But the searing memory of Jennifer and the children had incinerated any thought of happiness this little family at his table seemed to promise.

The next afternoon, he went to see Emile Thibedeau in his offices at the Palm Center Building in an upscale section of Avola's business district. But before Harry left home, he climbed onto his roof carrying a length of clear nylon fishing line, a hammer, a two-inch finish nail, and Thibedeau's letter double wrapped and taped in black plastic. He reached down the chimney a couple of feet and tapped the nail half its length into a crack in the mortar.

Then he lowered the bag down the chimney on the line and hung the looped end over the nail. After he'd done that, he clambered back down the ladder and went into the house and opened the flue in the living room fireplace. Sticking his

head into the fireplace, he peered up through the open flue to
see if he could see the bag. To his relief, it was resting against
the side of the chimney and invisible. He closed the flue and
vacuumed up the small amount of soot his work had dis-
lodged.

Harry had spent an hour that morning in the library
finding out all he could about Thibedeau Enterprises, Inc. It
wasn't much, but it was enough to convince him the company
existed for the purpose of allowing its owner to step behind a
corporate door and do things he could not do as a County
Commissioner.

He also suspected it was as CEO of Thibedeau Enterprises
that its owner had entered into whatever agreements had
been concluded between him and Boone when they made
their Avola Gold deal. But that was guesswork because
Boone's letter was simply addressed to Mr. Emile Thibedeau. As Harry rose silently in the cherry wood and brass-
fitted elevator to Thibedeau's fourth floor suite, he tried
without success to make up his mind whether there had been
evasion or simple indifference in omitting Thibedeau's titles.

A sleepy receptionist smiled him into a blue leather chair,
and rang her boss while he took in the deeply carpeted room,
which he told himself was big enough for a dance hall. And
the glass breakfront on the left hand wall, he guessed, a little
enviously, would have sold for more than everything in his
living room.

"Mr. Thibedeau will see you shortly," she said. Having
announced Harry's arrival, she went back to turning the
pages of a magazine which lay open on her computer keyboard. The chair sighed as he sat down in it, and that was the
last sound he heard, aside from the rustle of the magazine
pages, until a door to his right swung open and Emile
Thibedeau welcomed him to Thibedeau Enterprises.

Thibedeau was tall and angular. He wore an expensive gray suit and English shoes. His nails had been professionally manicured, and the polka dots on his silk tie were the size of fifty-cent pieces. His hair was silver and sparkled in the soft light. He was clean shaven, tanned, and shook hands with a strong grip. His eyes were close to the color of his suit, and their brightness, Harry decided uncharitably, was due either to dope or false candor.

By the time he sat down in front of Thibedeau's mile-wide desk, Harry knew he wouldn't buy a cheap watch from the man, much less a used car.

"This is an unexpected pleasure, Mr. Brock. What can I do for you?" Thibedeau settled back in his chair.

Harry bent his dislike into civility. "I'm sorry about Slade Hatfield. I talked with him not too long ago. His dying the way he did is a bad business."

Thibedeau looked appropriately grave and nodded.

"He was a good man and a real wizard with a marine engine. I'm going to miss him."

"Did you know Will Trachey at all?" Harry asked. "He was killed back in May. Shot to pieces the same way Hatfield was."

"Worked for Orville Boone, didn't he? Lived out your way, if I remember right."

Harry caught Thibedeau's switch to a less formal way of speaking. He decided to follow the Commissioner's lead and kicked back a little, let his legs slide out some, joined in.

"That's right," Harry said. "Bartram's Hammock. In a cabin belonging to Orville Boone. His widow's there now with her two children."

Thibedeau shook his head and put on an expression of understanding sympathy.

"It's always the women and kids," he said.

170

"You're right there," Harry agreed. "Was Trachey black-mailing you and Boone?"

There was perhaps three quarters of a second after he stopped speaking when Thibedeau sat as if he had been carved out of granite. Then he breathed again and very carefully returned the bronze paperweight he had been turning in his hands to the exact place on his desk from which he had picked it up.

"What the fuck are you playing at, Brock?" His voice was icy.

"You'd know, wouldn't you?" Harry persisted.

Then he pulled his feet under him, because he had been looked at a couple of times in his life the way Thibedeau was looking at him, and in those cases the men had intended to kill him. But Thibedeau suddenly relaxed and leaned back with a laugh.

"What a shithead," he sneered. "Pretending to be a private investigator. Working for that pissant Mendoza." He interrupted himself to laugh again. "Get out of here, Brock, before I decide to kick you through the door."

Harry stood up and looked across the desk at Thibedeau. The man was no longer afraid. He leaned back in the full comfort of his vulgarity, arrogance, and pride of place. But for a fraction of a second he had been unable either to speak or move, and in that frozen instant Harry thought he'd found his answer.

Chapter 15

Driving home, Harry reviewed his encounter with Thibedeau and decided he might have done more than set a cat among Thibedeau and Boone's pigeons. He was certain that as soon as he left Thibedeau's office, the Commissioner had called Boone. It was possible, Harry thought with a stir of uneasiness, he was going to find himself the center of some unwelcome attention. As soon as he was home, he called Jim Snyder.

"I had a talk with Emile Thibedeau this afternoon," Harry told him, "and I may have gotten a little carried away. I asked him if Willard Trachey had been blackmailing him and Orville Boone. He didn't like it and threw me out of his office."

"Damn it, Brock, you might just have got Katherine into a lot of trouble," the detective said accusingly, reminding Harry that while Snyder might not be the swiftest swallow in the flock, he wasn't stupid either.

He was also impressed by Snyder's outburst. Here was a new side to the man. Tucker's spoiled moonshiner theory was wearing thin.

"I don't see how," Harry said.

"Well, if you're right, Thibedeau's going to tell Boone about your visit, and Boone's going to think Willard told Katherine something. Then he's going to think Katherine told it to you. So guess where he's going to go to find out just what it was she told you?"

His voice was beginning to rise by the time he got to the end of his explanation, which was a long one for Snyder.

"Then I'm glad I called you." Now he had the response he was looking for, he set about shamelessly exploiting it. "You might want to be seen in public places with her a few times. It will be noticed, and that by itself will be protection for her, along, of course, with the reassurance of your manly presence."

He did not say what else he thought, which was that it might also put the iron into Boone and Thibedeau to learn the Sheriff's Office had an interest in protecting Katherine. It might lead them to begin worrying about what the police might know. He saw no reason to say he thought that any physical threat would come from Boone.

"Well, I might be able to do a little of that," Snyder agreed. Harry could almost see his ears turning pink. "Do you know you could lose your license making unfounded charges like that against a County official?"

"I only asked if Trachey had tried to blackmail him and Boone," Harry said.

The detective snorted in disgust.

"Are you holding out on us?" His voice was suddenly thick with suspicion.

"Not really."

"That's not much of an answer."

Thinking about the letter, Harry agreed it wasn't and hung up, feeling only slightly guilty. He wandered to the lanai door and stood there for a while, looking without his usual pleasure at the long afternoon shadows falling across the open part of his yard. In that unguarded moment he suddenly recalled with plunging spirits the moment at the table when Minna mentioned the sunset and what had followed.

How could I have made such a mistake? he asked himself. He glanced again at the feeling of happiness he had so briefly experienced and then suppressed it. He thought of his ex-wife and children haunting the table. It's done for you, Brock. It's over. Get it through your thick head.

At that moment, the pair of red shouldered hawks nesting behind the house zipped over the lanai like two barnstormers. Grateful for the distraction, he watched the two beautiful brown and buff birds burn through their elaborate, patterned mating loops, screaming passionately at one another and telling the world this was their home.

By the time they were finished blasting the silence to bits, Harry had recovered enough to ask himself again if Katherine had been lying to him about the letter. Then a new and disturbing thought hit him. If she knew Will had tried to blackmail Thibedeau and Boone, and that Hatfield had done the same thing, she had committed a crime in not telling the police. With the letter in their hands, the police might be able to make the charge stick.

And while that tape ran in his head, Harry reminded himself he couldn't withhold the letter from the police very much longer without putting himself in the soup as well. But, he told himself, scrambling for a justification for holding onto the letter, he also had a professional obligation to protect Luis Mendoza, item one of which was to get him out of jail. The letter was the best leverage he had to do that and to remove the cloud of suspicion enveloping Luis.

Also he suspected that Thibedeau and Boone were linked to Trachey and Hatfield's murders. But with only the letter for support, he knew the Sheriff's Department and the State Attorney's office would not make any move against either Boone or Thibedeau. To force them to act, he would have to produce more evidence.

★ ★ ★ ★ ★

The next morning Harry went again to see Mendoza. He repeated the clanging, echoing entrance into the jail and was put in the same low rent room where he had met Luis on his first visit. The prisoner shuffled in, looking fifteen years older.

"Jesus, Luis, what's wrong with you?" Luis's appearance shocked Harry into forgetting the claustrophobia the room had awakened in him.

"I've been sick," Luis said as he slumped into his chair. "I started bleeding last Saturday. It's an ulcer. At least I was put on a special diet and Prevacid every day. It's helped. No more half-fried potatoes and blackened peas for a while."

"Are you in pain?"

"No, just tired. I'm not sleeping a lot."

"I may have some good news." Harry said. "I can't give you the details yet, but some information has come my way that might help you."

"This have anything to do with Emile Thibedeau?" Luis asked.

Harry glanced toward the cubicle where the guard was sitting, slowly turning the pages of a copy of *George* with an expression of surprise and disgust. How the magazine had found its way in here was linked, Harry guessed, to the tabloid exit from life of John Kennedy, Jr.

"Don't use names." He was embarrassed by the dramatic whisper he was using. "How did you find out?"

"One of the guards said he'd heard you'd been messin' with the Commissioner. He urged me in the most serious way to tell you to keep the fuck away from Thibedeau if you want to stay healthy."

"Tell him I appreciate his concern," Harry said. Luis grinned. Harry was glad to see that Luis could still be amused.

175

"I will. We often talk. He shows me pictures of his family. It passes the time."

It struck Harry as a moment rich in irony. Luis was being serious and mocking at the same time, joking with a kind of wisdom he had not had before. Maybe, Harry thought, from time to time everyone should spend some time in jail. The idea revived his claustrophobia, and he quickly abandoned the theory.

"If I can develop what I have, there's a good chance," he continued, "I can get this horse off your foot. Let yourself feel a little relief, Luis. For the first time we've got motion in this case."

But to Harry's disappointment, he saw that Luis's spirits were not revived.

"Have you told Jeff Smolkin about being sick?" he asked. Luis shrugged.

"Tell him," Harry said. "He might be able to get you moved out of here. It's worth a shot."

They talked a few more minutes and then Harry left.

On his way home he picked up the mail and found among the trash a letter from Boone's attorneys Brimmer, Lawton, Childers, and Scope. It was signed by Arthur Brimmer and informed Harry that Boone was buying back his lease. Harry had five days to vacate the premises.

Harry was not surprised, but he was pretty sure that under Florida law, without just cause, dynamite couldn't vacate that lease. He went home, dug his copy of the lease out of his desk, and made a call to Jason Bryde just to be sure. By his own assertion, Jason had been lawyering in Avola since Flagler ran his railroad down the peninsula. But Bryde's exact age was a well-kept secret. Deep in his eighties was Harry's guess.

But whatever the truth was, Harry knew the judge had a wonderfully sharp mind, and ran his practice like a man of forty. He had been president of the Tequesta County Bar Association half a dozen times and was currently president of the Florida Bar Association.

His was also an active member of the board of directors of most of the conservation groups in the southern part of the state, and he was the founder of the Avola chapter of the Audubon Society, which is where Harry met him when he first moved to Tequesta County.

Harry told Jason some of what he'd been doing for Luis Mendoza and said he thought he'd gotten across Boone a little and was paying the price. The judge listened to what Harry had to say and asked to be read the relevant parts of the lease. When he'd heard enough, he told Harry nothing short of a major abrogation of the terms of the lease by Harry could break it, and that John the Baptist had more chance of making straight the path of the Lord than Boone did of evicting Harry from that house. Then he asked if Harry wanted him to send Jack Brimmer a letter instructing Orville Boone to go to hell. Harry said he did.

Bryde chuckled. "Good. I will derive an extraordinary amount of pleasure from writing it, and in the process I will twist Jack's tail a little over being a party to such skullduggery."

When Harry asked him to send along the bill, the judge said he'd let Harry buy the beer and the bait the next time they went bass fishing.

"It's a promise," Harry told him.

"Make it soon," Bryde said. "And, Harry, watch your back trail."

He hung up the phone, not needing to ask what the judge had meant. And despite the warning, he allowed himself to feel good that he wasn't going to lose his place. As always, it had cheered him just to talk with Jason Bryde.

After lunch Harry went to see Tucker. There were two or three things he wanted to run by his friend. Sanchez had stopped limping and woofed Harry up the yard in fine style. Oh-Brother! took his head out of the saw palmetto clump behind the hen house, where he appeared, improbably, to be studying the past works of Bonny and Clyde, and trotted over to greet him. The mule was chewing on a straw. And with his hat on and that straw in his mouth, there was a shaky moment when Harry thought the mule was going to speak to him.

But he limited himself to waggling his ears in greeting and taking off Harry's hat, carrying it to the house, and, to Harry's relief, giving it to Tucker, who stood waiting at the door. Forgetting himself, Harry walked along beside Oh-Brother! with a hand resting on the animal's shoulder, telling him and Sanchez about the alligator he'd just seen in Puc Puggy Creek. But he refused to allow himself to believe Oh-Brother! had taken off his hat as a reminder about people in glass houses, and so on. But, if not, why had he taken it?

"How tall is Oh-Brother!?" Harry asked Tucker after shaking hands.

"About seventeen-and-a-half hands," Tucker said. "That's about five-feet-ten inches at the withers, figuring four inches equals a hand."

"Top of the shoulders, right?"

Tucker looked pained but nodded and gave Harry back his hat.

"In Oh-Brother!'s view that hat's gone way past Good-will," Tucker said solemnly.

Harry put it on. Oh-Brother! shifted the straw in his mouth and regarded him thoughtfully. Sanchez barked once sharply and headed off purposefully around the house. Oh-Brother! cocked an ear at Harry and then followed Sanchez.

"There're reviewing Bonny and Clyde's stratagems over the past few months," Tucker said. He led Harry into the kitchen. "They're trying to find some pattern to their depredations and establish, if they can, an s.o.p."

Harry knew that was a load of rubbish, but, somehow, every time he got around Tucker and those two animals he began to believe Tucker's stories.

"When I was walking up the drive, Oh-Brother! had his head in the palmettos where Bonny and Clyde opened their tunnel," Harry said.

"That's it." Tucker waved a mug at him to indicate tea was coming. "I told him to let Sanchez handle that—because of the bad business over the tunnel collapsing, and Sanchez losing his way and getting kicked. But Oh-Brother!'s not a mule for nothing. So Sanchez hung back and let him do it."

"What have B&C been up to lately?" Harry steeled himself to take that first drink of tea.

"It's been quiet," Tucker answered. "But we're expecting a new onset any time now. What's brought you out here?"

Tucker passed Harry his mug of tea, trying to keep his face straight as he watched Harry take his first sip.

"I've got a letter. Two actually." Harry told Tucker the whole story, including calling Judge Jason Bryde.

"And you told Jim Snyder about the letter Katherine gave you," Tucker observed with a worried frown, "but you're hanging onto it."

"Yes," Harry said.

"Because you think the Sheriff's Department won't do anything about it?"

"It's more that I think the whole damned system won't do

anything about it," Harry said. Just thinking about that made him angry.

"The people on the State Ethics Commission are going to be deeply unhappy with Thibedeau when they've read that letter," Tucker responded. "Maybe you ought to give it to them."

Harry shook his head. "How's that going to tie Thibedeau or Boone any closer to the murders?"

"By itself, I don't suppose that letter would do much to fire up an Assistant State Attorney in Avola who had to get a grand jury to issue an indictment on a murder one charge." Tucker scowled and pushed a plate of brownies toward Harry. "All the same, the fact that Will Trachey and Slade Hatfield had that letter tells me it got them killed."

"After this, therefore because of this," Harry said glumly.

"I take your point. It's generally a damned poor way of reasoning. But in this case I'd say *post hoc ergo propter hoc* was on the money."

"So would I," Harry agreed, "but it doesn't get me any closer to proving Thibedeau and Boone are murderers. If they are."

Tucker sighed and poured more tea.

"When I'm putting in a garden," he said, "the hardest part for me isn't the digging. It's waiting for the seed to sprout. I figure you're waiting for the seed to sprout."

"And the letter's the seed?" Harry asked doubtfully. "Well, maybe you're right."

Harry started to get up, but Tucker put a hand on his arm and said, "Hold on, Harry. You gave me a warning a while back, and after I'd thought it over, I decided you were right. Oh-Brother!'s staying out nights. He's helping Sanchez keep an eye on things. Bonny and Clyde will just have to take their chances."

Harry noticed that Tucker didn't look happy about saying

the foxes would have to take their chances. But the old farmer rallied and went on making his point.

"I'd say Katherine is at risk, probably not as much as you, but at risk just the same. Before too long, we might think what to do about getting her some protection."

Harry told him what he'd said to Snyder.

Tucker responded with a grin. "That's a sly move. And it ought to keep the dogs off her."

"Let's hope so," Harry said. Then he asked Tucker if he thought she had been involved with Will and Hatfield's blackmail schemes.

"Well, she's got more brains than both of them ever had and credible deniability as far as Hatfield is concerned. I'm inclined to think Hatfield did steal that letter from her. But when it comes to Will, I'm not so sure. What's your take on it?"

"I'm stumped." Harry made the admission reluctantly. "I'm damned sure I don't want the police implicating her."

"So that's another reason you're hanging onto the letter?"

"For now."

"OK. But you remember, it makes you a target. We've already got two men down. I wouldn't want to lose you just when you and Oh-Brother! are getting on so well."

Harry ignored his comment about Oh-Brother! and said he'd be careful and walked home. He was still thinking about the conversation with Tucker when he reached for the handle on the lanai door. Then all the world he wasn't looking at rose up and struck him between the shoulders. He felt himself slam into the door, heard the wood splinter, and then nothing.

Chapter 16

Harry woke up to find Jim Snyder leaning across him, trying to put something under his back. Whatever he was doing hurt like hell, and Harry wanted to swear at him, but all he could manage was a whisper. Snyder lowered Harry's shoulder back onto the ground and began pressing on his chest. That hurt too and made Harry even angrier.

"What the hell are you doing?" he croaked.

"This here is a time for praying and not complaining," Snyder said.

His ears were red and his face was screwed up in a tight frown. He leaned down on Harry, still pressing his right hand against his chest and looking at his watch.

"You late for an appointment?" Harry inquired. He wanted to laugh and couldn't.

Then he wanted to close his eyes and sleep. Somewhere, a long way off, he knew he was hurting a whole lot. But it didn't seem to matter.

"Don't you quit on me, Brock," Snyder shouted and pressed down harder on Harry's chest. "Brock! Open your eyes."

"What are we doing down here on the ground?" Harry whispered. He was irritated Snyder wasn't going to let him sleep.

"Sweet Mother of God," Snyder exploded. "Are you still trying to be funny?"

"No," Harry said. "Get off me."

Snyder was breathing heavily. "Can't. You've been shot. I'm trying to keep you from bleeding to death."

That was ridiculous. Harry started to say so, but just then Katherine burst out of the house carrying an armful of towels.

"Katherine, what are you . . ." Harry whispered and passed out.

The bullet went in on the upper left side of Harry's back and came out his chest. It missed his heart and his spine and left a small hole going in and a considerably bigger hole coming out. But when the crime scene crew dug the slug out of his front door, it was still in one piece. Which meant Harry didn't have bits of lead along with bone slivers scattered through him. That was the good news. The bad news was that he lost the next three weeks of his life being questioned, operated on, bandaged, dripped into, wired, poked, prodded, and forced to do a variety of humiliating, painful, totally boring things. When they finally let him out of the hospital, he squinted in the sunlight like a spring woodchuck.

"Lab results tell us the bullet we dug out of your door came from a 9mm semiautomatic. Figuring the trajectory from the hole in the door and where Snyder found you, the person who shot you was probably standing at the rear left corner of your Land Rover. That would be what, David? Seventy-five feet from where he was hit?"

This was from Snyder, standing beside Harry's bed, peering down at him with a cheerful expression on his long face.

"Close enough," Herrera said.

It was the day after Harry was shot. Harry was a smiley face, pretty much wandering around in Wonderland. The nurse had given them five minutes, and Harry kept slipping away while they talked.

Herrera leaned forward, trying to get Harry to focus his eyes. "Brock, did you see who shot you?"

"No." It had taken Harry several seconds to process the question and then frame an answer. Herrera's face looked big as a moon. The thought of an olive moon made him smile.

"We're losing him," Snyder said. "Let me try again. Harry, Harry, try to remember. You were going into the house. Did you see anyone? Did you see a car?"

"No car," Harry said, "and it wasn't Mendoza."

"Jesus," Herrera said. "Will you stop screwing around?"

"It's OK," Harry whispered.

"What?"

But Harry faded. He eventually woke up to pain. Between bouts, during which all thinking stopped, he tried to remember whether he had heard or seen anything unusual before he was flung into the door.

"Whoever did it must have come up from the creek," he told Snyder. Snyder had overridden the nurses and brought Katherine into the room.

"Good guess," she said, sitting on the side of the bed. "Jim said C.I.D. found part of a boot print down by the water. Somebody had a boat in there."

"Probably waiting for you to show," Snyder said, his ears getting red as he spoke.

When Katherine sat on the side of Harry's bed, Snyder immediately began fidgeting and glancing nervously from the corridor door back to Harry. Sick as he was, Harry grinned at Snyder's agitation. Katherine also noticed the detective's uneasiness.

"Can you get me a root beer, Sergeant Snyder?" she asked.

"Surely can," he said and almost ran out of the room.

"This is your doing, isn't it?" Katherine said.

Harry feigned innocence. "Don't know what you're talking about."

"I've got a baby-sitter," she complained. "If I'm not working or sleeping, there's Jim Snyder. I'm lucky he doesn't go to the bathroom with me."

"A nice guy. Doing his job," Harry said.

It was Saturday and she was wearing her old shorts and a dark green blouse. As she talked to him, she tugged her braid. Harry couldn't decide whether he found listening to her talk or watching her pull her braid more delightful.

She made a failed effort to appear indifferent. "He's OK, for a hillbilly. You still got that letter?"

"Don't you breathe a word to Snyder about it," Harry said with what little force he could muster.

"I won't. Mr. LaBeau blames himself that you got shot. But I believe you were shot over that letter, just as you said might happen."

"You've been visiting." He did not want to talk about why he'd been shot.

"He came over with Sanchez and O-Brother! to introduce them to me and the kids. Oh-Brother! wears a straw hat!"

"I know, and don't ever make any cracks about it either. Did Minna and Jesse like them?"

"Yes, especially Sanchez. They fell all over that poor dog until Oh-Brother! pushed Sanchez away with his nose and let Minna pull his ears. I believe that mule was jealous of Sanchez because he was getting all the kids' attention. Then Mr. LaBeau put Jesse on his back. Then Minna. Oh-Brother! walked them around the yard with Sanchez leading the way. I swear that dog and mule talk to each other. Do you think that's possible?"

"That's not the half of it," Harry said.

Snyder came back with the root beer.

"Was the bullet that got me a match for the ones you dug out of Hatfield?" Harry asked.

Snyder looked pained and gave Katherine a guilty look. "I don't think a check on that's been done."

"Snyder," Harry said, "don't bullshit me."

Snyder rubbed a hand over his bristle cut and scowled at the wall beyond the bed.

"That's information I'm not free to give out. But here's some bad news I can share. Your house looks like wild pigs got into it."

Harry remembered what Trachey's place looked like and groaned.

"My painting stuff OK?" he asked. He was not surprised either by the news or Snyder's refusing to answer his question about the bullet.

"It's strewn around some," Katherine said. "Somebody was looking for something."

"You got any idea what they were looking for?" Snyder inquired.

"I've got a pretty good recipe for green tomato mincemeat," Harry said.

"Hey!" Katherine sang out. "Mr. LaBeau said he'd teach me how to make that."

"I got the recipe from him," Harry said.

Snyder started on Harry again, but the nurse appeared at the door and said, "Everybody out, except the one with the bullet hole in him." Which confirmed Harry's suspicion that a patient is not a somebody.

Herrera and Snyder together made half a dozen more calls on Harry over the next week. He enjoyed seeing them but not as much as he would have liked to see Katherine. He wasn't much help to Herrera and Snyder, and they let him know it. But he couldn't accuse Boone of shooting him without giving the police the letter. And he wasn't ready to do that.

Maria Benedict came to see Harry. She came in the evening and brought him a bunch of carnations bright as a rainbow. They lit up his bedside table like a lamp. She was dressed in black slacks, a gold blouse, and black sandals. Her hair shone like an onyx waterfall, and even the ghastly fluorescent ceiling light couldn't dim her beauty. Harry began to feel better the moment he saw her.

Harry thanked her for the flowers. "What's happening out there? This place seethes with rumor, but it's all about what's going on here. It's worse than a convent."

"Oh, shame on you," Maria cried. "Since when has gossip been gender-specific?"

"OK, a monastery. Look, I want you to do something for me. Find out from C.I.D. if the bullet that hit me and those pumped into Hatfield came out of the same gun."

"I'll try, but it won't be easy. They've put a tight lid on the investigation. I don't know why." Harry thought he did. "Now, no more business."

They talked for a few minutes about some new boardwalk construction at the Stickpen Preserve. Then she got up, told him to concentrate on getting better, and left.

Harry did improve, but the hours dragged. In the long night hours, his memory seemed to redouble its efforts to fill his mind with scenes from the bad times in Maine. They also reminded him of the passage of the years. He went from there to thinking about his life on Bartram's Hammock. For reasons he refused to examine, thoughts about Katherine became entangled with his feelings of loss and isolation.

Fortunately, Harry found a companion. His name was Charles Spiller, a twenty-five-year-old orderly from Barbados. He worked nights and was putting himself through the local branch of the University of Florida. He was majoring in plant science and planned to become a paleobotanist. Things were usually slow after midnight, and they talked. To his delight, Harry found the man had a quiet, penetrating sense of humor, a shining intelligence, and a profound curiosity about his new world.

Harry was interested in Charles's life in Barbados. Charles was equally interested in life on the Hammock. He was alternately shocked, appalled, and riveted by Harry's account of Tequesta County politics. At first Harry worried that he might be disillusioning Charles with his lurid tales of American political life.

The worry was unnecessary. Charles began reading the *Banner* with avid interest and asking questions of anyone with the time to listen. Before Harry left the hospital, Charles had a pretty good grasp of the issues driving County politics. Harry's concern that Charles might abandon botany for political science was equally ill founded. As a junior, he was starting his field studies on plant systems in fresh water marshes and was joining a team working in Big Cypress Swamp. He was committed.

Harry rode home in a taxi with his left arm still in a sling and found Tucker, Sanchez, and Oh-Brother! in the yard waiting for him. Harry didn't waste his breath asking Tucker how he knew he was coming. Harry went into the house with Tucker, expecting to find a disaster. But Tucker, with Katherine's help, had cleaned up whatever mess there was. He had also stuffed the refrigerator. A chicken was baking in the oven, the Sunday smell drifting through the house. There were clean sheets on his bed, and the floors and windows were polished to a serious shine.

"I'm thinking Boone or some of his people were in here," Harry said after thanking Tucker. He was looking at the way his paint gear had been strewn around, a muddle Tucker had wisely left for him to deal with.

"Or Thibedeau," Tucker added. Harry let that pass.

"They got Hatfield's bag. At least I didn't find it."

Harry had already checked the fireplace. The flue hadn't been opened.

"It's all right," he said. "The letter wasn't in the bag. I'm pretty sure they didn't get what they came for."

"Good," Tucker replied with a grin. "I'll be going. I've made you some potato pancakes and peeled a few carrots. They're in the chiller. The roaster will give you something to pick on." He brushed away Harry's thanks. "If you need any help with anything, you know where to find me."

"There's something else," Harry told him. "When whoever broke in here goes through that bag and doesn't find what they're looking for, they could think you've got it."

Tucker frowned and studied the toes of his work shoes. "That's possible," he said. "Or they may go after Katherine. Hadn't you better be thinking about getting that letter to the police?"

As Harry walked Tucker out of the yard, he promised himself that he would get the letter into Snyder's hands at his first opportunity. Then he found himself wondering what Sanchez and Oh-Brother! had been doing while he and Tucker were talking. Then he got a grip on himself and went back into the house to take the chicken out of the oven.

Just getting back from the hospital and walking around the house had tired Harry, and his shoulder ached like a cracked tooth. But he wouldn't allow himself to rest until he had his painting gear back in order. Only then did he make himself some coffee and get off his feet. He thought again about calling Snyder or Herrera and telling them about the letter and promised he would do it tomorrow.

Chapter 17

The next morning Harry was washing the breakfast dishes when Maria Benedict called.

"I'm going to give you this quickly," she said. "And you didn't get it from me. The gun that took you down was used on Slade Hatfield. The department doesn't have a clue who the perp is."

"Thanks, Maria. I owe you."

Harry had put in a very restless night, but by morning he had rethought what he was going to do with the letter and reached a decision. The plan scared him a little, but he pushed himself forward. After Maria hung up and before he could change his mind again, Harry put in a call to Jeff Smolkin, Luis Mendoza's attorney.

"How are your contacts with *The Avola Banner*?" he asked.

"Do you mean can I get something printed?"

"In tomorrow's paper."

"What have you got? Will it do Luis any good?"

"Bet on it."

"Then I can do it." Excitement raised the lawyer's voice. "Come on, Harry, what is it?"

"I'll bring it over."

Smolkin, a short, stocky man in his early forties with a hairline that had raced backward, was on his feet the moment Harry stepped into his office.

"Hey, Harry." He reached eagerly across the desk to shake hands, his dark eyes dancing. "Give me the good news."

Harry passed Smolkin the letter, and when he'd read it, he punched his fist into the air and shouted, "Yes!"

"Before you get too excited," Harry said, "what you're reading is a copy. I'm going to give another one to either Snyder or Herrera. I'm hanging onto the original because Thibedeau and Boone have a lot of chips they can call in. Some may be in the Sheriff's Department. Some, in the *Banner*."

"But if the *Banner* prints this letter, it can't be buried." Smolkin was too pleased to be worried by what Harry had said.

"Not as long as I can keep the original safe," Harry agreed. "Can you promise me it will be in tomorrow's paper? If you can't, I'm going to have to hide in the swamp."

"Don't worry." He dropped into his chair and flipped open a yellow writing pad. "This time tomorrow the whole damned state will know what those bastards have been doing. But first, I've got to have the provenance of the letter. How much can you tell me?"

"Enough, I hope, to break Luis out of jail." Some of Smolkin's enthusiasm had infected Harry.

From Smolkin's office, Harry went to see Katherine and told her what he'd done.

"I think I've sunk myself." She made a rueful face as she waved a hand at the surrounding space.

They were talking in the conference room where Harry and Snyder gave her the bad news about Hatfield. With a little help from Helen Bradley, they met without anyone other than Helen knowing they were together.

"This whole place may go into the tank," Harry agreed. "But I don't think Boone's interested in you. If he thought you had the letter, you would have heard from him by now."

Katherine heard him out, sat quietly for a moment, and then began speaking. "Orville came to see me after Slade was killed. He was real concerned. He kind of urged me to come into town for a while. I said we were all right. Then he fussed some more and gave me a cellular phone and said, 'You carry this. You hear?' " She looked at her hands and rubbed the place where her wedding ring had been. Harry waited. "He's been real kind," she said finally, "but he has his own way of doing things. It was one of the first things I noticed after coming here. He doesn't give out warnings. If you screw up, you don't get a second chance."

"How worried are you?" Harry asked. He thought he knew what Boone's concern was focused on, but he didn't want to press her for fear of making her more frightened than she was already.

"I gave you that letter."

"Yes, you did, but remember, only you and I and Tucker know that, and if you're asked, you're going to say that you gave that bag of Hatfield's to me without looking in it."

"Well, maybe I won't have to say anything," Katherine said. She straightened her back. "I'd better get back before I'm missed. Is your shoulder still sore?"

"A little."

"You watch yourself. I don't know why, but I've got a bad feeling about this whole thing."

"Is Snyder looking after you?"

"Well," she said, coloring a little, "he's trying to, but you know me, Harry. I'm about as easy to fence as water."

"How hard are you being on him?" Harry tried not be jealous of Snyder and failed.

"Harder than I should be, but a girl's got to have some fun." She leaned forward and gave Harry a quick kiss on the cheek. Then she jumped up and ran out of the room.

Harry sat for a while, feeling the kiss on his cheek and telling himself glumly to forget it. When he left the building he almost had, or so he told himself.

Harry drove back to the Hammock by way of the jail to see Luis, who shuffled into the visitor's room grimmer than a wet November.

"Jeff Smolkin is going to take that letter to the judge and, with what I've given him, make a strong case for releasing you." Harry hoped his news would cheer up Mendoza. But the man shook his head with a heavy sigh of defeat.

"It's a nice try, Harry, but they're not going be scared off. Half of Avola wants me convicted of anything that can be made to stick." He scowled at his hands and hunched deeper into his prison coveralls.

Harry tried again. "Even if Jeff can't find a judge to shake you loose, any grand jury the state can put together will take one look at that letter and throw the state's case out the window."

It was no use. Harry couldn't dent Mendoza's gloom. He left the prison thinking Luis might, actually, have good reason for thinking his problem wasn't solved and that Boone's letter would not save him from the electrical bonfire the state was preparing. Some of the gloom came from his being in jail. But it was true that the gun that killed Trachey was not the one used on Hatfield and himself. The Assistant State Attorney might argue that Trachey's murder was entirely separate from the Hatfield shooting and the attack on him. Even escaping from the jail into the sun and the fresh air failed to restore Harry's spirits.

Chapter 18

The next morning Harry picked up the paper a little earlier than usual. With some anxiety, he opened the paper on the bridge where the light was stronger. The letter was on the front page. Harry read the accompanying article, only vaguely aware of the surrounding chorus of croaking, piping, grunting, and whistling dawn voices rising from the surrounding swamp. The writer gave Jeff Smolkin as the source of the letter and established the alleged connection with Willard Trachey and Slade Hatfield.

The article then reminded the readers that both men had been shot to death and that their murders were still under investigation. Jeff was quoted as declining to say how he had come by the letter. And the paper gave itself some cover by saying that although the letter appeared to be genuine, neither Boone nor Thibedeau had acknowledged its authenticity, and both had denied any wrongdoing and refused further comment. Harry noted with satisfaction that while the blackmail issue was not raised directly in the piece; it rose from the account like the stench from a dead snake.

When he finished reading, he clapped the paper shut and said, "Not bad." He looked around at the creek and the brightening sky and added his affirmation to the general celebration of the coming day. By the time he got home, the mockingbird was belting out his songs in the wisteria and the cardinals were chipping wildly in the sea grapes. Even if all was not right with the world, the day had definitely gotten off to a good beginning.

He was finishing breakfast when Jeff Smolkin called, full of news and good cheer. "Forget it's Saturday, I've had a call from Eric Smith, the Assistant State Attorney who's handling Luis Mendoza's case," he said excitedly. "He wants to talk. The bad news is I may not be able to keep you out of the conversation. I can't lie to the A.S.A."

"Don't even think of it," Harry said.

"The letter safe?"

"As houses. Snyder or Herrera gets a copy this morning. But I'm holding onto the original."

"Great. Here's something else Smith told me. He's been getting unsourced reports that Boone has a major cash flow problem. Smith wanted to know had I heard anything. I said I hadn't. How about you?"

"No." Harry saw no point in saying Tucker LaBeau had said the same thing a few days ago.

"Well, whether the rumors have any basis in fact or not, when the politicians with connections to Boone read this letter, they will desert him in a bunch. It's going to be CYA, big time."

Then he said he hoped Avola Gold was headed for Chapter 11 and told Harry he'd see him on Monday.

Harry kept interrupting his Saturday morning chores to call the station house to ask if Snyder or Herrera was in. At about eleven the dispatcher said she'd just seen Herrera passing her window. Harry put two copies of the letter in a manila folder and drove to the North Naples Sheriff's Office. When he stepped into Herrera's office, the detective jumped to his feet and started shouting.

"I'll have your fucking license," he bellowed. He was leaning over his desk, his face suffused with blood. "That letter was supposed to come to me. You had no right . . ."

It went on for a while. Harry listened. "I gave a copy to Jeff Smolkin," he said when Herrera stopped yelling. "Here's yours and one for Snyder."

He dropped the folder on the desk. Herrera ignored it.

"I want the original," he said. He was still breathing hard.

"Nope. That goes to Eric Smith, if the Assistant State Attorney wants it."

"Harry, you son-of-a-bitch," Herrera said. He slammed his fists down on the desk. "Don't mess with me."

Harry put his temper in a tight rein. "I'm not messing with you, David. Nobody but Smith gets it. And Smith doesn't get it until I'm dead certain there's no way it can accidentally fall into the office shredder."

"Dead is what you're going to be if you're not damned careful," Herrera retorted. He dropped into his chair.

"That possibility has crossed my mind," Harry said flatly. "I take it Sheriff Fisher's already let you know how pleased he is the letter is published."

"He called."

"That would account for it."

"Account for what?" Herrera demanded. He was angry again.

"You'll think of it," Harry replied. "Make sure Snyder gets one of the letters."

As he left the station, Harry was not troubled by Herrera's shouting or the half threatening comment about his own demise. He dismissed them as the detective's response to being carded by his boss. But even cutting Herrera that slack, the man had still been angrier than the situation warranted. What gnawed at Harry was the feeling that Herrera was venting a personal anger. And he asked himself just how deeply did Thibedeau and Boone have their hooks sunk in the Sheriff's Department?

Chapter 19

The crash and groan of shattering glass and crumpling metal jumped Harry out of bed. As he ran down the stairs, the silence which had followed the crash was broken again by the tortured wail of crumpling metal. Harry reached the lanai in time to see a big, light colored car lurch away from the oak on the corner of his lot, gather speed, and fishtail away in the direction of the bridge. He kept on running until he reached the tree.

Chunks of bark were ripped away from the trunk and strewn on the ground. The exposed wood was deeply gouged and splintered. "Shit," Harry said. Then he noticed he was standing in what looked like hailstones but were nuggets of glass, strewn around his feet in a glittering heap. Harry guessed the car had lost a headlight and probably a side window.

He stood for a moment shivering in the cold air. Then the thought hit him. "Katherine!" he said.

He began to run for the Rover then remembered he had no keys and nothing on but a T-shirt. He raced back to the house, pulled on some clothes, and set out for the cabin. But he didn't get there. Reaching Tucker's place, he saw that most of the lights in the house were on. There was no way Tucker LaBeau would be up at three in the morning unless something was seriously wrong.

He swerved into the yard. When he jumped down, Oh-Brother! suddenly loomed out of the deeper shadows of the pecan trees, his head up and his eyes glinting dangerously. Harry caught his breath, but the mule checked his advance.

"What's wrong?" Harry asked him and immediately felt foolish.

The mule tossed his head and backed into the shadows again. Harry ran for the house. He found Tucker kneeling on the kitchen floor bent over Sanchez. Tucker was bandaging the dog's head. The towel under Sanchez's head was soaked with blood.

"He's all right," Tucker said without interrupting what he was doing. "The bullet grazed the top of his head. He's lost a little hair and hide and may have some concussion, but I've got the bleeding stopped. Scalp wounds surely do bleed."

Harry knelt beside Tucker. "How did it happen?" he asked.

At the sound of Harry's voice Sanchez thumped his tail a couple of times on the floor but showed no inclination to get up. Tucker finished tying off the bandage, patted the dog's shoulder, gathered his extra pads, scissors, roll of gauze, and bottle of hydrogen peroxide, and scrambled to his feet.

"Somebody tried to burn me out," he said. "I suspect if he'd succeeded, you would be coughing and scrambling for a bedroom window just about now."

"I'd better look in on Katherine," Harry said.

"No need," Tucker told him. "I checked the road. That car never went any farther than here. Tracks are plain."

Harry felt a rush of relief. "A car ran into that big oak on the north corner of my front yard. Whoever was driving probably came from here."

"Time's right," Tucker said. He put away his gear while they talked, and rinsed off his hands and dried them on the roller towel next to the sink. "Whoever was in that car is in bad shape. Probably why he went off the road."

Tucker's nightshirt was partly tucked into his overalls, which were hanging by one strap fastened over his right shoulder. He was barefoot but had what looked like a green and white striped cotton nightcap on his head. Harry tried not to stare at it.

"Come with me," he said. Tucker grabbed his flashlight off the counter and led the way around to the west side of the house. "Look at that." He pointed his light at a pair of three-gallon cans and a litter of drenched rags lying scattered in the grass along the side of the house.

The stink of spilled gasoline hung heavily in the air.

"What stopped him?" Harry asked.

The sight of the overturned cans and the wet rags were such raw evidence of malevolent, vicious intent, and bespoke such danger that Harry wanted to grab them up and fling them away from the house. But they were evidence and he curbed his impulse.

"Sanchez and Oh-Brother! caught him." Tucker went on in a matter-of-fact way. "I figure he was just about ready to set her off."

"Did Sanchez's barking wake you?" Harry asked.

Tucker was moving away from the house, toward the road. Harry followed him, glad to get away from the cans and the rags and the stench of gasoline. Tucker had a couple of dozen orange trees just west of the house, and they went a few yards into their dappled shade before he stopped and answered Harry's question.

"No, but the man's yelling did. He got this far before Oh-Brother! and Sanchez brought him down. From the racket it must have been quite a set-to. He finally managed to get to his gun and fire a couple of shots. One of them grazed Sanchez."

The ground was ripped and trampled where Oh-

Brother!'s hooves had torn up the sod and sunk into the soft earth. Harry thought of Oh-Brother! coming toward him out of the dark, and the hair prickled on his neck.

"You're telling me that mule attacked whoever it was out here?"

"Of course," Tucker said in surprise. "I told you he was staying out nights."

"And he and Sanchez ran the guy off."

"They did a lot worse than that." Tucker chuckled. "You should have heard him holler."

"You never saw him?"

"Nope. It was all over by the time I got out here." Tucker pointed his light through the trees toward the road. "I didn't see him, but he went that way. My guess is he was in pretty bad shape. Of course, he was lucky with that shot. He knocked Sanchez down. That let him crawl off. You see where he dragged himself. Once Sanchez was off his feet, Oh-Brother! wouldn't leave him. He was standing over Sanchez when I got here. The burner must have pulled himself onto his feet because I heard the car go right after I found Sanchez."

"I saw it," Harry said. "Cadillac. In the moonlight it looked white to me."

"Orville?"

"That would be my guess."

"It's been a night," Tucker said wearily. "Earlier on, Bonnie and Clyde hit us. Killed Beauregard and some of the hens. Dug into the hen house under the wire."

"I'm sorry about Beauregard." Tucker had been fond of the old rooster.

Tucker raised a hand and dropped it. "He put up a good scrap."

Harry turned and found the mule standing beside him,

sprinkled with moonlight, a tall, darker shadow in the shadow of the tree. "Oh-Brother!'s here."

"I know. He's just being protective."

"He's lost his hat."

Tucker shook his head. "It's in the stable. He never wears it at night."

When he left Tucker, Harry drove to Katherine's cabin. The cabin was quiet and dark. There was nothing to be gained by waking her and the kids. So he drove home and called the Sheriff's Office and made a report. He was transferred to CID.

"Boron," a weary voice said. Procedure had slipped with the hours.

"Why are you calling this arson?" Boron asked when Harry finished. Harry wanted to ask if he'd been listening, but settled for repeating what he'd already told the officer.

"And you don't know who was in the car."

"No."

"OK." Boron gave a long sigh and hung up.

Graveyard shift. Halloween all the time.

Chapter 20

Harry snapped awake wondering if the phone had been ringing while he slept or whether it was only part of the nonstop nightmares that had sunk their claws into him once he closed his eyes. Then he remembered the trouble at Tucker's. He was thinking about that as he went to check the phone. The message light was blinking.

"Hey, man," a soft voice said. "How you doing? Sorry for the hour, but something really weird has been happening. Can't say more on the phone. I'm here till seven a.m. You really should know about this."

Harry's brain was still fogged with sleep, and it took him a moment to recognize the speaker. It was Charles Spiller, the orderly he'd gotten to know in the hospital. He looked at his watch. Five a.m. He hesitated for only a moment before making up his mind. He found Spiller in the almost-deserted hospital cafeteria eating his breakfast.

"Hey, man," Charles said, half rising to shake his hand. "I guessed right. You're still an early riser. You want something to eat? They do fine here with the scrambled eggs. The coffee won't kill you."

"What have you got?" Harry asked. He put his tray on the table and sat down, the aroma of freshly cooked eggs rising around him.

"You be the judge," Charles said. He wiped his mouth with a napkin and pushed away his plate. "Around four this morning, I got called to help lift a big white dude out of the back seat of an unmarked police car onto an ER gurney. He looked like he'd been in a fight with a gorilla. His clothes were ripped into strips and the blood was everywhere. His head was wrapped in a T-shirt bandage, but I could see enough of his face to know he looked familiar. Sheriff Fisher checked the man in under the name of John Doe."

Charles stopped to see if Harry was showing any interest. Harry had forgotten about his eggs.

"Keep talking," he said

"Gets better. The Sheriff said there'd been an automobile accident and there wasn't going to be no trouble about insurance. This was Sheriff's Department business. Everybody was going to keep their mouths shut about this citizen until they heard from him. Then he went along with the gurney to the O.R., talking to the man, telling him to hang on and so forth, and calling him Orville, forgetting his name was John. Right then I knew where I'd seen that face before. Less I'm mistaken, what we got here is Mr. Orville Boone."

He paused to ask Harry if that was worth getting him down there at sunup?

"It sure as hell is," Harry said, grinning as if he'd won the lottery. "Is there any more to this story?"

"The best part. The Sheriff had to leave him at the O.R. and go back to the waiting room, but I hung around until one of the nurses I know came out. She saw me and broke out laughing.

"I asked her what was funny, and she said, 'John Doe must have had a collision with a wagon being pulled by a wild mustang and a mean dog because there's the prints of a horseshoe on his caved-in ribs, fractured right thigh, and the side of his head. And there were really big dog bites on his left calf and his right buttock.

" 'He's concussed, got multiple lacerations, broken ribs,

and a fractured femur, but I guess he'll live. For certain, he's going to be a while mending and sore for a lot longer.' " Charles took a long breath. "What do you think happened to him, Harry? And what's the Sheriff doing calling him John Doe? Man, this is some place. We Bajans don't know we're born."

Harry was almost too excited to talk, but he calmed himself down enough to answer Charles. "I think I know what happened to Boone and why Fisher put him in here under the name of John Doe. I can't tell you yet, but I will." Harry got to his feet. "Thanks, Charles. You just made my day, and I didn't have to shoot anybody. I'll talk to you."

Driving back to the Hammock, Harry kept thinking, Find the car. Find the gun. And before he reached the hump-backed bridge, the thought hit him that Fisher had probably hidden Boone's car by having it hauled to the County impoundment lot. That would be the quickest way to control access to it. Harry knew he was going to need help finding out if the car was in there. As soon as he walked into the house, he picked up the phone again and called Jeff Smolkin at home.

Smolkin answered on the fourth ring.

"Boone's in the A.C.H. under the name of John Doe," Harry said.

"No shit!" he shouted.

"Sheriff Fisher put him into the hospital about four-thirty this morning in pretty bad shape." Harry's sense of urgency sharpened his voice. "Call your contact at the *Banner*. Get him on the story and find out what's happening. I'm going to try to find his car. The Sheriff said his John Doe had been in an automobile accident, but that's not what put him in the hospital."

Then Harry told Smolkin about Boone's attempt to burn out Tucker LaBeau.

★ ★ ★ ★ ★

The call made, Harry realized he was hungry. Over breakfast, he reviewed the events of the last eight hours with considerable satisfaction. Despite Boone's attack on Tucker and the disappearance of his car, Harry continued to feel energized by what had happened. The letter had broken the logjam. Boone had broken cover. And if it was Boone in the hospital, it sounded from what Charles Spiller had said that Boone would be helpless for a long time. That had to be good. One threat removed. Katherine and Tucker were now a lot safer, he thought gratefully.

Eager to share his information with Tucker, he washed his dishes, gave the rest of the kitchen a lick and a promise, and went to see how the old farmer was getting along. He found him laying one inch wire mesh in a trench he had dug in front of the hen house door. When the wire was laid, Harry grabbed Tucker's shovel and buried it for him.

"There's nothing like closing the barn door after the horse is gone," Tucker said with a wry grin as they stepped back to survey their handiwork.

He looked tired, and Harry was painfully reminded that Tucker was an old man, a fact he seldom remembered in his company. As he helped Tucker put away his tools, Harry told him about his visit to the hospital.

"The Sheriff," Tucker said, shaking his head sadly.

The two men had come out of the barn and were standing watching turkey vultures circling upward over Puc Puggy Creek on a column of warm air.

"The bad news," Harry said, damping down his earlier optimism, "is that without the gun Boone used on Sanchez, we're no closer to proving Boone killed Trachey and Hatfield than we were before he tried to burn you out."

"It could be in the car," Tucker said.

"Possibly. I'll find out tomorrow."

"Where are you going to look?"

"I'll start with the police impoundment lot over on Mechanic Street. But I've just thought of something. Boone might have dropped that gun out here last night."

"Good thought. Let's look."

Boone's trail to his car was easy to follow, but they found no trace of the gun.

"Do you think Fisher would have been foolish enough to get rid of the gun?" Tucker asked.

"Probably depends on how many IOUs of Fisher's Boone's got in his pocket."

When he got home, Harry called Judge Jason Bryde. He told him about Tucker, about the car crashing into the oak in front of his house, Charles Spiller's call, and what the nurse had said about Boone's injuries. "And I think Fisher put Boone's car in the police compound, and without some help, I'm not going to get in there. Tucker and I couldn't find Boone's gun, so I'm guessing it's still in the car."

"For Fisher's sake, I sincerely hope he hasn't disposed of the weapon," the judge said. "I could get you into the compound, but let's do this another way. I know Eric Smith pretty well. When I've finished talking to him, I believe he will go in there for a look himself. I'll be with him."

Harry broke into a grin of satisfaction. "Thanks, Judge. That's way better than my doing the looking."

"Don't thank me yet, Harry," Bryde replied. "First, let's find out what Fisher has stashed in the impoundment."

When Harry put down the phone, he felt washed out. It could have been the relief at knowing the Assistant State Attorney was going looking for evidence which, if he found it, would put Boone away for good. Harry decided to relax and let the judge work his magic. Something about his decision niggled at him, but he forced his mind away from the annoyance.

The *Banner* buried the article on Boone in the back pages of Section A, and Harry had to go through the paper twice to find it. At least, he muttered when he found it, it's not in the Classifieds. The short piece was headed, "Local Business Leader Hospitalized." The writing had been heavily edited and mentioned Boone's name only once.

The description of his injuries was brief and not specific. In a tortured paragraph from which most of the important details had been excised, the writer managed to say Boone's injuries were not the result of an automobile accident. Harry swore. Somebody at the *Banner* was doing Boone's laundry.

Just then the male red-shouldered hawk jetted over the roof and blasted him with a string of raucous cries. It seemed an appropriate response. Harry cheered himself with the thought that, given cause, the court could pry the record of Boone's injuries out of the hospital.

Chapter 21

Still feeling restless, Harry drove over to see Tucker. Snyder's car was in the driveway, and when he reached the house, having been escorted to the back door by Oh-Brother!, Harry found the detective sitting at the kitchen table, a mug of Tucker's evil tea in front of him. Sanchez was laid out on a folded green blanket beside the back door, his head still bandaged. He thumped his tail at Harry and lifted his head a little in welcome.

"He's better than he's letting on," Tucker said, giving Harry a stage wink. "Sit down. Tea's coming."

Sanchez groaned pathetically. Snyder grinned, but Tucker kept his face straight.

Harry sat down at the table. "Was Herrera here?"

"No, but the crime scene people have been and gone. Efficient. Thorough," Tucker said. "Still no sign of the gun."

"Dave has done something unusual," Snyder added.

He drank some of the tea and gasped for breath. Tucker watched him critically, but Snyder recovered his voice and went on, trying, Harry thought, not to sound offended with his partner.

"He cleared his desk this morning and left without saying a word to me. And when I asked the super what was going on, he gave me a dirty look and said Sergeant Herrera had asked for some leave time. He said he had no further information. It puts me in the pickle barrel and no mistake."

They talked a while about Herrera's departure, and

Snyder opened up enough to say he thought Herrera was having family problems. Then they talked some more about the arson attempt on Tucker. By the time Harry got home it was almost six o'clock. The heat of the day was relenting, and he had a shower and a cold beer in mind. But he walked into the house to find the phone ringing. It was Jason Bryde.

"I made the call," the judge said. "Smith and I found the car. The trunk reeks of gasoline, and there are some rags in it. It looks as though cans had been piled in there, but they're gone now. It looked to me as if somebody, I won't say the Sheriff, had done some cleaning."

"Any sign of a gun?"

"No."

Despite his belief that Sheriff Fisher had probably thrown it in a canal, Harry decided to let the judge play that one any way he wanted. Bryde did not say what he was thinking about the missing gun, and Harry didn't press him. Instead, when he was finished talking with Bryde, Harry called Smolkin and gave him the news. "Pass it on to Luis with my congratulations."

Finding Boone's car was good news, and Harry allowed himself to feel good about it. In the next couple of hours, he thought, Fisher would have his hands full explaining himself. Crime scene people would soon be swarming like ants over the vehicle. With Eric Smith and Jason Bryde looking over their shoulders, it was unlikely the Sheriff would make any further efforts to interfere with the evidence.

Harry was on his way to the refrigerator for a beer when the phone rang again.

"Have you had your dinner, Mr. Brock?" Abigail Blakeley asked when he picked it up.

"Just thinking about it." Harry swore silently at his lack of style.

"I know such short notice borders on insult, but would you consider having it with me? I do want very much to talk with you."

"I'll pass consider and go directly to yes," Harry said. "Where do you want to eat?"

"Would you risk eating here with me?"

"Yes," he replied. His answer came so quickly it surprised him.

"Shall we say seven-thirty?"

"That's fine."

He hung up the phone and immediately thought of Katherine. He did not want to think of Katherine. He had been very deliberately avoiding Katherine. Snyder was looking after her as if she was a national treasure. Harry pretended he was pleased. But the truth was he missed Katherine. And for the first time in many years he felt lonely. Missing her made him angry. He ran up the stairs to shower and change, forcing her out of his mind.

Abigail poured Harry a second martini. "I have a tape I'd like to share with you. Thanks to that letter in the *Banner* linking Emile Thibedeau and Mr. Boone in a votes-for-money scheme, Avola Gold stock has, to use my husband's colorful phrasing, been flushed."

Harry smiled as he took his drink. "I can cope with my disappointment."

"I'm relieved." She gave him a seraphic smile.

Dinner bore no relationship to what Harry's kitchen produced. And that did not count the silent Thai cook who appeared in the candlelight and vanished from it like a slightly sinister wraith, putting down and taking up dishes. The wine did not come from the supermarket.

When the meal was over, Abigail moved them to the lanai.

She led him to a white couch, then floated down beside him in a cloud of gold cloth, her pale hair gleaming in the soft light. On the river below the house, boats with their running lights winking and dancing on the water passed with a remote and pleasant murmur.

"I believe this . . . collapse will mean whatever hopes Mr. Boone had for continuing with the Avola Gold project are almost certainly dead," she said.

"A lot of money has been lost by people who don't like losing money," Harry replied.

She nodded and drew the hem of her dress across her ankles. She had taken off her shoes and pulled her feet up onto the couch.

"Shall we listen to the tape?" she asked.

"Why not?"

When she came back with a player and several tapes, Harry asked, "Are you taping your husband's business calls?"

She smiled and set the player on the glass coffee table. "Not here. I'm doing it in New Jersey. I have a secure phone here. I've left the rest as they were. He's welcome to listen to my chit-chat."

"And he won't suspect you've caught on." He was troubled by what she'd just told him but wasn't sure what, if anything, he should say about it.

"How astute of you, Harry. Here we go." She punched a button on the machine and returned to the couch, bringing her perfume and her irony with her. Harry found both of them attractive, but he forced his attention away from her to Joe Speroni's rasping New Jersey voice.

"Our friends are not going to like coming up empty. Those dickheads Boone and Thibedeau have really screwed up this time."

Another voice with less accent but just as harsh interrupted. "What say we reissue the Avola Gold paper under another name and pump the hell out of it?"

"If it was just the state and county courts we were dealing with down there, I'd say go ahead. But the Governor is fucking around with a federal investigation. Sean Fergus, his State Attorney, recently quashed a complaint against that asshole Thibedeau. So he's got paint all over him, and from what I hear, the Governor is shit-face over it."

With a hiss of annoyance, Abigail bounced up and snapped off the player. For once she sounded really angry. "Disgusting!" Her voice was icy. "Absolutely disgusting!" She caught herself, straightened up, and gave a forced laugh.

She tilted her head at Harry and managed a smile. "Tangled webs," she said.

"These friends . . ."

"Yes," she said and held out a hand to him. "Aren't they wonderful? Will you walk with me?"

He saw that beneath her beautiful and beautifully maintained surface, she was quite seriously upset. Whether it was anger or pain that was causing it, Harry couldn't tell. He put down his glass and joined her. She slid an arm under his.

They stepped through the lanai door. "There's a paved walk down to the river. Shall we brave the night air? I need to do something. If I don't move about, I feel as if I will burst. I am so annoyed and so ashamed. But, there, I apologize. You have troubles enough."

"They don't make yours any less real," he said.

"Well, thank you, Harry. It's very kind of you."

And she went on talking. As they set off down the brick path, Harry fell into step beside her, their bodies moving in a common rhythm. Harry listened, enveloped in her voice, her perfume, and her warm, physical presence. In addition to the interest he took in what she was saying, he was intensely and very pleasurably aware of her arm linked with his and her hip brushing his leg.

"My husband has been deliberately dishonest," she said. "And he's consorting with known criminals, people who would kill you as quickly as look at you. And these poor idiots in Avola like Mr. Boone and Mr. Thibedeau have fallen into a snake pit and have no glimmering of their situation."

Harry looked up at the velvet night and the wash of stars drifting across the sky. "Couldn't have happened to two nicer people," he said.

She followed his gaze and gently squeezed his arm.

"It is beautiful, isn't it? I am so very sorry for having been such a fool."

Harry put his hand over hers. "I can't imagine you ever being a fool."

He realized a bit late that his words were spoken with such fervor they were almost a declaration of love.

"What a wonderful thing to say, Harry." She turned and slid her arms around him and kissed him. He put his arms around her and returned the kiss.

"I'm sorry, Harry," she said when they stopped.

"For kissing me?" He felt very disappointed.

"No. For no longer being young."

"How old do you think I am?" he asked. "And how old was Calypso when Odysseus was shipwrecked on her island?"

"Old enough to have known better," she said, "and thank you for the flattering comparison. But I can't offer you immortality."

"Thank God."

She laughed and took his hand.

"What are you going to do with those tapes?" They fell into step together, his uneasiness returning.

"When we're done with them tonight, they're going into my attorney's bank. And they will stay there until I need them."

"For what?" he asked.

"Leverage, Harry." Her voice hardened. "Joseph Speroni and I are going to part company. And when we do, he is going to pay for linking me to that rabble of hoodlums and criminal conspirators he calls his business associates."

"Do these tapes name names," he asked, "in ways that could be used in court against some of these people?"

She gave a grim laugh. "A cookie jar full."

Harry stopped and faced her and grasped her arms. "Then don't, for the love of God, tell anyone else you have them. Most especially not your husband."

"Harry, are you trying to frighten me?" she demanded. "If you are, please stop it."

"Abigail, listen to me. You do not threaten these people without an army surrounding you. Most especially, you don't turn a divorce action against your husband into an occasion for revealing the details of these crooks' scams and extortions. Hasn't your attorney told you how risky that would be?"

"How lovely, Harry," she cried. "You're being protective! You must be the last gallant man left standing."

She was looking at him, laughing happily, her eyes full of starlight. She was beautiful. His restraint collapsing, Harry kissed her. It was even better than the first time.

She leaned back in his arms. "Harry, I think we should go in. I know it's dark, but I do have the shreds of a reputation to think of."

He could not help laughing. "But your being funny is not going to alter facts," he said, trying to sound serious. "What you have done is extremely dangerous. Have you got enough information on your husband to do whatever it is you're going to do without having to use these tapes?"

"More than enough." She gave him another quick hug.

"Then get those bugs out of his office. With any luck, neither he nor anyone else will ever have to know what you've done."

"Excellent advice, Harry," she said. "I've got everything from them I need anyway. Now, we are going to forget all about things unpleasant and decide what we'd like to drink when we get back to the house. You're not in any hurry?"

He told her she had the rest of his life.

"Good." She gave him a conspiratorial smile.

Chapter 22

The next morning Harry slid out of Abigail's sleepy embrace and went home expecting to be a much happier man. But he soon discovered new dissatisfactions. For one, the passing of midnight had done severe damage to the Rover, not that it was in any worse shape. The post-midnight Harry now found himself deconstructing his romantic perception of the horrid old crate. He went into the house and ate a solitary and unsatisfying breakfast while trying to decide what this new involvement with Abigail meant.

He began by telling himself that what had happened meant nothing more than that two consenting adults had drunk a little too much and had a great night in bed. But despite the tough talk he admitted that the pleasures of the night had underlined and intensified his feelings of isolation. Attempting to find some comfort in his blessings, he listened to the mockingbird singing outside the kitchen window and was not cheered. He tried to add to the list, and Katherine's name came up.

Warning himself to stop being an idiot, he decided to work, starting with an update on Boone. After that he would talk with Jeff Smolkin. And after that he thought he would check in with Helen Bradley. He got out of the house as fast as he could. On the way through the door, he asked himself if he was actually missing Abigail or just feeling lonesome. Of course I miss her, he said fiercely to the Rover as he jumped into the driver's seat. Of all the damned dumb questions.

He refused to talk to himself all the way to the Avola Community Hospital and ran upstairs to ask about Boone. The duty nurse told him Mr. Doe was scheduled for release on Thursday. And, yes, the police had been talking to him. It was the nurse's guess that they were trying to find out who had been the cause of his injuries. Poor man, he was going to be a long time recovering. Provoking shocked protests from the nurse, Harry said he hoped so. He left, rejoicing in the knowledge the police had their hooks in the bastard.

Helen Bradley greeted Harry warmly and came around her desk to shake hands. She was wearing a white tailored blouse and a narrow navy skirt. Her thick hair was pulled back in a dark orange ribbon, and she looked to Harry, as always, quietly in control of her world. He admired that in her and sat down with pleasure. Around them, Harry imagined he could feel the offices humming efficiently, despite Boone's condition. He said as much and she winced.

"I'm afraid the business world runs without a heart, Harry," she said, failing to convince him she was heartless. She pressed a button on her telephone and asked her secretary to bring them coffee. "But, of course, you know that," she said. "Thanks for coming. You give me a good reason to stop thinking about numbers. What does bring you here?"

"I stopped at the hospital." He paused briefly while the secretary passed them mugs from a tray. "Boone is being discharged on Thursday. What's he going to find when he gets out?"

She regarded him for moment or two without speaking, then set her mug on the desk; the heavy jade rings she was wearing caught and held the light as she spread her hands on the desk.

"You're working for Luis Mendoza, right?" There was a chill in her voice.

"Yes."

"And what is it you expect me to tell you?"

"No more than you want to, but I hear Boone is stretched tight as a piano wire. And I also hear the Avola Gold shares are blowing around the county landfills with the rest of the airborne trash."

"Wait," she said. She got up and closed the office door and came back to sit beside him in the second visitor's chair. "I hear the same thing." She leaned forward, elbows on the arms of her chair, turning a ring on her finger. "I'm circulating my resume."

"Is it that bad?"

"Worse." She looked away from him with a frown that he read as both angry and worried. "Yesterday, two of the worst looking men I've ever seen in my life came in here unannounced. No one knew who they were, but they went through the building from top to bottom, and when they were finished, they went into Bob Blanchard's office and stayed there an hour."

"He's CFO?"

She nodded. "I always thought Bob was a tough guy, but when they let go of him, he looked as if he'd been run through a food processor. All he could say was, 'I'm quitting. I'm quitting.' "

"They were from out of town."

"Oh, yes. And when they spoke to me, I understood only about every third word. Given what I managed to understand, it's just as well. They were the kind of trouble I never even imagined in Avola."

Harry got to his feet when Helen had finished. He hoped Abigail took his advice and pulled the taps on her husband's phones. She was another one who didn't know what bad really was.

"Thanks for talking to me," he said.

She pushed off the desk. "I hear you were shot. Are you OK?"

"It didn't improve me a whole lot, but I'm still walking."

She laughed.

"I know you've got your hands full already, but if this place folds, could you help Katherine find somewhere . . ."

"No problem, Harry. She's come along well here. I'll do what I can."

"Thanks," he said. "Have you been on any Audubon outings lately?"

"No. Things have been in too much turmoil here. I'm about worn out."

"Well, you watch yourself," he said. "Let me know when you get a new address."

"I'll do that." She smiled. "Maybe we can walk another strand. Meanwhile, here's my card. My home number's on it."

Her phone began ringing. She made a rueful face, and Harry left. When he reached the main entrance doors, he met Snyder coming into the building. His ears turned bright red when he saw Harry, and the blush gradually spread to his face.

"Caught you," Harry said.

Despite his own confused feelings about Katherine, he had come to like Snyder. Perhaps it was his youth or because he thought that the world was a better place than Harry did. The country was still in him, and every so often it shone through, clean and refreshing.

"There's some things I want to tell you," Snyder said, "but not here."

"I'm not hard to find." Harry assumed he wanted to talk

about Boone. "How's Katherine and the kids?"

"They're good. I can't get to see them as much as I'd like."

"That Ford of yours goes past the house fairly often," Harry replied, just to see him turn red again.

"I get out there when I can," Snyder admitted with a grin.

"I've got a question for you," Harry said. "Has anyone in the Department found Boone's gun?"

Snyder shook his head.

"I suppose they swept his car."

"With a vacuum cleaner," Snyder frowned. "They didn't find anything but the blood that probably came from Mr. Boone. Still, he's in a lot of trouble."

"I believe you," Harry answered.

Harry's next stop was Smolkin, Barrett, and Klein. After a short wait, Jeff Smolkin walked him into his office, talking a blue streak.

"Hold it," Harry said when he shut the door. "Start over. It may be attention deficit, but I haven't followed you."

Smolkin waved Harry into a chair. "Age takes its toll,"

"On second thought," Harry said, "I'll begin. First, Boone's gun has gone missing. It may be Fisher's doing, but no one's going to prove it. Second, a couple of representatives from Boone's New Jersey backers visited his office yesterday. They gave his CFO a very bad time before they left. My guess is by the time Boone gets out of the hospital, he will find his operation under new management."

Smolkin's eyes popped and he gave a low whistle.

"The collapse of Avola Gold stocks?"

"I think so. They're probably looking to recover their investment."

"Best thing Boone could do would be to take refuge in Chapter 11," Smolkin said. "Courts would lock whatever there is up. At least it would keep it away from the grease balls."

"They'd just take it out of his hide," Harry said. "I think he's better off letting them get it from the business. How's Luis?"

"You may be right. I was just going to tell you," Smolkin said throwing up his arms in his excitement. "Cronin has forced his release."

"About time," Harry said. "Who's Cronin?"

"Judge Rebecca Cronin," Smolkin said loudly. "Queen of *habeas corpus*. My Joan of Arc. Enemy of false witness and unwarranted incarceration. She jumped him out of there."

Harry couldn't help laughing. Here was one happy man. "What about the murder charge?"

"I think Eric Smith is going to drop it, but I don't have the official word yet. And I don't know what prompted Judge Cronin to move so fast, but whatever it was, it was potent."

Judge Jason Bryde, Harry thought with satisfaction.

After talking with Smolkin, Harry went home feeling very good. Too good. On the way, he thought of calling Katherine then squelched the impulse. You're not going there, he told himself. So forget it. That left Abigail, but the impulse died before it got a hold on him. I don't have to call anyone, he muttered glumly as he bounced over the bridge onto the Hammock. Once home, he found himself thinking about Boone's gun. Then, surprisingly, he thought of his conversation with Helen Bradley and what she had said about the visitors. A light clicked on. Had they gone to see Boone?

He called the hospital and got the charge nurse on Boone's floor. She remembered him and remembered the two callers who insisted on speaking to Mr. Doe. Harry thanked her. Boone had to be sweating that gun. And he was fairly certain the "investors" wanted Boone out of jail and functioning on their behalf. So, if Fisher hadn't taken care of it or if Boone hadn't thrown it in Puc Puggy Creek on his way off the Hammock, what would be more natural than telling the two goons where it was and letting them dispose of it?

Harry turned over the possibilities in his mind and came to the depressing conclusion that, like it or not, the gun was gone. Period.

Chapter 23

The next morning Harry called on Tucker to see if he was all right. There was no reason to think he wasn't, but ever since Boone had tried to burn him out, Harry had been concerned about him. And because he didn't know where Boone's visitors from New Jersey had gone, he was also worrying about Katherine and decided to take a look around her end of the Hammock to make sure she was safe.

"I've got something to show you," Tucker said as soon as Harry finished congratulating Sanchez on his quick recovery.

Sanchez was on his feet when Oh-Brother! led him around to the back porch, but as soon as Harry said recovered, Sanchez' legs folded under him as if he'd fainted, and he fell to the floor with a pitiful groan. Oh-Brother! turned his head away and trotted around the corner of the house.

"He's embarrassed," Tucker said, *sotto voce*. He nodded toward the departing mule. "He's very disappointed with Sanchez. I've told him not to be so judgmental, but you know mules. Puritans, every last one of them."

Sanchez opened one eye as Harry followed Tucker off the porch and gave another groan. Tucker pretended not to hear and quickly led Harry away.

As soon as they were inside the hen house, the old farmer pointed proudly at a young barred rock rooster, which, except for being a lot smaller, could have been Beauregard's twin. "Well, there he is."

"What are you going to call him?" Harry asked.

"Longstreet." Tucker was beaming. "It's going to take a cool head to lead this flock. And we don't need any more Pickett charges in here. He's going to learn that when the Gray Assassins slide in the door, it's time to take to the rafters. Beauregard never did appreciate the value of tactics. His approach was always: The enemy is in front of me, and I shall strike him. Oh-Brother!'s working on this one."

At the sound of his name, the rooster cocked one eye at Tucker and stared at him intently.

"Any more night riders?" Harry asked as they emerged into the fiery sunshine.

"No," Tucker said. "Bonnie and Clyde are enjoying their victory, but they'll be back. I just hope Longstreet is a quick study."

Tucker and Oh-Brother! walked Harry to the Rover.

As Harry got in behind the wheel, Tucker gave him a warning. "Were I you, I'd start thinking about Emile Thibedeau. He'll be planning something."

Harry nodded, but his mind was already elsewhere. Finding Tucker well and busy, he had gone back to wondering what the two enforcers from New Jersey were up to. He made a quick tour of the north end of the Hammock, giving the area around Katherine's place a close look, without finding any evidence of stalkers. Satisfied, he went home.

Chapter 24

At noon on the following Monday, Snyder and Katherine stopped by to tell Harry the crime lab had confirmed the traces of gasoline in the trunk of Boone's car. But there were no clear prints on the gas cans the police had taken from Tucker's yard.

"Rumors at the station are that the Sheriff will not press charges," Snyder said. He was carrying a tray of iced tea onto the lanai under Katherine's critical gaze.

"What about Boone's injuries?" Harry pulled chairs around the table. "What's the Sheriff's Department got there?"

"Snyder says that's being kept under wraps," Katherine said.

They were beginning to sound like a married couple, and the fact she was calling him Snyder made Harry very much less happy than he was pretending.

"What's funny?" she demanded.

She was on her way to the cabin from work and was wearing a lavender dress and low-heeled shoes, her working clothes. Her braid was twisted around her head. Harry thought she was looking lovelier every day. Just for the pleasure of seeing Snyder's ears light up and giving himself some additional grief, Harry started to say he was wondering what they were doing out here at noon time, but his tongue balked.

"How long have you been calling Snyder 'Snyder'?" he asked instead.

She turned away from him too late to hide her blush. Snyder lit up like a stop sign.

"You call him Snyder," she protested.

Snyder groaned with embarrassment. Katherine broke into a delighted laugh.

"You're not safe off a lead, Harry Brock," she cried.

Harry fetched a plate of cookies, and by the time he got back, the two of them were sitting on the porch bench looking very somber.

He put the cookies down on the low table in front of them. "There wasn't time to get into a fight," he said.

"We've got something to tell you, Harry," Snyder said. "It's not very good news."

Katherine finished the statement. "Maria Benedict and Dave Herrera have left together for Costa Rica."

"You're right," Harry said, "It's not good news." Then he added, "I hope they'll be happy." But he thought it was damned unlikely.

Snyder grunted and rubbed a hand over his face.

"What's that supposed to mean?" Katherine demanded.

"Dave's got a wife and house full of kids," Snyder said. "And more family than you can shake a stick at."

"Had, Snyder," she said. "Had."

Snyder shook his head. "They'll be with him no matter how far that plane flies, and if Maria doesn't know it now, she'll find out soon enough."

Katherine gave Harry a raised eyebrow look. When they left, Katherine, still looking somber, gave Harry an extra long hug.

"I'm not going anywhere," Harry said.

"I'm glad to hear it." She regarded him with a serious expression.

Harry watched them drive away and tried to tell himself

they made a good-looking couple. "An attractive young couple," he said aloud, as an added reminder, but he said it without conviction.

Shortly after they left, Harry called Jeff Smolkin.

"Can the hospital and the people who treat an injured patient be compelled under law to tell the court the nature and extent of the person's injuries?"

"You're thinking about the Boone indictment," he said.

"This isn't for attribution," Harry said. "It's information I need."

"Because you've heard Eric Smith isn't going to indict the son-of-a-bitch."

"Any truth in the rumor?"

"There may be. And while going after the hospital records may prove intoxication or other drug use, there's nothing substantial enough to prosecute for arson or attempted murder or even intent to do grievous bodily harm."

"Those records will show Boone was bitten in the ass by a dog and kicked by a mule. Wouldn't that do it?"

"Maybe. But proving the injuries were made by Tucker's mule and his dog would be a gamble the Assistant State Attorney might not want to take."

"Retribution if he loses."

"Big time."

"Look, I'm going to see Luis this afternoon. Any news there?"

"No."

"Smith can't be thinking of putting him on trial?" Harry demanded.

"I wish he would," Jeff responded. "I'd blow him out of the water."

When Harry reached Luis's house, there was a moving

van in the yard, and four men were carrying furniture and taped boxes out of the house. Harry found Luis in his study, cleaning out his desk. "What's going on?"

Luis had aged. His hair was whiter than it had been before he was arrested, and his face was gaunt and an unhealthy gray. He seemed to move in a constant hunch as if he was trying not to be seen.

He brushed his hands together. "We're moving, Harry."

"Where are you going?"

"Not far, and you know why," he replied. "We'll stay in Avola until this is over. I've leased a place for us over in Wyandotte until the case is settled one way or the other. Then, unless I'm in jail, we'll leave Florida together. If I am, Theresa and Gisele will probably go to Puerto Rico. Theresa has a sister there who has said she would be glad to have them."

"You're not going to jail, so forget that." Harry tried to sound confident. "But I would sure as hell hate to see you leave Avola. We need you here, Luis."

Mendoza smiled wanly and shook his head.

"Thank you, Harry, but you know as well as I do, I'm finished here. What kind of life would there be for us? My influence is gone. I'm a jailbird. Innocent or guilty, I am ruined. My only hope is to move away and start over. If I can."

Harry knew he was right. The bastards had destroyed him professionally in Avola.

"I can no longer pay you, Harry," he continued. "I'm sorry. It looks as though you're out of a job."

"Like hell I am," Harry countered. "I am going to pursue this until either I'm put in one of Tucker's compost piles or Boone is hanging by his thumbs. Don't you worry about paying me. You've paid me too much already for the damn little I've done for you."

Mendoza laughed. "You've been very effective," he said. "If it hadn't been for you, I'd still be in jail. So you have my gratitude and my thanks."

He put out his hand, and Harry shook it.

"If I can find that gun, we'll nail the son-of-a-bitch." Harry made the point to say something positive. He did not think it could be found.

Snyder called on Wednesday to tell Harry the two visitors from New Jersey had vanished.

"Everything takes so long in this system," Snyder complained. "By the time authorization was granted to bring them in for questioning, they were long gone."

Harry tried to ease Snyder's guilt. "They wouldn't have told you anything."

"You're right. I've got something else. It's final. No charges are going to be filed against Boone. I hear his alcohol count was up around two point five. And there was cocaine in his system. Assistant Attorney Smith wanted to go after him, but Attorney Fergus said it wasn't worth the trouble. I doubt Chief Fisher will press for a trial. He's too busy to take a full breath as it is."

Am I surprised? Harry asked himself and knew the answer.

"How's Katherine and the kids?" he asked.

"Katherine's OK, and the kids are fine. But it's a mercy they have a summer day program to go to. They are getting to be too much."

Snyder had passed quickly over Katherine, and Harry wondered what Snyder was finding "too much" about Minna and Jesse.

The next morning the *Banner* had a front page story saying Commissioner Emile Thibedeau was under scrutiny by the State Ethics Commission for influence peddling and related charges. The commission, the article said, was "responding to filings by several Avola citizens. Among those filing charges was Luis Mendoza, recently released from jail where he had been held while the Assistant State Attorney's office in the 21st District considered bringing murder charges against him in the deaths of Will Trachey and Slade Hatfield. The Assistant Attorney's office had declined to comment on his release or the status of the charges."

Harry put the paper under his arm and walked back to the house, surrounded by the boisterous early morning chorusing of birds, crickets, locusts, cicadas, frogs and even, he noticed, the hopelessly late rumbling of a still horny alligator, trying to extend its mating season. He listened with pleasure to the throaty racket as he walked along the sandy track. But mostly he wondered how he was going to find out who killed Trachey and Hatfield. Having read that the state was pursuing charges against Thibedeau made him wonder if he was not just wasting time and energy.

It came down to this: Boone would walk away without being charged with murder, attempted murder, or arson. Thibedeau would, at worst, be issued a warning by the Ethics Commission. Boone and Thibedeau and a fair number of their buddies had lost some money. That was comforting. In fact, Boone's businesses just might go under. Better still, Luis was out of jail. But probably the State Attorney's office would eventually let Thibedeau and Boone slip away.

Deeply dissatisfied with the outcome he had visualized, Harry stopped on the bridge to watch the wavering flight of a dozen ibis crossing the immense crimson disk of the sun. Taken out of himself a little by the beauty of the morning, he toyed with the possibility that it was time to declare victory and walk away from the investigation.

He took a deep breath and thought of Maria and Herrera. Were they brave or foolish? He asked but got no answer. Then he thought with even less satisfaction of Abigail Blakeley. What should he do about her?

"What do you want to do?" he asked aloud and silenced the frogs under the bridge.

His question startled him and got his feet moving. Why should I do anything? he demanded as he strode off the bridge. I don't have to do anything, he told himself with fine conviction, but he couldn't shake the uncomfortable feeling Abigail was walking beside him, regarding him with one of her quizzical smiles.

"Now what?" he demanded querulously of the telephone as he came into the house and found his message light blinking. He punched the message button.

"Perhaps you're still in bed, Harry," Abigail's voice said. "But I doubt it. It would be too self-indulgent, I think. I expect you're fetching your paper. Anyway, I'm up ridiculously early, and there's something I want to discuss with you. Give me a call, my Dear."

He called her, expecting to hear another chapter from the misdeeds of her husband Joe Speroni.

"I want to talk with you, Harry," she said, "and I don't want to do it here or on the phone."

Her voice had none of the playfulness he had heard in her message.

"Is something wrong?" he asked.

"Not exactly. No, there's nothing wrong, but if you can give me some time, I do very much want to talk with you."

He thought for a moment and said, "Shell Mound Park on the Seminole River is a pretty place with benches and a nice river walk. It's on the north end of Fourteenth Avenue."

"In half an hour?"

"Yes."

She was standing beside her Jaguar, waiting for him.

"What a lovely spot," she said, taking his arm.

They walked into the park through the bougainvillea-draped entrance arch. The arch opened onto an expanse of carefully tended trees and grass and a winding, white shell path along the green bank of the river.

"Sit or walk?" Harry asked, pausing in front of a varnished wooden bench.

"Walk, I think," Abigail said, turning to kiss his cheek and give him a bright smile.

She was wearing pale gray slacks, sandals, and a light blue blouse. Her hair was tied back with a gold ribbon, and she was, Harry thought, absolutely beautiful.

They moved off together. "You worried me," he said. He was not fooled by her bright manner. "What's troubling you?"

She started to protest, then squeezed his arm and gave a forced laugh in which he heard neither humor nor delight. "I have something to tell you and something to . . . ask you? Offer you? I'm not sure which."

She shook her head and looked out across the river. A gleaming white trawler, its brass flashing in the sun, with *Nantucket* painted in black letters on its stern, passed them slowly, leaving no wake, on its way to the Gulf, its heavy engines rumbling gently.

"The blue waters are calling," she said. The boat slipped by on the ebbing tide. "And someone is answering the call."

The words were spoken with such sadness that Harry stopped short and turned her to face him.

"Abby," he said. "What is it?"

"Perhaps we should sit down," she said.

"I'm planning to leave Avola in August, Harry," she said when they were seated. Tears suddenly welled up in her eyes. "Oh, damn. I promised myself I wouldn't."

He dug in his pocket and pulled out a handkerchief and gave silent thanks that he had picked up a clean one before leaving the house.

"God, Harry." She was laughing and crying at the same time. "You're giving me your handkerchief. Do you know how impossible that is?"

"Never mind the handkerchief. Is this for good?" He was not prepared for the pain her news brought with it.

She wiped her eyes and sat holding the handkerchief crushed in her hands.

"Probably."

"I will miss you," he said. "In fact, I'm going to miss you a lot."

"And, if it comes to it, I'll miss you, Harry." She turned to him, speaking earnestly. "But we don't have to be separated. And I most sincerely hope we won't be."

"But you said you're leaving."

"Yes."

Then she grasped his hands and said in a rush, "Come away with me, Harry."

The handkerchief tumbled to the ground unnoticed.

"I can't do that, Abby," he said. "I . . ."

"I don't mean for a fling." She gripped his hands more tightly. I mean for something far more serious than that."

Her proposal left him shaken. He had no idea it was coming and was completely unprepared for it.

He struggled to create some space. "Abigail, I couldn't. I mean, I don't have . . ."

She gave her head a quick, impatient shake.

"The money?" She frowned. "Harry, I have more money than we could ever spend. The world is ours. We can live wherever we want, do what we want to do, and we will want for nothing. My Dear, do you understand?"

She released his hands and sat straight-backed, waiting tensely. Over their heads a mockingbird began singing, repeating each of his songs three times, as if he was practicing. Harry did not know he was hearing the bird, but its singing became a part of the memories he kept of the moment.

"Are you asking me to marry you?" He made an effort to get some control over his racing thoughts.

"No, but I will marry you, if that's what you want."

"I don't know what to say, Abby." He felt almost stricken.

"What do you want to say?" she asked quietly and recovered one of his hands.

"What do I want to say? I don't know, Abby. It's so sudden . . ."

But he did know. He wanted to say, Yes. They had the world before them. A new life. It would be the end of loneliness. Then what was stopping him? Why not just say yes? Go for it, Harry, he told himself.

He tried to speak, but the words couldn't come. And in that moment Katherine's face slipped into his mind. Her image was so clear and so vibrant he thought she was going to speak, and in that instant he knew what was blocking him.

"I'm sorry, Abby." It seemed to him the words were being torn out of him.

"Why, Harry?" she demanded.

"I don't love you, Abby."

He did not say that he loved Katherine Trachey, but he knew it for the first time and knew it absolutely. Abigail's offer had made him confront the possibility of leaving Katherine forever, and the shock of it had forced him to acknowledge the truth.

"Harry," she said quietly. "You don't have to love me to make this work. And unless you love someone else, don't throw us away. We could be so happy together."

Looking at her, he knew she was right. Without Katherine, they could have been happy together. Abigail Blakeley was a beautiful, intelligent, charming woman. He had never known anyone else like her. He thought in that moment it was unlikely Katherine would ever love him. She would, in all probability, marry Jim Snyder. It was what she ought to do. But the knowledge changed nothing. Sadly, he shook his head.

"I can't do it, Abby," he said. "I am in love with someone else. It just wouldn't be fair to you or me either."

"Oh, damn it, Harry." She snatched the fallen handkerchief off the path. Then her tears spilled over, but she fought them, saying over and over, "Oh, damn, damn, damn it!"

Chapter 25

Saying goodbye to Abigail Blakeley had been very hard. And the hours after Harry returned home were even harder. He may not have loved Abigail the way he loved Katherine, but they had been lovers. And now she was gone, Harry was beginning to understand how much he would miss her. As he had done for years when he was seriously disturbed, he got out his painting gear.

When he finished painting, Harry put his canoe into Puc Puggy Creek and spent the rest of the day sketching and photographing. When he paddled home in the waning day, he had enough images of alligators, wading birds, clumps of white swamp lilies, and yellow willow overrun with morning glory and moonflower vines to keep him painting for six months. But he had no clearer idea of how he was going to get through those six months than he had when he got home from saying goodbye to Abigail.

At two the following morning, he was awakened by a steady thumping on the front door. He pulled the pillow over his head, but the thumping went on. Swearing, he pushed himself out of bed, pulled on his shorts, grabbed his gun off the night stand and ran downstairs without turning on a light. It was Tucker.

"This is a hell of a time of night to be calling on anybody," he said, "but something's not right down the road."

He didn't have to say, "Katherine's," for Harry to know

where he meant, and the shotgun he was carrying said as much as the worried look on his face about what kind of trouble he was talking about.

"Come in," Harry said. "Tell me what's wrong while I put on some clothes."

"I was having trouble sleeping," Tucker said. Harry ran back upstairs and Tucker raised his voice to make himself heard. "So I took a walk around the place with Oh-Brother!, to see if the night air might make him sleepy."

Harry ran back down the stairs, shoving a handful of shells into his shorts' pocket.

"A big car with its lights off slid past not making as much sound as a healthy locust buzzing. If it hadn't been for Oh-Brother!, I'd have missed it. He knew it was coming before it was in sight and called my attention to the road. Sure enough, there it came ghosting along in the moonlight, soft as a feather."

"Any idea who it was?" Harry asked as they climbed into the Rover.

"Nope. Couldn't see inside, but I decided to get you."

"Where's Oh-Brother!?" Harry asked.

"He's home looking after Sanchez. He wanted to come, but I told him somebody had to look after the place, and I couldn't be in two places at once. He wasn't hearing of it until I agreed to get you."

"Smart mule," Harry said.

They passed Tucker's farm in the Rover, making a lot more noise than the mystery car.

"We need a plan," Harry said.

"Got one," Tucker answered. "We leave the Rover turned sideways partway down the track to the cabin. We go the rest of the way on foot and come up on the cabin along the shaded side of the clearing. The moon's like a floodlight tonight."

The big car Tucker had seen was sitting in front of the cabin. It was a black BMW.

"Recognize it?" Tucker asked.

Harry shook his head, but he thought of the two visitors from New Jersey, who had mysteriously disappeared, and his stomach lurched. There were lights on in the cabin, but the only sound, aside from the light wind, was the medley of swamp songs pouring out from the Stickpen west of the cabin. With Tucker watching the front door and the back corner of the cabin, Harry got across the open spaces between the trees as fast and quietly as he could and inched along the side wall until he could look in a window.

The windows on his side of the cabin were chin high, and the curtains had been pulled, but there was still a space through which Harry could see some of the sitting room area. Katherine was seated on the couch with her hands and her ankles tied with what looked like clothesline rope. Her face was pale and drawn but her head was up, and she looked anything but daunted. Minna and Jesse were huddled beside her.

At first Harry didn't recognize the tall man standing facing her. He was wearing a light gray blazer and dark trousers. He stood with his hands in his pockets, apparently comfortable with his situation. Harry could hear the rumble of his voice, but he couldn't see his face or hear what he was saying. Then the man turned his head slightly. It was Emile Thibedeau.

Under his breath, Harry said, "Oh, shit."

Whatever was going on in the cabin had reached some sort of stalemate, or else Thibedeau was waiting for someone. Harry thought of the Rover and eased back to Tucker.

"It's Emile Thibedeau," he said. "Katherine's sitting on the couch with her ankles and wrists tied. The kids are with her and seem to be OK. Thibedeau was speaking. I couldn't hear what he was saying, but I got the feeling he was waiting for something or somebody."

"If it's somebody, they're going to find the Rover," Tucker said. "Might be the right time to hide it in the bushes."

"Good idea," Harry said. "I'll get it out of sight."

When he got back, there was a lot of shouting and yelling coming from the cabin, and Tucker had vanished. Harry ran back to the window just in time to see Thibedeau slap Katherine across the face hard enough to knock her sideways onto the couch. She struggled to sit up, shaking her head to clear it, an angry red welt spreading across the right side of her face.

Minna and Jesse were crying and trying to pull Katherine upright. Thibedeau was half bent over her, his back to the window. Then Tucker, who must have slipped into the cabin through the back door, suddenly appeared behind Katherine. He raised his shotgun and shouted, "Hold it!" loud enough for Harry to hear him.

Thibedeau's right hand swung up holding a gun. He fired over Katherine's head. Tucker's shotgun flew up, and he fell behind the couch. Swearing, Harry pushed onto his toes, hitched his right shoulder up, and punched his gun through the glass. Just as he had managed that, the wind blew the curtain across his line of sight and a bullet exploded the last of the glass and whined over his head. Harry dropped down, cursing his stupidity and scraping glass slivers off his face. Getting himself killed was not going to help Katherine. Another bullet banged out through the side of the cabin about a foot from his shoulder. Thinking Thibedeau might make a run for his car, Harry sprinted for the front of the house.

Nothing. The front door was shut and, while Harry crouched behind a tree, it stayed shut. The cabin was silent.

The waiting gave Harry time to curse himself for his tunnel vision. Tucker had told him to watch out for Thibedeau. But he was so focused on Boone, he hadn't listened. Now look at the mess his mistake had put Katherine and the kids in.

He shook himself loose from his guilt and began thinking about what to do. Thibedeau had Katherine and two kids in there with him. Tucker was down, and if Harry burst into the cabin, he would either be shot coming through the door or find Thibedeau holding a gun to somebody's head. Harry backed deeper into the trees, keeping out of the moonlight as he retreated.

Harry had almost reached Thibedeau's car when he heard a car coming along the Hammock road. In that moment he guessed who Thibedeau was waiting for. Who else but those two missionaries from New Jersey? They hadn't left Avola. They had only dropped out of sight.

Harry risked a full out run through the moonlight to Thibedeau's car. The key was in the ignition. The instant the engine caught, he reversed straight up the track. The front door of the cabin flew open, and Thibedeau ran onto the porch and began shooting. Harry floored the gas pedal and swung himself around in the seat. The windshield exploded into a shower of glass pellets. More bullets smacked into the car. His side window shattered. Then he was swallowed in the brushy growth crowding the track.

Harry gunned the BMW in a snaking path along the track, pushing the car as fast as he could hold it in the road. He expected Thibedeau to come running and shooting, but he was not pursued. Before he reached the Hammock road, he saw the bounce of headlights on a clump of sea grapes and slammed to a stop. He switched off the engine and jumped out of the car. He caught a flash of light as he swung the door shut and looked down to see he was sprinkled with popcorns of glass. He shoved the keys into his pocket and ran for the cabin, sparkling like the rhinestone cowboy.

The cabin was in darkness. Harry swore fervently. He had hoped to edge from one window to the next until he could get a shot at Thibedeau. Harry stayed in the shadows as he moved across the front of the cabin and placed himself where he could see the cabin door and the opening where the track spilled into the yard. He didn't have much confidence in his quickly worked out plan, but he had to get Thibedeau out of the house, and he figured he had less than five minutes before the Bobbsey Twins brought two more guns to the party.

He ran around the cabin and dodged into the lean-to shed and paused to let his eyes adjust to the increased darkness. He saw an old tin pail. He grabbed it and the stepladder leaning against the cabin wall and went back into the trees in a crouching run and kept running until he reached the water. Turning west, he trotted through the trees until he came to a pile of palm fronds and other brush that had been dragged back there and piled up. He shoved his gun into his belt and began breaking up the driest palm fronds he could find and stuffed them into the bottom of the pail. Then he dodged back toward the water until he found a stand of willows. Working swiftly, he stripped their branches until he had filled the pail with green leaves.

Satisfied, he hurried back to the house and located the bathroom window. Working quietly, he opened the stepladder, placed it under the window, and went through his pockets until he found a book of matches. Carrying the pail, he climbed onto the stepladder and reached down into the pail until he felt the palm fronds. He struck a match and dropped it into the dry fronds, waited an instant for the flames to spurt, and let the green leaves tumble back over the crackling flames. A funnel of gray smoke rolled out of the pail.

"Right," Harry said to the pail as he pulled out his gun.

He scrambled up the stepladder and beat the glass out of the window with his gun. Katherine screamed, and the kids started yelling and Thibedeau was shouting at them to shut up so he could tell where the sound was coming from. "Keep yelling," he whispered. He heard a door crash open as he shoved the pail through the window and lowered it until it came to rest on the back of the toilet. The bathroom was filling with smoke before he pulled his arm back through the window.

He jumped down from the stepladder just in time to hear the front door bang open and hear Katherine shouting, "Run, run!"

The kids! Harry sprinted for cover. Thibedeau must have run into the bedroom and made for a window because he heard a sash crash open and two blasts from his gun followed him into the shadows. Harry picked up speed and went through the cypress along the edge of the water like Hiawatha. If Jesse and Minna had made it out of the house, he wanted to be there to grab them and get them away from the front yard before Thibedeau or his helpers could catch them.

There was also a chance Thibedeau would break cover and give Harry a chance at him. He didn't. He was sticking with Katherine. A bird in the hand, Harry thought. But the kids were already at the boat landing when Harry found them. They were crying and looking back at the cabin and dragging their feet but still going. Harry gathered them up and got them back into the shadows and quieted their crying.

"He shot Mr. LaBeau," Jesse said as he padded along behind Harry into the trees.

Harry was carrying Minna, who was clinging to him like a limpet.

"I know," Harry said. "But it's going to be all right. And right now I want both of you to listen to me very carefully."

He had managed to get them about fifty yards into the woods behind the cabin. Picking up Jesse, he waded very slowly and carefully into a big saw palmetto tangle, holding their bare legs above the saw-toothed leaves. When he reached the center, he put them down carefully in a small open space and put both hands on the ground and waited and waited a little more. Nothing. Good. No fire ants.

Then he sat down and pulled them into his arms.

"Do you remember when we looked at the rat snake?" he asked.

"I do," Jesse said.

Minna only nodded, but she was listening.

"And you remember we had to be very quiet when we moved the branches so we could see it?"

"It was a prince." Minna wiped her eyes with the backs of her hands.

"Sure," Harry said. He gave Jesse a little shake to keep him from contradicting her. "I'm going back to get your mother and Mr. LaBeau. While I'm gone, you have to be very, very quiet so the man who's keeping your mother in the cabin won't be able to find you. OK?"

"I don't want to stay out here," Minna said. "I don't like this place."

"It won't be for long, Minna," Harry said. "Jesse will look after you."

"If I had a cat, I wouldn't be afraid," she said a little more loudly.

"She's been trying to get Mom to let her have a kitten." Jesse sounded weary.

"If you stay here with Jesse and keep very, very quiet, I'll get you a kitten," Harry told her. "What color do you want?"

"Black and white," she said. "But mostly white."

Then a heavy voice began shouting Thibedeau's name. The two night visitors had found the cabin.

"OK," Harry said. "Black and white. Mostly white. Now, sit down. Don't make a sound. If you hear anybody coming close, don't move and don't answer if they call your names. When I come, I'll say it's me. Promise you'll be quiet?"

They both nodded.

"Good," Harry said and gave them a final hug. "I won't be long."

Harry waded out of the tangle and began to think of some way to lessen the odds. Three against one was not good. He got back to the cabin as quietly as he could and stood in the shadow of the trees on the water side of the building while Thibedeau shouted from the front door to the two guns in the yard. One was tall. The other was short. Both were dressed in street clothes, and both had guns in their hands. Thibedeau told them about Harry and the two kids, making no effort to speak quietly.

"We'll take care of it," the bigger one said.

"Yeah," the short, fat one chimed in with a pleased chuckle. "Where are they going to go? It's all woods."

"And when we get back, we'll take care of the one in there," the tall one added. He pointed his companion one way around the cabin, and took the other.

"Short and Tall take a walk in the Stickpen," Harry muttered. He retreated a little deeper into the trees, thinking the swamp might do some of his work. The two gunmen met behind the cabin, then stepped into the moonlight, and began squinting into the trees.

"What's all the fucking racket in there?" Short asked in a loud voice.

"Fuck the racket," Tall answered. "Let's get this over with."

He walked purposely into the trees, moving in Harry's direction. Harry fired a little over his head and showered him with oak bark and Spanish moss.

"What the fuck . . ." He ripped off three shots in Harry's direction.

But Harry was already behind a big royal fig feeding another shell into his gun. Tall was shouting at Short by this time and telling him to get his ass out there and make a sieve of whoever was doing the shooting. Short had stumbled into a clump of sea grapes and was swearing and crashing around trying to untangle himself. When he did, he must have tried to push his way through a saw palmetto because he began yelling as if he'd been attacked by hornets. Harry grinned. Good old South Florida.

Tall pushed ahead and Harry backed away from him. When he showed signs of slacking his pace, Harry put some more bark in his face. Short was out of the palmetto and was trying to run to catch up. It was a noisy business and required a lot of swearing. Harry led them away from where Jesse and Minna were hiding and drew them onto a point of land that jutted several hundred yards into the swamp.

Harry looked around to locate himself and figured they had gone forty or fifty yards onto the point. He could no longer see the cabin lights, which Thibedeau had switched on after Harry's smoke bucket diversion. And the trees were thicker here, reducing the moonlight to narrow shafts and sparkles occasionally falling onto the forest floor.

Harry began to move more quickly, making enough noise to draw them on. When he'd gone as far as he wanted to, he eased himself into a big clump of coffee bushes and lay down, praying he hadn't dropped onto a fire ant nest. Then he shouted, "You clowns couldn't find your ass with both hands."

"You son-of-a-bitch," Tall shouted and charged straight past Harry, followed by Short, puffing and swearing.

They were both shooting and shouting threats. When they were past him, Harry got up and brushed himself off while they went crashing ahead. He was almost back at the cabin when behind him he heard several shots, muffled by distance.

Good, he thought. Maybe you'll shoot each other out there. He thought there was an equally good chance they would just wander into the swamp and get themselves lost. That possibility pleased him. When he reached the palmettos where he had stashed the two kids, he said quietly, "It's me. Harry."

No answer. That scared him until he waded into the tangle and found them lying next to one another sound asleep.

For a moment he savored his relief, then checked to be sure they were warm. He paused for a moment to listen to their slow, steady breathing. Satisfied, he backed out of the tangle, still asking himself how he could separate Thibedeau from Katherine.

Chapter 26

In his eagerness to get back to the cabin, Harry almost walked into Thibedeau. Harry was pushing through a stand of maple saplings when to his right he caught a flash of Thibedeau's white shirt as the man stepped through a shaft of moonlight. Harry eased himself out of the maples, swearing silently at his carelessness.

From the shadow of a big cabbage palm, Harry listened to Thibedeau moving toward him and concluded the last spatter of gunfire had drawn him out of the cabin. Harry considered edging around the palm and risking a shot. But the chance of hitting Thibedeau through the tangle of maples was very slim. Instead, he pressed himself against the trunk of the palm and waited.

Thibedeau stopped. For a very long minute, Harry lost him. When he finally saw him again, Thibedeau was edging back toward the cabin. Harry swore silently. He wanted him in the open. If Thibedeau got into the cabin, it was stalemate again.

Stooping very slowly, Harry felt around on the ground until he found a rock. He straightened slowly and stepped to the left, still keeping the cabbage palm between him and Thibedeau. Then he tossed the rock back into the maples. A moment later it crashed through the branches and leaves and thumped the ground.

Harry did not wait for Thibedeau's response. He gambled the man would, at least for a moment, freeze in place and sprinted for the cabin. Running in thick woods at night is a noisy business. Before Harry had gone ten yards, Thibedeau was shooting at him. Harry choked down his fear and picked up speed, hoping Thibedeau didn't catch him in a patch of moonlight.

Gasping for breath, Harry broke out of the trees and bolted for the cabin. He threw himself through the door, fell to the floor and kicked it shut. "It's me," he shouted as a bullet smashed through the door and zipped over his head with a splintering whine.

"Are the kids OK?" Katherine shouted.

"They're safe," Harry said, scuttling in a crouch to a window and peering out. "Get onto the floor. Stay quiet. Thibedeau's right behind me."

He expected the air in the cabin to start buzzing with lead. But Thibedeau stopped shooting. Harry crawled back to the door, locked it, and made a dash on his hands and knees to where Katherine was still tied up.

"That son-of-a-bitch," she said. "If he so much as touches those kids, I'll pull his head off. So help me, Lord Jesus, I will."

"Stop hollering," Harry said. "I've got to be able to listen." He turned off the lamp beside the couch and began untying her. "The kids are safe. He's not going to get hold of them. Is Tucker dead?"

"Oh, God, Harry, I think so," she said. "He went down as if lightning struck him. He's somewhere behind the couch, and I haven't heard a sound out of him."

When she was free he put his arms around her. Holding her made his heart pound even harder. "We need to be as quiet as we can. Thibedeau will be planning how to get in here. If we're lucky, the other two are good and lost. If we're not, they'll soon be back here mad as hornets." He let go of her. "How are you? Can you move around?"

"Yes," she said. "I'm OK."

"Good," he replied. "While I check on Tucker, you call 911."

She threw her arms around him and clung to him a moment, then slid to the floor and crawled to the phone.

Harry slithered back to where Tucker was sprawled on his back with his shotgun angled across his neck. Behind the couch where Tucker had fallen, it was black as the inside of a boot. Harry couldn't see well enough to tell where he was shot, but running his hands over Tucker, he couldn't find any blood on his head or upper body.

"The phone's dead," she said. "But my cell phone's in my bag."

She scuttled away. A moment later she was talking to the dispatcher. She crawled back and said in a loud whisper that help was coming but they were short of officers and there had been a bad accident on I-75. "The dispatcher promised to do her best."

"Great," Harry said. "I feel a lot better."

"And safer," Katherine added.

"That too," Harry said. He grinned.

Just then it came to Harry that Tucker's face was warm. He put an ear down to his mouth. "He's breathing!" Harry said. "He's alive."

"Tucker," she said and gave him a shake. "Tucker, wake up."

Nothing.

"I don't get it," she said.

"Well, he's not bleeding," Harry said. "At least I don't think he is."

The diagnosis was cut short by a flurry of gunshots, and the shattering of glass as slugs ripped through the cabin. One blew the lamp beside the couch off the table and whined away like one of the bullets in a Class B western. Katherine put her hands over her ears, but she didn't scream.

"Cocksucker!" she shouted when the barrage stopped.

That brought on another burst of shooting.

"Don't even breathe loudly," Harry whispered.

"Sorry," she said.

They crawled back in front of the couch.

"You're not," he said.

"What?"

"Sorry."

She gave him a jab in the ribs.

"We can't stay in here," he said. "We're like ducks in a shooting gallery. And if those two thugs come back, it will be worse."

"Hey," she said. "I've got a gun. Orville gave it to me when I moved in here."

"Can you use it?"

"Sure. I can shoot bottles off a fence post real good."

"Have you got any ammunition?"

"A couple of boxes."

"Get them," he said. "We just improved the odds."

She went on her hands and knees into the bedroom and came back with a .32 revolver stuck in the waistband of her shorts and a box of shells in each hand.

Harry was checking the windows and she was sitting cross-legged on the floor loading the gun when the handle on the back door began to rattle and a small voice said, "I want to come in."

Katherine started for the door, but Harry grabbed her. "I'll go. You stay down and whatever happens, stay out of the line of fire from the door."

He scrambled to the door, eased off the lock, snatched the

door open, grabbed Minna, and pulled her behind him and scooted to the side, his gun drawn. He had expected Thibedeau to come bursting into the room gun blazing. He didn't, but before Harry could swing the door shut, Thibedeau had blown two more holes in it. He must have heard her voice and come running.

"I don't like it out there," Minna said. She wriggled in his arm. "It's scratchy."

Katherine scuttled across the floor and grabbed her.

"Honey, where's Jesse?" Katherine asked. She tried to keep the stress out of her voice but didn't make it.

"Asleep," the child said. "I'm thirsty."

"Believe me, Thibedeau hasn't got him," Harry said, "and if Jesse stays where he is, nobody will find him."

From somewhere north of the cabin came the sound of shouting.

"Those two bozos have wandered close enough for Thibedeau to hear them," Harry said. His stomach sank.

There was a shot.

"He's signaling them," Katherine whispered.

"Right. He'll wait a minute and shoot again so they can orient themselves on him. I'm going outside."

She grasped him by the arm. "I don't like you going out there alone."

"We can't just stay here," Harry said as gently as he could. "If those two hired guns find their way back, we're done for."

He thought it was likely they'd set fire to the cabin, but he didn't want to say that with Minna listening.

"If I'm outside, I may be able to keep them occupied until the police get here," he said quickly. "While Thibedeau's thinking about getting those two out of the swamp, I can slip out of here without him noticing."

"Shoot first and ask who it is second," she said. "Whoever

251

comes in here is going to get turned into a colander."

"Just don't shoot me."

"No chance. You take care, you hear?"

"I hear you. Wait a minute after I've gone, then close the window. Do it fast."

Harry chose a front window and slid out feet first. As his head went over the sill, she gave him a parting kiss on the cheek. He was so surprised he almost forgot there was a good chance morning might find him floating face down in Puc Puggy Creek.

Thibedeau fired two more shots at intervals of a couple of minutes, which was the way to do it. Harry got himself into the trees without sounding like a stampede of buffaloes and cheered himself with the thought that over the water in the cypress swamp, sound would bounce around like a billiard ball. Short and Tall could still be wading towards I-75.

Five minutes later, while Harry was working himself around the cabin, looking for Thibedeau, they waded out of the water huffing and swearing loudly at one another. When they saw Thibedeau, they began on him. Harry had made it to the edge of the water and was crouched in deep shadow, watching them from about fifteen yards away. They could not be seen from the cabin, and Thibedeau was not being careful.

When they stopped swearing, Thibedeau said, "He's inside. What do you want to do? I've got six shells left. So unless you've got a lot of ammo, just blasting them out of there isn't going to work."

"Fuck that," Short said. "Torch the place."

Thibedeau may have hesitated three seconds, but no longer than that.

"OK. There's a mower and a chain saw in the lean-to on the back of the cabin. There's probably gasoline."

"Let's do it," Tall said. "We've been way too long as it is.

Larry will go with you. I'll give you cover."

"Larry," Harry said to himself and stood up.

The three men had turned away from the water toward the cabin, and when they stepped into a small opening in the swamp cypress, Harry shot Tall because he was the biggest target. The man went down without a sound. Larry was fast. Before Harry was all the way back into a crouch, bullets were showering him with bits of bark and cypress needles.

For the next ten minutes, Harry backed away from the cabin, moving deeper into the trees. Thibedeau and Larry had separated and were following him. He retreated only when he knew where they both were, and, without firing, he allowed them to get closer and closer to him. He knew it was much safer to be drifting back from his pursuers than running from them in the dark, provided he kept track of both of them.

Then he lost Thibedeau. He experienced a cold trickle of fear but decided to even the odds by taking out Larry. Then he would be able to concentrate on Thibedeau. Harry reminded himself that although Larry blundered through the woods like a blind cow, he could shoot. Harry moved in front of him and stopped behind a big bay tree, gambling he would pass it because the area around its base was free of undergrowth. Larry obliged. He broke into the opening, muttering under his breath, and walked right past the tree. Harry swung the barrel of his gun against the gunman's head and struck him again as he slumped to the ground. Then he picked up Larry's gun.

That left Thibedeau. Since losing sight of him, he had not heard so much as a swish of branches sliding over cloth to tell Harry where he was. Harry stayed in the shadow of the tree and waited, listening hard. Then he heard the welcome sound of sirens. They were some way off, but he guessed they were over the bridge and on the Hammock road.

At that moment Thibedeau stepped around the tree with his gun held in front of him with both hands. Harry caught the glint of moonlight on the barrel and let his knees go. As he fell, he twisted toward his attacker, and pulled up his gun. He and Thibedeau fired at the same time. Harry rolled onto his knees. But his target had vanished.

"Where the hell . . ." he gasped and struggled to his feet, expecting every moment to be shot. Nothing. And no sign of Thibedeau.

Harry gathered his courage, sucked in his breath and went around the tree in a rush. He almost fell over Thibedeau, sprawled face down on the ground, his white shirt glowing in the moonlight.

Just then Jesse began calling Harry's name. Harry could see both of Thibedeau's hands. Wherever his gun was, he wasn't holding it.

"Thibedeau," he said.

There was no response. Harry nudged him with his foot. Nothing. He bent down and rolled him over. His body was completely limp. A wide, dark stain covered the front of his shirt. Thibedeau's eyes were closed. Very gingerly, Harry pressed his finger against Thibedeau's neck. There was a pulse.

Harry stepped away from the body and eased the hammer down on his gun. It was over.

Jessie called again, and Harry shouted, "I'm coming."

By the time he got the boy and carried him back to the cabin, making a wide detour around Thibedeau and Larry, the yard was full of police with lights, and Jim Snyder was inside with Katherine.

Chapter 27

The doctor finished examining Tucker and let the medical team lift him onto a gurney. "He's probably got a concussion. His eyes are going to be blacker than a raccoon's." He went off with the medical teams to collect Thibedeau, Larry, and Tall. The doctor was right about Tucker's eyes. The bullet that felled the old farmer had struck the breech of his shotgun. Flattened by the impact and most of its force spent, it ricocheted and struck him between the eyes. The blow cracked his skull and knocked him unconscious without penetrating his head. A Sheriff's deputy found the flattened chunk of lead where Tucker fell.

The biggest surprise for Harry in the following days came from Jim Snyder.

"It's definite," he told Harry. They were in Snyder's office going over Harry's statement concerning the cabin shoot-out one last time. "It was Thibedeau's gun that killed Slade Hatfield and wounded you," he said with satisfaction.

"And you're going to tell me he didn't have a permit to carry it."

Snyder's ears reddened. "I'm sorry to say that it was this department that issued him the permit."

Harry laughed. "I probably knew that. What are you going to do now with your time?"

Snyder shook his head. "I'm up to my neck in new cases. It doesn't end."

Harry stood up and shook the policeman's hand. "Good

luck, Jim. I wish you well."

"Much obliged," Snyder said.

He smiled and gave Harry's hand an extra shake without knowing that Harry was thinking more about him and Katherine than about his work. It had been painful for Harry to say as much as he had, and he left the office with a feeling of relief that did little to dispel his gloom at the prospect of Snyder and Katherine riding off into the sunset together.

Tucker was not surprised to learn that Thibedeau had shot Slade Hatfield and Harry with the gun that was registered with the police.

"Never occurred to him he might be caught," Tucker said. The farmer was sitting in his hospital bed the upper part of his head wrapped like a mummy's.

What Harry found hardest to live with was his own failure to consider Thibedeau as a serious danger. And his carelessness had damned near killed the four people he cared most about. It made him groan to realize it had happened because he had let his hostility toward Boone, the big, bad developer wolf, who was dragging a brush chain across southwest Florida, unhook his judgment. Of course, Harry admitted, cutting himself some slack, when Boone had tried to burn out Tucker, he just stopped thinking, period.

"It's still not clear," Tucker said, "what Boone's role was in the events leading up to the shoot-out at Trachey's cabin. You figure he knew what Thibedeau was doing? Was he a willing accomplice?"

"Yes and yes," Harry said at once. "He's refusing to cooperate with the police, but despite his lawyer's best effort, the judge tells me he will almost certainly be charged as an accessory to murder. I hear Thibedeau is sharing as much of the responsibility for what happened as he can."

Harry paused to study Tucker. "Is my talking tiring you?" he asked.

"I'll let you know when I've had enough," the old farmer said. "Get on with it."

"OK." Harry suppressed a grin. "It does look as if Thibedeau's the real sociopath in the bunch." He rubbed his own nose in the unpleasant reality of his blindness. "Thibedeau liked his Rolex, his English shoes, his silk shirts, the big cars, and expensive women. He liked power and the connections it brought him. He was not about to let a couple of losers and their friends spoil his party. I suspect he went after Katherine because Boone was too badly cracked up to stop him. Boone may have been the one keeping him off her from the start of Willard's blackmail scheme.

"She told the police that Thibedeau refused to believe Willard and Hatfield hadn't given her more damaging letters. He seemed to be most concerned they would be used to anchor the ethics charges against him. He told her he would kill her if he didn't get them."

"We should take some satisfaction in this," Tucker said. "None of them would have gotten out of that cabin alive if we hadn't come along. His calling in the two heavies makes that clear. But he failed, and despite all the Wild West stuff nobody died."

Harry finally, if reluctantly, agreed he had done something right.

"And they're all going away for a very long time," Tucker said. He leaned back against the pillows and closed his eyes.

Tucker was in the hospital for nearly a week. Oh-Brother! took his absence stoically. The only evidence of his concern was his refusal to wear his hat while Tucker was away. Sanchez's sufferings were a lot more public. He moped, refused to eat, and lay on the back porch and groaned whenever Harry came in sight. He declined all of Oh-Brother!'s gambits to get him on his feet, and insisted on having his bandage put back on his head.

Harry told Tucker. "I'm not surprised," Tucker said. "He's a lot more emotional than Oh-Brother! That comes from having been brought up in a Latino family."

When Tucker came back from the hospital, Katherine moved in with the kids to take care of him. The blow to his head had produced some balance and other problems that were slow to go away.

"And he wanders a little," Katherine told Harry. "Sometimes he gets me mixed up with someone he must have known a long time ago."

And since Snyder spent a lot of his free time with Katherine and the kids, Tucker acquired an extended family that seemed to suit him right down to the ground. Sanchez and Oh-Brother! recovered their spirits with Tucker's return and greeted the arrival of Minna and Jesse with enthusiasm.

Although Harry had mixed feelings about the arrangement, he went over every day to work in Tucker's garden, feed the animals, and deal with the barn and the hen coop. Sanchez and Oh-Brother! with the kids on his back usually greeted him, and the parade would stop long enough for Jesse and Minna to report on their latest group project and then go on its way, Sanchez's tail waving like a flag and Oh-Brother!'s ears waggling like semaphores through the holes in his hat.

A few days after Tucker came out of the hospital, Harry visited Luis Mendoza at Wyandotte and found him waxing his car in his garage. He was dressed in pressed jeans and a white, short-sleeved shirt that looked as if it had just come out of its wrapper. His loafers gleamed with polish. His garage was cleaner than Harry's living room.

"Harry," he said with a broad smile, "it's a pleasure to see you."

Harry had never seen him looking better.

"Congratulations on having all the charges against you dropped," he said. "The wheels of God and so on."

"Thank you. It is a great relief. But you are a hero, my friend! You deserve the gratitude of the whole city. I am proud to know you." He pumped Harry's hand as he spoke and grinned with pleasure.

"I'm no hero, Luis," Harry said. "Thibedeau damned near punched my clock. What's happening with you? Are you the same unhappy guy I saw moving out of his house a while back?"

"Yes and no," Luis said with a relaxed laugh. "We are going to the West Coast. We found a place south of San Francisco, close to the ocean. I sold my business in Avola and am buying one out there very much like it."

Harry suspected the vagueness of the address was deliberate.

"Can't persuade you to stay here?" Harry asked.

He shook his head. "There is no life for us in Tequesta County. We would have no peace." He spoke calmly but Harry did not miss the bitterness. "None of us. Especially our daughter. It's much better that we go."

Reluctantly, Harry agreed and said so. But as they shook hands, he couldn't help thinking Tequesta County was losing a good citizen and a tireless and compelling advocate for a world that had some green left in it.

One morning after Harry was finally done with the last of the police work connected with the shootings, he finished his chores on the farm, and instead of going home, which he had been in the habit of doing, he decided to visit with Tucker. He did not admit he wanted to see Katherine more than he wanted to see Tucker, but that wasn't surprising because he had not admitted avoiding her by going straight home every day. He found Tucker and Katherine sitting in the deep shade of the back porch shelling beans. A steady rattle of beans fell from Katherine's hands into the enamel basin on her knees and Tucker was working beside her, looking happy as a man could whose eyes were encircled by rings of bruises in fading shades of yellow, purple, and green.

"You've got to work if you sit down here," Katherine said. She gave him a welcoming smile and pointed at a three-legged stool. When he sat down, she pushed the basket of beans towards him.

She was dressed in sandals, her old denim shorts, and a blue sleeveless blouse. Her braid was wrapped around her head, and Harry couldn't think of any way to make her look lovelier. He feasted his eyes on her and concluded that since Willard's death she had matured into a beautiful woman. There was a stillness about her that had entirely replaced the wired intensity of the old Katherine. Looking at her made Harry's heart ache, but he told himself he was getting used to loving someone who did not love him.

Harry pulled up the stool and starting to shell along with them. "Boone's selling the Hammock to the State. Who would have believed it? My lease won't be renewed."

"Mine either," Tucker said.

"But this place belongs to you," Harry protested. "Boone can't . . ."

"No, Boone can't touch this place," Tucker agreed with a placid smile.

"Then what . . ." Harry demanded.

"Keep working," Katherine said.

260

Tucker smiled cheerfully. "Nothing discouraging. I arranged things with the state so that I stay here until I die. Then they take the place and do what they want with it."

"The woman who talked to Tucker about it said they might turn it into a farm museum," Katherine added. "She said there can't be a dozen places like this left in southern Florida."

Harry looked in astonishment at the two of them. His mouth must have dropped open because Katherine asked him if he was catching flies.

"No. Somebody could have told me this was going on," he protested.

"I just did," Tucker said.

"Did you get a letter?" Harry asked Katherine.

"Yes, but I don't have to leave right away. It's not a problem." She shot Tucker a glance and then looked at Harry, giving her head a slight shake.

"Then it looks as if the Hammock's safe." Harry did not want to let his concern show.

"Yes," Tucker said.

He leaned back in his rocker and looked out into the woods. The late morning sun leaked through the canopy, dropping long yellow shafts of light into the cool shade. A pair of bush jays, screaming lustily, darted among the tree trunks and hanging vines, flickering in and out of the dusty light.

"Always making a fuss." Tucker watched them with an indulgent smile.

Katherine and Harry looked at him, their hands still.

"Bonnie and Clyde have cubs," he said after a moment's pause.

"How do you know?" Harry asked.

"Saw Bonnie yesterday. She was on her way to Puc Puggy to catch some crabs. She's got a family."

"Did she see you?" Katherine asked.

"Oh, yes. She stopped and looked at me with one paw lifted. I waved and she went on her way. She and Clyde grow thin as rails this time of year. The cubs and this hot weather pull them down."

"Well, at least the cubs will have a place to grow up in," Katherine said.

"Yes," Tucker said.

Katherine and Harry went back to shelling beans. They worked without talking, the sound of the cicadas and locusts, the creak of Tucker's rocker, and the crackle of the dry pods providing a peaceful background sound. Tucker fell asleep. Harry worked quickly, unaware of what his hands were doing, trying to convince himself that being with her this way was good enough. But he knew it wasn't. Not nearly. His heart felt heavy as a stone.

After a while Katherine stood up and said quietly, "How about some tea? Come and help me make it."

He trailed into the kitchen after her.

She put on the kettle and turned to Harry. He was leaning against the table. "I know I'm being selfish to say it, but even though the bad stuff seems to be behind us, I'm not nearly as happy as I expected to be." She spoke dispiritedly and more as if she was making a confession than complaining.

"What's wrong?" he asked. He expected to hear it was about her job at the Boone offices. Helen Bradley had already left. "I thought you and Helen were working on something."

"It's not that." She shook her head impatiently.

"Something wrong between you and Snyder?" He tried to keep any of his own feelings out of the question.

"There's nothing to go wrong between Jim and me." She snatched a cloth off the sideboard and regarded him with exasperation. "Sometimes I think you're blind as a bat. Do you think Snyder and I have been sleeping together?"

"Well . . ." he stammered.

"Well, nothing," she snapped.

She threw down the cloth and folded her arms as if she was keeping herself from hitting him.

"Do you love him?" he asked. The question scared him.

"No I don't and he doesn't love me and that's not going to change for either of us. It's a damned cold world when nobody but your kids love you."

At that moment, just as the kettle began to sing, all of Harry's good intentions disintegrated and fell off him like a shed skin.

"I love you," he said. "Not that it could make any difference to you. But I do love you."

For a moment she stared at him as if he'd lost his mind, or so he thought, but the next instant, she flung herself across the space separating them and threw her arms around his neck.

"Harry!" she screamed, as they sent the table scattering across the floor.

Harry finally caught his balance enough to wrap her in his arms.

"Say it again!" she cried.

"I love you, Katherine," he said. He laughed as she gave another rebel yell.

"And I love you." She kissed him so hard they banged into the table again and shoved it with a crash against the wall. "Oh, God, Harry. I love you."

Tucker stuck his head in the door and said, "Are you two wrecking the place?"

"Tucker!" she shouted. "I owe you five dollars. Harry loves me."

Tucker laughed and lifted his hat in a salute. Sanchez and

Oh-Brother! appeared with the kids, who rushed into the kitchen clamoring for food and drink. When they had been fed, Tucker put his arms around Katherine and Harry and said, "We ought to do something to celebrate."

"I know what let's do," Harry said. "Let's take the Rover and go looking for a black and white kitten, mostly white."